This
Old
World

❧

STEVE WIEGENSTEIN

Blank Slate Press | Saint Louis, MO

Blank Slate Press
Saint Louis, MO 63110

Copyright © 2014 Steve Wiegenstein
Book 2 of the Daybreak Series

Manufactured in the United States of America
Cover Graphics: Shutterstock, iStock (Getty Images)
Set in Adobe Garamond Pro and Americanus Pro
Cover Design by Kristina Blank Makansi

Library of Congress Control Number: 2014946276

ISBN-13: 978-0-9858086-3-1

For Sharon and Anna

This
Old
World

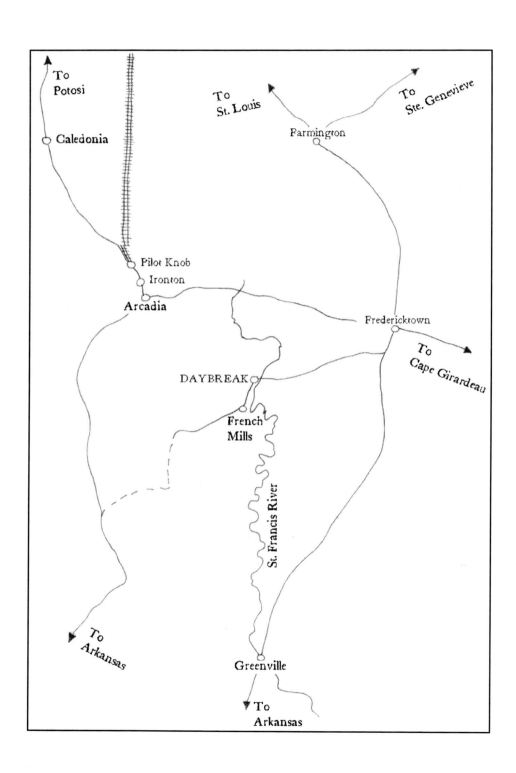

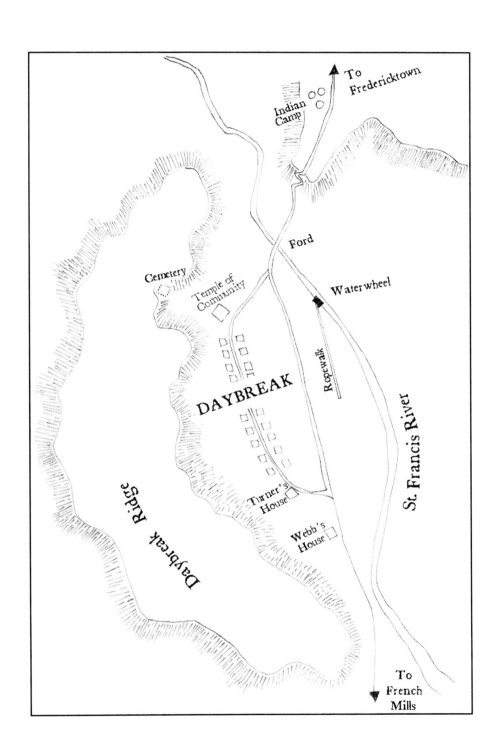

This old world is full of sorrow,
Full of sickness, weak and sore.
If you love your neighbor truly,
Love will come to you the more.

We're all children of one father,
We're all brothers and sisters too.
If you cherish one another
Love and pity will come to you.

American Folk Hymn

Chapter I

Charlotte Turner stood beneath a redbud tree and watched the last six chickens of Daybreak scratch for morsels among the henbit carpeting the cemetery. They'd been kept in a coop for all the years of the war, far enough into the woods that the sound of their clucking couldn't be heard by a passing raider, then brought down to scratch whenever the weather allowed. Any sign of trouble and she could shoo them into the forest within moments.

A wren sang overhead. Charlotte loved the sound of a wren in the morning, a bird she had heard since childhood but never known by name until she came out to Daybreak and began accumulating knowledge of the world. Life in the forest had taught her much—plants that heal, plants that harm, songs and calls and what they meant. It troubled her that more knowledge was out there to be learned, knowledge she hadn't mastered, plans unfulfilled, projects uncompleted, good things undone. But the war had come, and those plans and projects scattered like straw in the wind.

She shook off the thought. Life before the war was a dim memory. Almost like a child's tale, the memory of a group of settlers coming to this remote Ozarks river valley to create a community of equality and sharing, like the Brook Farm and New Harmony communities that had gone before them, only this time they would make a go of it. But now they had been four years struggling for survival since the war had begun in earnest and the Federals had ordered all able-bodied men from the valley. Hens without roosters, scratching for whatever nourishment they could find beneath the leaf litter. Four years of growing food, hiding it, parceling it out to the children, retreating to Harp Webb's old saltpeter cave whenever there was news of raiders in the area. Four years of escape plans and fear. When Price brought his army up from Arkansas last fall, trying to take St. Louis in some sort of desperation move, Charlotte had never been more glad they lived miles from the main road. As the Federals retreated, they burned towns and farms, and the advancing rebels had gobbled up what remnants they could find. From Pocahontas north to Fredericktown was a swath of burned ground and hunger.

From where she sat she could see sprouts encroaching into the northern fields, the ones last cleared from forest. Someone needed to cut those sprouts or else that field would be lost within the year. But who? Emile Mercadier could try, but at his age it would take him half a day to cut one sprout. Newton was nine, old enough to work, and he did his best. But they needed him for planting and hoeing the vegetables. If that crop didn't get planted and tended properly, there would be worse awaiting them than the loss of a newly cleared field.

No wonder she spent time in the cemetery. They would all be in the ground soon enough. Her sister Caroline, dead in childbirth out in Kansas. Her mother soon after. Caroline's husband, lost at Chickamauga, now a part of the earth in some lonely Tennessee hollow. Her father in the soil of Virginia. Hard enough to learn of his death, harder still to know he would lie forever in a rebel state. Adam, here beneath her feet, along with all the others from the early years of the settlement who had coughed or bled or suffered their way into the arms of the earth. And James, where was James? Charlotte recalled the day he had walked out toward town to enlist, not taking a horse for fear it would be confiscated, leaving her behind with a child in hand and another in the womb. She had approved of the enlistment then, encouraged it even, what with Sam Hildebrand roaming the countryside and carrying a grudge for the part they had taken in the fight that had taken eight of his men. Better to face a visible enemy in the daylight than to live in permanent fear of Hildebrand's rifle from the forest. But the years had been so long. She hadn't heard from him in nearly a month. Had he found his own bitter mouthful of dirt?

Dark thoughts, dark thoughts. Charlotte closed her eyes. The more she reflected, the more she saw a trail of incompletion all along her path, from childhood forward——the piano lessons abandoned, the reading list never finished, and Daybreak itself, ragged and half-empty, although she had to give some credit for that to the Federal troops and the guerrillas. Perhaps, though, they had only accelerated the inevitable.

She opened her eyes and stood. This was not the time to moon about lost opportunities. She needed to chase the chickens into their homemade cages, plant lettuce and radishes, sweep the woods for lamb's quarter and dock, pull an onion from its hiding place and get it clean for tonight's soup. She needed to endure another day.

At the ford where the road to Fredericktown crossed the river, a man with a pack on his back and a walking stick in his hand waded through the water. Charlotte smoothed her skirts and squinted into the distance. This was the first traveler they had seen in days. The occasional military patrol, old folks in wagons, sometimes a refugee family—but a man alone and on foot? Charlotte watched as he reached the near bank. He sat in the road and took off his boots, dumped out the water, and resumed his walk. When he came to the fork, he stopped.

He was wearing a blue kepi and what looked like a Union soldier's coat, but that meant nothing. The rebels and bushwhackers wore them, too. But on foot like that, he had to be a Union man. No one else would be so foolish as to walk though this part of the world alone.

The man had a black beard and from this distance what appeared to be black hair streaming out from under his cap. He still stood at the fork in the road, either thinking or waiting for someone to come out. Charlotte decided it might as well be her. She chased the chickens into their pen and headed down the hill.

She passed behind the Temple of Community, its broken windows still boarded over from the fight four years ago. Who could afford glass these days? And the weekly meetings had faded into memory, with the men all gone. When something needed deciding, they just met in someone's house or in the cleared ground in front of the Temple. The four houses closest to the river, the ones most prone to flooding, were empty now. They used them for storage, as if there was anything valuable to store.

Perhaps this man had come to her with news of James. Perhaps this was the moment she had been dreading, when she heard of his death, in battle, or by disease, or amputation, or one of the thousand ills that can befall a man, the moment when she would have to stand and hear some claptrap about the sorrowing heart of a grateful nation.

No. That always came by letter, if you were lucky enough not to have read the name in the newspaper beforehand.

She stopped in the road about six feet in front of the man. She could smell him from where she stood. His overcoat was stained, more dirt brown than blue, and he had a Springfield rifle slung over his shoulder with a piece of rope.

They regarded each other.

"Lee's surrendered," the man said.

"It's about time," said Charlotte.

She waited. But the man seemed to be in no hurry to announce his business.

"We can't feed you," she said after a minute.

"Didn't ask."

"So you didn't. But you'd not turn down a meal if offered, I wager."

"No, ma'am. That's the soldier's first rule."

"What's your regiment?"

"Eighth Missouri."

She should have known by the thick Irish accent.

"I mustered out clean," he said. "I can show you the paper if you like."

He gestured toward his knapsack, but she waved him off impatiently. She could feel the eyes of everyone in Daybreak on her. She wasn't sure how it had come to be her job to size up every potential threat, but somehow it had. If he had not come to beg a meal, what had he come for?

"You have a woman among you, a woman named Kathleen Flanagan," the man said.

He said it more as a statement than a question. Charlotte narrowed her eyes, suspicious. She remained silent.

"She was keeping my child for me," the man went on. "My name is Flynn. The child's name would be Angus."

So that was it. Charlotte looked up at the sky.

"You'd better come on in, then," she said at last. "Your son is here."

She led the way into the village. This was not going to be easy. Everyone had gotten accustomed to the idea that little Angus's father was gone, never to return, moldering in some field somewhere or simply off to start a new life now that his wife was dead. Marie Mercadier had been caring for the child for three years now, nearly four.

"So you know," she said over her shoulder, "Mrs. Flanagan's not Mrs. Flanagan any more. She's Mrs. Mercadier now."

"A woman her age," Flynn said.

"She can be old and still crave happiness."

Charlotte glanced over her shoulder, but Flynn gave no sign of what he was thinking. She stopped and faced him before they reached the first houses.

"You have heard about your wife?"

He nodded.

"I'm sorry."

"Got the letter in Tennessee. Not much to do about it by then. Might as well keep fighting. I would have come home when my three years ran out, but we were in Carolina by then, with all the tracks tore up behind us. Had to fight our way north."

She turned to face him again. "We all have our stories about the bad things that happened to us in the war. Not to play you down any, but just to tell you."

"Oh, I get your point," he said.

"My name is Turner, by the way. Charlotte Turner."

"Husband out fighting?" He read her expression. "How long since you've heard from him?"

"Not quite a month. A month almost."

He nodded. "That will happen, ma'am. You get to fighting, and days will go by. You shouldn't put nothing to it."

"Oh, I don't." She left it at that. She did not want to tell this stranger the feeling she had, the feeling she believed in as much as she believed in her own self, that if Turner were to die, out on the field or in some back-line hospital, she would know it that minute. She would feel the shock, no matter the distance or the time. And she had not felt that shock. Therefore he was still alive, somewhere, and heading her way.

It occurred to Charlotte that she was becoming a creature of signs and omens. Perhaps it was the hunger. She hoped she had not changed so much as to be unrecognizable when James came home, like some she had seen—crabbed, clenched women who never met someone's eyes, whose instinct to protect and conserve had crossed over into some kind of madness. A woman in French Mills had died that way last year, growing suspicious and inward, hoarding food, and hiding from everyone, even her neighbors, until the silence and darkness of her house led those same neighbors to push down her door and find her dead in bed, starved, with bins full of food in her kitchen.

They had reached the pump in front of the Temple of Community. Charlotte stopped. "I'm sorry," she said to the man. "I didn't mean to be so unfriendly. It's not very Christian of me."

"You're entitled," Flynn said. "I'm a stranger. Don't know as I could tell you who's Christian and who's not these days."

As they stood, people emerged from their houses and came out to see the stranger, confident now that Charlotte's presence had marked him as harmless, if perhaps not friendly.

The former Kathleen Flanagan, who had returned from St. Louis early last year and married Emile Mercadier, stepped out of the group and came close. "Michael Flynn?" she said.

"The same."

"Lord have mercy," she said. "You've come back."

"I'm on my way, anyway," Flynn said. "Still another couple of days to go."

"Good Lord, son, we haven't heard anything from our old settlement in three years. You won't find nothing down there."

"I'm going anyway. That's our land. Where's the boy?"

Kathleen's face became blank. "He's well. You needn't worry about him." Flynn's gaze darted around the circle of townsfolk. "He's not here," she added.

"Bring him, then. I can make a dozen miles or more today."

Kathleen stepped closer to Flynn. "I have wiped your nose with my apron too many times to be talked to like that," she said. "Now you listen to me. You are that boy's pappy, and his mama is gone, God rest her. But before you just show up from nowhere and claim the child, you need to think. Can you feed him? Can you dress him? To be honest about it, son, you'd frighten the boy. What you need right now is a meal and a bath."

Flynn's face clouded with anger, but he held his tongue. "I'd have you bring me my son," he said after a moment.

"And I'd have you take a bath, and a meal, and then talk sense with us." Kathleen turned to two girls hiding behind the skirts of Frances Wickman, their mother. "Sarah, Penelope, go fetch water from the well and put it in the kettle at my house. This gentleman will want plenty of hot water."

Penelope muttered something under her breath, but had the sense not to say it aloud. The girls darted off.

"So this is what happens when we leave the women behind," Flynn said. "They take over."

"Something of the sort," Charlotte said.

"Well, ain't you pert," said Flynn.

"I've been called worse."

But Flynn followed Kathleen to her house, where the girls had been filling the kettle, hung on a tripod over a firepit out back. Some of the townspeople followed, while others returned to their homes. Kathleen placed some kindling on the smoking coals and blew them back into flame.

"You go on inside," she said. "There's a washtub on the floor."

Flynn walked toward the door but stopped and turned. "I almost forgot to say," he said. "The war's over."

"Well, that's good," Kathleen said. She turned back to the fire as the children ran off, squealing, with the news. She watched them leave. "I hope you're telling us the truth."

"Oh, I am," he said. "Couldn't believe it myself at first."

"Help me with this, Charlotte," Kathleen said. They took sides and lifted the hot kettle off the flames, shielding their hands with rags. As they carried it into the house, more townspeople came running to hear the news. "Let him have his bath, and then we'll hear all about it," Kathleen told them. She shut the door behind them, and together she and Charlotte poured the hot water into the washtub.

"We'll step outside now. You take your time," Kathleen said.

By now, the news had passed through the village and people were running to the Mercadiers' house. Emile Mercadier had been in the barn, mending tack, and hobbled in as fast as his arthritic legs would allow, a hole punch still in his hand. "What this man says, is it true?"

"I expect so," said his wife. "I knew him before the war, down at our colony in the wilderness. He was not a liar. A Black Irish hothead, but not a liar. I doubt if he has changed much since then. You might find him some clean clothes."

Charlotte and Kathleen walked up the dirt lane that ran through the center of the village. They did not speak, but both knew where they were headed: the Temple of Community, where Marie Mercadier had tried to keep some trace of civilization going for the last few years by holding school for the village children.

They found her there, the room empty, benches overturned as children in their haste had dashed from the building at the news of the war's end. She was wiping off slates with a damp rag.

"Angus's daddy has come back," Kathleen said, but from Marie's look it was clear she had already heard.

"I've cared for that boy going on four years now," she said, not looking up. "I nursed him at my own breast."

"I know, honey," said the older woman. "It ain't fair, and I know it."

"Now I hear he wants to take him down in the wilderness, where your settlement used to be. Nothing's there, and you know it."

"We'll talk to him. I have known this man Flynn since he was a pup."

"Can't take a five-year-old boy into the woods like that. Does he think he's still in the Army?"

"I know, honey," Kathleen said again.

"Do not try to soothe me!" Marie snapped. "I am not a child, to be cooed to and soothed. I have brought up this child. He is mine in every way but blood."

That was when Charlotte spoke up. "I know, Marie. But the law is on his side, even though he is a stranger to us, and to Angus as well. Perhaps he'll listen to reason in time. Where is the boy?"

Marie looked glum but had no reply. "He was here till a little while ago. When all the children ran out, he tagged along. Probably wherever they are. Look for Newton and Adam, and he'll be there."

They left her with her schoolbooks and walked out into the noonday light. At Mercadier's house, halfway down the village road, the crowd of villagers was waiting in the street for Flynn to emerge. Charlotte and Kathleen joined them. Sure enough, the boys were in a tight knot at the front of the crowd—Charlotte's sons, Newton now seven and Adam almost three, and Angus between them at five.

Charlotte went up to them. "I need to tell you something," she said to Angus, taking his hand. "Walk over here with me."

She was about to lead him to a quieter spot, the doorway of the Wickmans' house nearby, but before they could pull away from the throng, Michael Flynn emerged and stood on the Mercadiers' step, dressed in some of Emile Mercadier's castoffs. He was clean and his hair was wet, but his wild beard still stuck out from his face in all directions. He surveyed the crowd.

"Is the war over?" someone called out.

"Mine is," Flynn said.

"What have you heard?" Mercadier said.

"Lee's done. Johnston's done."

"What about Smith?"

"Smith I wouldn't know about." He stepped down into the circle of people toward Charlotte, who was still holding onto Angus's hand. "This the boy?" His gaze was intent, his expression hard to read.

Charlotte turned to the child. "Angus," she said, "this is your father."

In an instant the child pulled free of her hand and darted off through the crowd like a sparrow through the forest. He rounded the corner of the house and was gone. They stood in awkward silence.

"Well, come and eat," Kathleen said into the empty moment. "This will take some time. Let's go to the Temple, everyone."

"Temple?" Flynn said. "What the hell kind of place is this?"

Charlotte followed, listening as Kathleen explained Daybreak to him—the community's philosophy, the sharing of wealth, the weekly meetings, the pure democracy—all of which was true, at least in the abstract, although since the war had taken most of the men the abstract ideals of their social order had given way to the daily labors of survival. Hearing the pride in Kathleen's voice reminded Charlotte of the reasons they came out here in the first place. They were going to remake the world one little village at a time, following James's ideas of sharing, democracy, and social equality. So the dream had not taken shape in the last few years. Whose had? Flynn listened politely, but Charlotte could hear the skepticism in his questions.

She hung back from the group, watching for Angus to reappear. He wouldn't go far, not with all the hubbub going on. Nothing to eat at noontime but hoecakes anyway, so why hurry inside? Besides, Charlotte was feeling strange. She felt disembodied, not entirely real, as if she were merely walking through this world and not inhabiting it. She lingered in the street and watched everyone file in, then walked to a limestone slab that they had brought up from the river and placed on logs to make a bench beside the pump. She sat, feeling the warmth of the sun on her back and the cool of the stone underneath her.

Sure enough, Angus appeared a few minutes later, sidling up beside Charlotte from behind. He leaned over her shoulder and rested his chin. Neither of them spoke for a while.

"I don't need a father," Angus said eventually. "Josephine doesn't have a father."

It was as if he instinctively found the most painful thing to say. Of course Marie's little girl Josephine had a father, but it was Charlotte's own husband, and they had never found a way to tell the children of this complication.

"Well," she said. "You have one, anyway. I don't know anything about him, but he's here."

"Don't need him. Mother and I do just fine."

"Honey, we've talked about this before. Your real mother died, and Marie took you in. This man is the only real kin you've got, and you're the only kin he's got." Angus did not reply. After a while, she added, "Let's go in and eat. Everyone's inside."

"He in there?" To her pause, he said, "Not hungry."

"Well, I am," Charlotte said. "Hold my hand, and I'll sit beside you."

They walked into the Temple, where the benches and tables were spread out on the main floor as they always were, with plates and utensils, and everyone eating in groups of six. Even with a war on and little food on the table, Charlotte had insisted that the community keep its tradition of common dining.

Frances Wickman had gathered dandelion and dock in the morning, so they each had a small mess of boiled greens on their plates beside the cakes. The boys, who paid no attention to their food, were crowded around Flynn, peppering him with questions. But he had little to say, chewing on his hoecake with fatiguing deliberation.

The Mercadier family, old Emile and his autumn bride Kathleen, and Emile's daughter Marie, with her little Josephine clinging to her side, ate in silence at one table. Marie's gaze burned at Flynn, but he ate as if oblivious. Angus pulled from Charlotte's hand and squeezed between Marie and her father at the table, ducking his head to avoid being noticed. Charlotte served herself and sat down directly across from Flynn, scooting her sons apart to make room.

"Mr. Flynn here fought in a lot of battles," Newton told her.

"I expect he did," Charlotte said.

"But he won't tell us if he killed anybody."

"You boys need to leave this man alone. He's trying to eat his food."

The children frowned but obeyed. They lingered at the table, swinging their feet, until Charlotte excused them and they scurried out the door.

"Fine boys," Flynn said.

"Yes," said Charlotte. "They and Angus make quite a trio." She put down her fork. "Mr. Flynn, you should think long and hard before taking your son away from here. He has grown up here. He has friends and loved ones."

Flynn tipped his head to look at his son, squeezed in on his bench, while giving Charlotte a sideways glance. "I don't discuss family matters with strangers," he said.

"Fair enough," said Charlotte. "But let me tell you this. I remember when your group went through before the war. Must have been eighty of you, all headed for that settlement down south. But since Price came through, there has not been a single soul come up that road from the Irish colony. You take Angus down there, it'll be the two of you alone. That settlement is gone."

"I said I don't talk about family business!" Flynn shouted, half rising from the table. "I appreciate you people caring for my boy, and I'll pay you. But I will do what I please." He slammed his fork onto his tin plate and pushed back the bench. "I will wait outside."

In the silence that followed Flynn's stormy departure, Angus began to cry. He clung to Marie's side as Charlotte stood up, her face hot.

"He has the law on his side, you know," she said to the Mercadiers' table. Kathleen nodded. Charlotte walked out to the landing in front of the doors, where Flynn waited on the slope below. Standing there, she could not help but remember Harp Webb lying on the very spot where she now stood, a bullet in his belly, and her rifle hot in her hands. She looked out across the fields to the river.

"A final word, and this is not family business," she said. "We had a rebel for a neighbor, owned a thousand acres south and across the river. Killed in the war. When the provost-marshal auctioned off his land, our community bought it up. If you don't like what you find down south, I'll sell you a forty or an eighty across the river, fine land but it's uncleared. You don't have to say yes or no, just know that it's here. That young one has been with us since he was a baby, and it will break our hearts to see him go. So if you don't find what you're looking for down there, come back and be our neighbor."

She walked past him and did not look back. She did not want to witness the tearful farewell, the crying, the whimpering, the arguments and recriminations. She went to her home and shut the door. About an hour later, she glanced out her window to the road south and saw Flynn walk past, knapsack and bedroll tied and trim, looking neither to left nor right, and Angus trudging ten feet behind him. Angus carried a sack which she knew had to contain a week's worth of food, and he had a bundle of clothing tucked under his other arm.

That night she wondered how far they had gotten. The next river they had to ford was the Black, twenty miles down; it would take them two days at least. Adam was too young to understand Angus was gone, probably for good, but Newton knew it; he was subdued and went to bed quietly. At least she could comfort herself that Flynn was experienced at making the best bed of rough terrain.

Sometime in the middle of the night Charlotte heard the front door latch open and close. She sat up in bed with a start. Could Angus have run off and found his way back? It hardly seemed possible.

For a moment she thought she might have dreamed the sound. But then there was the clump of shoes on the floor. A grown man, from the heaviness of the footfalls. Charlotte held still, her mind racing. Perhaps Flynn was not such an honest man as Kathleen Mercadier had thought. He'd have no luck finding anything of value here. But she had mentioned buying the land; perhaps he thought they had a stash of money.

The footsteps stopped. Charlotte listened.

She held herself still, barely breathing. For long minutes there was no sound. Flynn—or whoever—did not seem to be moving. For once Charlotte wished for a pistol.

But she had no pistol, and after another minute she decided that she had had enough waiting. She stepped out of bed, put on her robe from its hook behind the door, and found the box of phosphorous matches she kept on the shelf. Usually she lit her lantern with a stick from the hearth, but this was no time to be spare. She lit the lantern, dropped the globe, braced herself, and stepped out into the front room.

Just inside the door, fast asleep on the floor, his uniform caked with mud and his beard a woolly mat, still wearing his boots, lay her husband, James Turner, his head propped up on his pack, a sword and rifle laid on the floor beside him. Charlotte watched him for a moment in the lamplight. His face was thin and drawn beneath the thick fur of his beard.

He was so changed, not just from the war, but from the passing of the years. She remembered the first time she had seen him, so big and magnetic, back in Kansas. He was broad and robust, irresistible, exuding confidence like a cloud. The man who lay on her floor now was gaunt and brown, and the only cloud that might rise from him was dust.

She wanted to cry, to kiss him, to fall on his neck, to ask him how he had gotten home and what had happened to him since he had last written, to hear from his lips the story of how her father had died in battle. She wanted to show him his sons, the one he had never met and the one who would barely remember him. She wanted to bathe him and feed him with her own hands.

But it could wait. She blew out the lantern and let him sleep.

Chapter 2

When Turner awoke, his boots were off and a small boy had pulled up a wooden chair next to his waist, watching him intently, his feet dangling. He was skinny and towheaded, with his hair cropped close to his scalp. Turner scooted himself to a sitting position against the wall. His legs felt heavy.

"You sure do sleep a long time," the boy said.

Turner blinked. It was full morning outside, and leaf-shaded light came through the cabin's window. "What time is it?" he said. The boy shrugged.

"I caught a rabbit this morning," said the boy. "We're gonna to eat him tonight."

"That's a good thing."

The boy shrugged again and hopped down from his chair. "Mama says I'm supposed to remember you," he said. "Maybe I do."

"I remember you."

"Oh, yeah? What's my name?"

"Your name is Newton."

With a suspicious look, the boy walked to the door and lifted the latch. "I guess you're my daddy after all," he said. "Mama said to call her when you woke up."

"No!" Turner cried out, surprising them both with the vehemence of his voice. "I'm not fit," he said, trying to cover. "I need to wash up and shave, anyway. People oughtn't to see me looking like a vagabond."

Newton stayed at the door. He pursed his lips. "She saw you last night," he said.

"That she did. But in the broad light of day, I'd rather be more presentable."

Turner stood up and rubbed his face. It felt greasy. The train from St. Louis had arrived in Pilot Knob at three in the afternoon yesterday; he should have stayed the night there but couldn't stand to wait. So he had started out walking, forded the St. Francis at Sebastian, and then cut through the woods, foolishly, forcing his way through underbrush in the dark of night. When he finally broke out of the forest into a pasture, he knew somehow that he was behind Krummrich's old farm. The house and barn were burned; Charlotte had written him about the bushwhackers. But at least he knew where he was—on the road to Daybreak, five miles from home. There could be no stopping. He had no idea what time it was when he finally crossed the ford and reached his house, but the stars were bright and the moon was down.

"Guess there's water in the washbasin," he said, more to break the silence than anything. He walked into the bedroom and stood at the dresser. His first thought when he looked in the mirror was *old*. His hair was still sandy, but his face had darkened; it was deep brown and thin, with discolorations across one cheek—powder burns, maybe. He looked like an old man. Perhaps he had become one without noticing. Newton followed him and stood in the doorway.

"Razor's in my pack," Turner said. "Can you bring it?"

A half hour later, he felt more like himself, and had a washbasin filled with whiskers and dirty water. He stepped out the back door and tossed it into the grass. "All right," he said to Newton, who had watched him in silence the whole time. "You can go fetch your mother."

The boy dashed off, and Turner returned inside. He noticed for the first time that his Army coat had been hung from a peg on the inside wall and brushed down; she must have removed it along with his boots while he slept. His sword and rifle leaned against the corner.

Turner felt ill at ease in the house, too dirty and rough to be within walls after so many years of camp cots and ground sleeping, unworthy of such cleanliness and order. He wanted to sit on the bed, but his clothes were too dirty, so he walked back into the front room and sat on a chair. And yet as uncomfortable as he felt, at least he was home.

That face in the mirror, so haunted and haggard. Was it a face that anyone would want to see in the morning? The thought came to him that she might be just as beaten and worn, indeed probably was. The bright-eyed woman he had left behind—how much of that person remained? He could feel a hollow place inside himself where once a great well of enthusiasm and energy had bubbled. No reason to imagine she hadn't been similarly damaged. Her letters through the years had been as observant as ever, but it was hard to know what wounds might lie beneath her calm words.

She would want to know about her father. He had written her that he had been killed in battle, and that his death had been quick and painless, but she would want to know more. And what could he say that wouldn't cause anguish? Nothing. He had been standing there with him, behind the lines outside of Auburn, Virginia, as he wrote out the day's orders. They were backing up toward a railway, trying to keep the rebels from turning their flank. As always, they heard the rifle ball before they saw anything, the sucking hiss that, strangely, always frightened most when it was a single sound rather than the thousands that flew during battle. It whistled past Turner's ear; Newton Carr was turned to him, a word half-begun, when the ball hit him in the eye, smashed halfway into his head, and dropped him dead to the ground.

No sniper could have made that shot. They never learned whether it had come from their side or the rebels. Turner had always suspected that it was one of their own, a man tamping his rifle musket, perhaps, or an accidental discharge while shouldering, but it could just as easily have been a rebel firing in the general direction of their lines, hoping for a lucky hit—quartermaster hunting, they called it. All Turner knew for sure was that at one moment they were in calm conversation and the next moment his father-in-law was dead at his feet with part of his head missing.

What would he tell her? Nothing, preferably. This tale would serve no good. But he knew Charlotte—she would ask and ask, wanting to know everything. Well, she could just do without that.

And Marie. He had kept thoughts of her out of his mind as much as possible during the long trip home. They would only confuse him further, and he felt confused enough already. But the moment was here, when he would have to unearth those thoughts and decide.

The silence of the empty house was comforting. Sometimes after a battle he couldn't hear for three or four days, communicating only through notes. That silence was oddly comforting as well. There were plenty of sounds he would just as soon not hear. A quiet, empty house was fine.

So here he was, back in Daybreak. Now what? Pick up where they had left off? Husband, father, leader? It didn't seem possible. It would be like becoming thirty-five again, and he wasn't thirty-five any more.

He didn't feel like thinking about it. He just wanted to sit in the quiet. The deafness after a battle wasn't really silence; it was a ringing roar that drowned out everything else. But this—this was true quiet. A good place to let his mind sit empty.

He thought about the boy, his son. A foot and a half taller than when he had last seen him. All right. Seemed like a good enough boy. He had felt the boy's curiosity this morning, the desire to see everything about him, to watch and ask. He wanted to hear about the war; boys always wanted to hear about the war. But he had managed the politeness not to pester him. That was good. His mother had raised him right. But what about the other one? What about Adam?

On the train to St. Louis, boys had swarmed like gnats, fingering his captain's bars and peppering him with questions: Had he seen the surrender? Was he there? Did he know Grant? They knew all the names of the generals and the battles, had read about them in the newspapers, he guessed. Turner hadn't meant to be harsh to the boys. He had opened his mouth a time or two to speak. But nothing came out, so he turned his face to the window until they drifted away.

The door opened, and the brightness of the light from outside made him wince. And there she was.

Charlotte stood in the open doorway a moment, the light haloing her hair and body but leaving her face in darkness. Then she shut the door quietly and stood with her back against it.

Turner stood.

"You're back," she said.

He said nothing. He walked toward her tentatively and reached out his hands. She took them and for a moment that's how they stood, at arm's length, just touching fingertips. He thought about coming close to kiss her, but something held him back.

She was altogether too thin. Her face was drawn and lined. Turner waited for something beautiful, something eloquent, to say to her. He had always been able to find the words he needed. But this morning he dipped into the well of his mind and came up dry. He simply stood.

Then the spell was broken and she was in his arms, holding him tight with a grip that could break bones. He could feel her fingering his scrawny ribs and shoulder blades.

"Stars in heaven, I have missed you," he whispered.

"And I you," she whispered back.

They said nothing else, for there was nothing left to say, nothing that mattered, anyway. They stood pressed together in the dim indoor light.

Several minutes went by as they silently embraced. Then she pulled away and looked him in the eyes. "You must meet your new son," she said. "Not so new anymore. Adam turned three this month."

"I know. I toasted his birthday with the men."

"So is it 'major,' now? Will we all have to start calling you 'major'?"

"Brevet major. They put me back at captain as soon as they got a real soldier to take over."

He averted his eyes. Take over after her father was killed, that is. Here he was talking about Colonel Carr already, if only by implication. So much for his resolve.

Charlotte pulled him toward the door. "Everyone's wanting to see you," she said. "We're all so proud of you. You and all the men."

Turner resisted for a moment, feeling unready to face anyone. But her pull was insistent, the happiness on her face clear, and he found himself on the doorstone in the bright morning light.

They were a meager lot now, fifteen or so adults and a handful of children, gathered in a semicircle around the front of the house. There was John Wesley Wickman and Frances, and those two girls must be their twins, Penelope and Sarah, Sarah skipping around in circles and Penelope propped against her mother's knees, her legs splayed out at a strange angle. It looked to Turner that the girl's hips, malformed since birth, had not gotten any better. Wickman stepped forward and shook his hand.

"Welcome home, friend," he said.

And there were all the wives and sweethearts of the Daybreak men still gone to the war, Mrs. Prentice, Mrs. Shepherson, and all the others, their eyes haunted and darting. Some of those wives were widows now, and Turner tried to recall Charlotte's letters—which ones had lost their husbands and which ones were waiting for a return. And there was Emile Mercadier. Good Lord, he had aged! He leaned on a cane, and his hair was now wispy and white. Something seemed to be wrong with his eyes—they were gray and cloudy, and Turner noticed that he stood with his hand resting lightly on the shoulder of his wife.

And there, at the far edge, trying her best to look away, was Marie, with Josephine standing beside her solemnly, holding her hand.

Turner tried to look away as well but found his gaze returning to her again and again. She would not meet his eye.

He knew words were expected of him. "My friends, my fellow citizens——" he began. And now what to say? He felt empty. "It's good to be——I've missed——" He fought to keep his eyes from returning to Marie and managed to keep his focus on Josephine instead. "I have missed you all," he stammered out. "I am so happy——"

Then, nothing. He was out of things to say. He found the latchstring to the door behind him and stumbled inside.

Turner's heart was pounding. Of all the moments to feel afraid! During the war he had been afraid many times but had never retreated, never fled.

He returned to his chair at the table and sat down, wiping sweat from his forehead. The townspeople outside were no doubt perplexed——perhaps he should try to go out again and talk to them. But he could not. They would have to wait until tomorrow.

Charlotte came inside after a minute. "Are you all right?" she said.

"Of course I'm all right. I just——I don't know. I just didn't feel like seeing everyone all at once. It was a bit too much." He forced a smile.

Charlotte said nothing, but her expression was dubious. "I'm sure it's strange, being back here," she said. "You've gone through a lot."

Turner knew she was only making an excuse for him, but he didn't mind. Perhaps he deserved a little coddling for a while. "I'm the first man back, then."

She nodded, a little hesitantly. "One of the boys from the Irish colony was through here yesterday. But other than him, yes."

"What news is there?"

"Not much, beyond what I wrote you. Jesse Wilson died early. Prentice was exchanged but had to go back to the fighting. He didn't last a month after that. No news from Schnack."

"And Charley Pettibone?"

Charlotte grimaced. "He walked down the road and then he was gone. At least Prentice would send letters to his wife and children, but a young single man like Charley? And with a regiment mustered in Arkansas, we never even read about them in the newspaper. He was fighting on the wrong side. We may never know."

The cabin door opened, and Newton peered inside.

"It's all right," Charlotte said. "He's all right. You can come in."

Behind Newton, holding his hand, was a boy of three. He had bright blond hair and eyes that were shockingly pale and blue, the blue of the noonday sky.

"You must be Adam," Turner said.

Without a pause, the boy climbed onto his lap and kissed his newly shaved cheek. "You have had a hard, hard time of it, is what Aunt Marie says," he said, pronouncing the word "Aint," country style. "Aunt Marie says you're my daddy. Is that so?"

"It is."

"Angus's daddy came and took him away. Please don't do that."

Newton grabbed Adam's arm and tried to pull him off Turner's lap. "Adam is talking nonsense, Mother. Make him stop."

But Adam clung to Turner's neck. "I like it here, Daddy. Don't take me away!"

Turner gently disentangled the boy's arms and stood him on his feet, pressing him between his knees. "I'll not take you away, son. I like it here, too. I'm not taking anybody anywhere."

The boy would not be still, though he had enough sense not to squirm. But his eyes darted, and Turner could tell he wasn't listening. Newton continued to tug at him until Turner held up a quieting hand.

"Do you hear me, son?" he asked.

Adam finally nodded his head. "Yes, sir."

"All right, then. You boys need not concern yourselves."

Charlotte shooed the boys outside, and they tumbled out the door in a flurry of pokes and recriminations, rivals already. She and Turner regarded each other.

"We have a lot to catch up on," she said.

"No hurry," Turner said. "I don't know where to start, anyway." He looked down at his hands. "The boy is a fine-looking lad. Quite a talker for his age."

"Marie's been schooling them."

"*Aunt* Marie?"

"Adam took to calling her that because he knows he's some relation to Josephine. All the children picked it up, and I think she likes it."

"Do you mind it?"

Her face was fixed. Turner had seen versions of that face many times in the past few years, the survivor's face, the face of someone who could not allow lesser troubles to claim the attention due to greater ones. "I don't have time to mind it. The crops, the bushwhackers."

"Have they still been bad?"

"The crops or the rebels?" Charlotte sat across the table from him and took his hands. "The crops, not bad for what we can do. But there are so few of us, we can't manage the fields. The rebels, bad enough for a while, but there's not much left for them to steal. They've mainly gone south and west. You hear of Hildebrand coming through once in a while, but he's stayed away from here. There's quite a nest of them over toward Kansas."

"Well, that should be ending soon." He watched her face and knew she was waiting for more news about Colonel Carr. "I don't want to talk about your father right now," he said. "I am sorry. I am sorry for his death. You know I am. But I don't want to tell you any more about it. Maybe another day."

"All right. We can talk about other things."

A burdening silence fell between them. Turner groped for a thought. For two weeks now, the only thing in his mind had been *get home, get home*. Now that he was home, nothing else rose up to fill the place where that thought had been. He took a breath. Patience, patience.

"I haven't gone mad from the war. I want you to know that. I just couldn't think of what to say out there."

"Of course not."

Not that he hadn't seen it happen, or been close to it himself. There were so many ways to go battle-mad, and he reckoned he had seen most of them. Men would freeze in place, or fail to lift their weapons, or they would stand up from a safe position, cursing crazily into a hail of fire; they would grow deaf or immobile or have phantom pains; they would flee the field, forever shaming themselves and risking execution, even with an officer waving a sword in their faces. Or they would grow sullen and crafty, inward; he had come close to executing a man from his regiment only weeks before the Surrender. They had all known the Surrender was coming; it was only a matter of time. But that didn't stop the man from breaking. He had gone for water and come back with a horrid case of poison ivy, reported himself unfit for duty. It was obvious he had rubbed it on himself, for his palms and face were covered with the rash, and Turner was about to order him shot on the spot. Something in the man's blank gaze and indifferent expression stopped him. It would be like shooting an ox.

And himself? He had felt that sensation steal upon him as well. In him it took the form of insensibility, a dull lethargy that made him feel heavy and stupid, bovine, ready to die. There was the time on the hillside in Virginia——

Turner realized that he had gone away for too long, that Charlotte was still sitting across from him, expectant in the silence, while he refought his battles. He smiled at her in embarrassment.

"I'm sorry," he said. "I was off somewhere."

"So I see," she said with a smile in return, embarrassed as well. "I imagine you need some rest."

"Maybe. Or maybe what I need is activity, and lots of it."

"No shortage of that. The sprouts are taking over the fields, and the rope mill is falling apart. A lot of the houses lost shingles last winter. We've done what we could."

"Well, then." Turner took his hat and went to the door. Everyone had left; in the bright day he stood on the doorstone and looked out at Daybreak. In the distance he could see figures in the fields, some with hoes, some weeding by hand. It looked as though Charlotte had set them all to growing vegetables in the lower fields. Smart move.

The May morning reminded him of a day just a year ago, a foggy morning, when he had watched from the right as Upton sent twelve regiments against the rebel lines at Spotsylvania, massed shoulder to shoulder, screaming insanely, and with orders not to fire until they reached the breastworks, for firing would mean stopping to reload, and the imperative was speed at all costs. So forward they ran to their deaths over the swampy ground. It was no time for reflection, but Turner had found himself wondering how they all had gotten here, sane men, creatures of reason, singers of songs, now pressing the bodies of their wounded brothers into the mud as they advanced. Those were sounds to be deaf to——the blast and rush of canister, the cries of men, the abominable clanking of steel against steel, and the unmistakable, sickening slide of steel into flesh.

But now he had returned, and they would rebuild Daybreak. They would start anew. Except——

Except there was nothing to believe in about Daybreak any longer. What point was there in talking rot about cooperation and sharing? Men were beasts. Might as well admit it and be done. When they had come out here in the fifties, the world seemed ripe with possibility, human nature capable of improvement, a new social order ready to emerge. The great experiment was to have shown the rest of the country this path, but instead the country took a path of its own, and their pastoral dream now seemed like a relic from an antique time.

And yet what else was there to do? There were children to feed. Life had to go on as before, but it could not go on as before.

Might as well go cut sprouts. Standing in the sunlight Turner wiped his face with his hand. When he pulled his hand away it was wet, and his face was wet.

"Well, I'm a fool," he said.

But he was still crying, and he couldn't seem to make it stop. He had gone through the war unhurt, but here he was on his own doorstep, and he could not get to the door behind him, could not step off into the shade of the yard. He was stuck here on the stone, and he could not, could not, could not make it stop.

Chapter 3

Marie Mercadier had almost finished the school day when Michael Flynn showed up at the Temple door with Angus. It had been a week and a half since he had left. Flynn held open the door, and Angus walked quietly into the room, sitting at his usual spot on the second bench.

"Mind your teacher," Flynn said, then shut the door.

Angus looked neither to left nor right at the curious children who were trying to get his attention. He sat quietly on the bench. Newton Turner handed him a slate and chalk.

Marie tried to keep the class going for another few minutes but couldn't concentrate. So she let everyone out early and sat beside Angus.

She embraced his skinny body, stroking his hair. Angus didn't respond but let her hug him all she wanted. He was dirty and had some scratches on his face and arms—from pushing through underbrush, Marie guessed—but looked all right otherwise.

"Did you make it all the way to the Irish colony?" she asked.

"Yes, ma'am. But there wasn't anybody there," he said.

"Have you had anything to eat today?"

"No, ma'am. Daddy said we'd eat when we got here."

"Well, then."

She took his hand and led him to her house in the center of the settlement. There wasn't much food for him at the moment, but a lard sandwich would do. He devoured it eagerly, and when Marie took his shoes off and had him lie down on his old bed for a nap, he made no murmur. Within minutes he was sleeping.

Marie stepped out of her house and tried to think. She felt a great need to be sensible and cool at this moment, to keep her emotions from getting the better of her. She had never spoken of Angus as her son, though she had raised him and loved him, but she could not permit herself the illusion that this Irishman had come to return him. He was too stubborn a brute for anything like that. No, now was the time to take a leaf from Charlotte Turner's book and let her head rule, size up the situation and decide what was best. That was Charlotte's great strength, keeping her head. Charlotte had led Daybreak since the war began, and Marie had never seen her panic or lose her composure, not even when raiders came through looking for food, valuables, or enemies to kill. She hadn't seen Charlotte act emotionally since——

Well, since the day she had discovered her in the act of nature with her husband. Of all the losses Marie had suffered after her liaison with Turner had become known—the cost to her reputation, the pain to her father, the separation from Turner—the one that surprised her most had been the loss of her friendship with Charlotte. Charlotte said she had forgiven her, but the tension between them had never gone away. And how could it?

Marie told herself sometimes that she had been a foolish girl, old enough to know better to be sure, but swept away by the thrill of romance into a liaison before she had time to think. But she knew that was not the truth. If all she had wanted was romance, plenty of amorous young men in the colony would have accommodated her. She had wanted James Turner and no one else. Wanted him with all the knowing intent of a full-grown woman. Call it selfishness or love, it was her own choice, and both she and Charlotte knew it. So it was hard to imagine Charlotte entirely forgiving her, since she had not entirely repented. Marie had thought a few times about leaving the colony, taking Josephine and going west somewhere, covering the trail with a story about how Josephine's father had been killed in the war, but she had never gone through with it. And of course there was her own father to think of.

Charlotte and the Irishman passed by in the wagon, heading north out of the village. Now where the devil were they going? Marie strolled to the end of the houses to watch them as they crossed the ford, taking a tiny pair of spectacles out of her dress pocket to help her see in the distance. She knew it was vain, but she hated putting on the spectacles; they made her eyes look big. Flynn tied up the horse and wagon to a tree a few feet on the other side of the river and helped Charlotte down; they started walking through the brush. Well, if they wanted to collect ticks and chiggers by the basketful, let them. And why was she giving him the royal tour anyway? Bringing Angus back to the village didn't make him their friend all of a sudden.

Off in the other direction, in the north fields, she could see Turner at work with his grubhoe, creeping his way through the rows of corn, with Josephine right behind him. She followed him wherever he went these days, wordless, as if watching a particularly interesting moth. Marie liked this new interest sometimes—it was good for Josephine to get to know the man, and good for Turner to find it within himself to acknowledge her, and someday they would find a way to tell her that he was her father—but most of the time it bothered her. After five years of Josephine's constant presence, it was troubling to have her attach herself so suddenly to someone else.

As for Turner, he had sneaked a couple of moony looks but had not managed to speak to her yet. Just as well. She didn't have the words for him. They had parted well, with no sense of harshness between them, and Turner's letters—always addressed to Josephine—had never crossed into impropriety. And in truth, Turner had spoken to almost no one since his return. He emerged from his house, went to work, ate in silence.

As Marie stood in the street, she became aware that her father had come up beside her. Strange, how as his eyesight failed he had become quieter, more inward, moving around the colony like a drifting apparition. Stranger still, how effortlessly they had changed positions in life. He had always been her fierce protector, even in the dark days after scandal had enveloped them all. But age and infirmity had come upon him faster than she had ever imagined, and now she found herself drawn into the role of his guardian, although his sense of the geography of the colony was so keen that he hardly needed guidance. They stood together in the quiet morning.

"So the boy's come back," he said. "Newton and Adam will be glad of that."

"I know what you're going to say," Marie replied. "Don't get too attached. We don't know what's going to happen. This father of his could decide to take him away again."

"Then I won't say it." He smiled blandly in her direction, his blue eyes clouded with blobs of gray.

"Good. Where's Kathleen?" she said more softly.

Mercadier shrugged. "Tending to something. You know that woman, always busy."

Marie smiled. A fiend for work, Kathleen was that. "How did you ever persuade that fine woman to marry you, anyway?"

Her father smiled at the familiar rally. "It's the fiddle, *cherie*. A good fiddler always has his pick of the ladies."

"If you say so."

"It's what drew your mother to me, or so she always said."

"And I always thought it was your charming manners and your good looks. And of course your fortune." She took his hand to guide him over the threshold of their house so he could find his way to his bedroom. Angus was still asleep in his old bed in the front room but did not stir. The children might not need their naps nowadays, but their grandfather certainly did.

She stopped her thought. Grandfather? Josephine's grandfather, yes, but not Angus's. She knew what they all were saying was true—that she had no claim of law on the boy, although she had loved and cared for him all these years. As though caring was a mere accident, and this man could sashay in from nowhere and dismiss it all. A damnable law for a contemptible world, a world built by men, where a moment's spasm in the darkness counted for more than the daily labors of hand and heart.

Marie shook off her anger. All right, so Flynn had the law. She had the school, and the village, and the boy's affection. She would find her way.

Once Mercadier had settled in for his rest, Marie went looking for Kathleen. She was never hard to find; there was the kitchen or the fields.

This afternoon she was in the kitchen of the Temple, chopping onions into fine slivers. Marie took a knife and began to help. There were a few old potatoes on the cutting board as well. Another night of soup.

Kathleen seemed to read her thoughts. "We get all our men back," she said, "and there'll be some proper farming done around here again."

"I surely hope so," said Marie.

"Oh, just you watch. And Mr. Turner, he'll come around, wait and see. He's no fit man now, but he'll come round."

"Think so?"

"Oh, child, can you doubt it? I remember when we first came through here in fifty-seven. Father Hogan was convinced you were all a pack of loons, or devil-worshippers, maybe, giving over all your possessions to a man you hardly knew. Just because he had wrote a book. Several sermons we heard on the topic of following worldly deceptions. But I could tell you was people of sense, and your Mr. Turner no flim-flam, either. That kind of thing don't change."

Marie chopped onions and didn't reply. It would be a fine thing for the Daybreak community to return to itself, no question. But whether it could—whether there was still enough idealism left in its people, left in the world—that was no certainty. And as for Turner, she hardly knew what to think. No flim-flam, well, all right. But would she want him to return to the man he was before the war? Maybe. She still thought of their times together, not that she wanted them to return, but Lord, there was something to be said for the words of an eloquent man. Words of love or words of leadership all flowed from similar springs.

She looked up to see that Kathleen had stopped chopping and stood with her knife paused midair. For a moment she wondered if she had spoken some of her private musings aloud, and felt herself start to blush, but instantly she saw that Kathleen was not looking at her but into the distance, her eyes narrowed, listening.

"Horsemen," she said.

Marie listened as well. Sure enough, she could hear the faraway creaking of tack. Her mind raced. Where were the children? Horsemen only meant soldiers or bushwhackers these days.

Together they went to the Temple windows and peeked out, each woman instinctively keeping her body behind the wall. Marie pulled out her glasses for a better look. Five men had crossed the ford and were riding into the village slowly, spread out. They all had rifles but kept them in their saddle scabbards. They were young, lean as saplings, and they rode with the easy slouch of long practice.

"What do you think?" Kathleen said.

"I think I know one of those boys," said Marie.

She stepped out into the open area in front of the Temple and stood waiting, with Kathleen behind her. The horsemen came at a slow walk as if they were on a Sunday excursion.

"Hello, Charley," she said as the first man stopped.

It was Charley Pettibone all right. She thought she had recognized him. He had grown the ghost of a beard, and his light brown hair was long and pulled back. He removed his hat and put it on his thigh.

"Miss Marie." He nodded to Kathleen. "Ma'am."

Marie knew this man was the Charley Pettibone of the old days, jovial, gabby Charley, the flirtatious boy from Arkansas who had alternately amused and annoyed her with his outrageous teenaged gallantry, but she couldn't help shuddering at the sight of him now. Old Charley had disappeared. The man who slouched on his horse was lean and predatory, like a gar in the river, all bones and teeth. And a rebel. They killed rebels, and rebels killed them.

"Coming back to Daybreak, are you?"

Charley looked off at the ridge behind her. "Well. I don't know."

Marie didn't know, either. A rebel among them? Living and working? She wasn't sure she could abide it. "The war's over."

He shrugged. "Guess so. I hear Jo Shelby's took his army down to Texas, gonna keep up the struggle from down there. Or Mexico maybe."

"You wouldn't go to Mexico, would you?"

Charley shrugged again and looked away. "Mr. Turner make it through the fight?"

Marie pointed to the fields, where Turner had seen the men and was walking in. Even from this distance, his movements seemed to her reluctant and pained.

"I missed you all sometimes," Charley said.

She didn't want to say everything that was on her mind—that at first, when Charley had gone off to join his Arkansas regiment, it had all seemed like a young man's lark, to be settled within a few months and patched up over iced cream, but that as the years went by and the roll of the dead steadily grew, those feelings were replaced by the dread and hatred of wartime. When she read in the newspapers about the great battles, she hoped Charley hadn't gotten killed, but only in a general sort of way, the way one hoped for anything to end with as little harm as possible. But if he had been killed, would she have mourned? Not much. But now was not the time to dredge that up.

"We missed you, too," she said.

Pettibone's companions shifted restlessly on their horses. Marie thought them a hard looking lot, although none of them looked more than twenty-one or twenty-two. One in particular had a gaze that never rested for long, glancing out from under a flop of greasy black hair, and when it landed on Marie she felt a chill.

"You said these people would have food for us, Pettibone," the black-haired man said.

"We don't have much," Kathleen said. "But what we have we'll share. Tie up your horses and come inside."

By now Turner had reached them, Josephine trailing behind. "Well, Charley," he said, reaching up to shake his hand. "Good to see you're still on the side of the living."

"I'm all right here, then?"

Turner cast a furtive glance around. "Well, I'm not the one to say," he said.

Kathleen took another step forward. "Like I said, step down and have some food. We have soup in the pot."

"Pettibone, you said these people would have hams and chickens," the black-haired man said.

"Once upon a time, and in some future time, but for now we're off that diet," Kathleen said. "Everything's been stolen."

"Blame it on the reb, eh?" the black-haired man said. "I know that game."

"I'd say both sides done their part," Kathleen said, her chin set.

"I ain't staying around for thin-man soup. I'll go on a ways, maybe shoot a coon."

"You go right ahead, son."

"I ain't your son."

"That's a fact."

Charley interrupted them. "Boys, I think this is where you and I will part," he said, stepping down from his horse. "If that's all right with you folks." Turner just blushed and looked away, and Marie studied the ground. Charley shook hands with the other four riders. "Here's what you do. This road will take you over three rivers, and after the third one you're in Arkansas. First town is Pocahontas. Good luck to you."

The men rode away as slowly as they had arrived, and the group watched them round the bend in the road. "That one fella's a bit of a hard case, ma'am," Pettibone said to Kathleen.

"I'm a bit of a hard case myself," she replied.

"I can see that, yes, ma'am."

Marie looked around and discovered that Turner had gone back to the fields and was once again hoeing a row of corn. "You may need to give Mr. Turner some extra time, Charley," she said.

"Oh, that's all right." Now that the other riders had disappeared, some of Charley's insouciance seemed to return. "I seen 'em get like that sometimes. Just need a little quiet." He lowered his voice to a whisper. "How about the other boys? Any news?"

"Colonel Carr was killed," Marie said. "Prentice, too, and Jesse Wilson. Haven't heard about anyone else."

Pettibone's face fell. "Good men, good men," he murmured. "We always had a thing we would say—you'd walk past a man who had fallen, and you'd say, 'Somebody's darling.' Not a superstition, really, just something you should say. Sort of the right thing to do."

Kathleen patted him on his arm, and in his face Marie could see the young whippersnapper who had first shown up at the colony as a fifteen-year-old orphan, his belongings in a bag over his shoulder, his fear papered over with bravado.

"You were a lot of places, then?" Marie said.

"Oh, yeah. Pea Ridge, Corinth, Pittsburg Landing, Atlanta, Chickamauga, all the way to Bentonville. Richmond in Kentucky, that was a good day for the Fighting Fifth."

"So what now?"

"Now, I start the rest of my life. Them boys, they were wanting to carry on the fight, but me, once I topped the hill to Daybreak I thought, the war's over. I'm done."

Some of Marie's animosity fell away from her, hearing the fatigue in Charley's voice. He was right. The war was over. Time to bandage wounds and try to rebuild. "Well, there's plenty to do around here, and plenty of empty houses. Pick one and move in. And maybe you can bring Mr. Turner out of himself a little."

"Anybody in Mr. Webb's old place?" Marie shook her head. "Maybe I'll plant myself there, if everybody in the colony agrees."

"We haven't had a community meeting in months. Perhaps you could just talk to Charlotte."

"All right," Pettibone said. "Don't really matter. I ain't exactly got a lot of possessions to put down anyplace."

As they spoke, the wagon came back across the river, with Charlotte and Michael Flynn side by side on the seat. Charlotte pulled up to where they stood and looked at Charley for a moment before recognizing him.

"Well, Charley Pettibone," she said. "You survived."

"All my arms and legs still on me, too," Pettibone said.

"This is Michael Flynn." The two men shook hands, although Marie noticed Charley eyeing Flynn's uniform coat with suspicion. "Mr. Flynn here has acquired forty acres across the river."

Flynn gave a tiny nod. Looking at Marie, he said, "I wasn't my proper self last time I spoke to you, miss. I should have thanked you better for watching

Angus all these years."

"No luck on your colony, then?"

To her surprise, Flynn covered his face with his hands, and when he pulled them away, his jaw was working. But his voice was steady. "No, miss. Not a soul, not a sign. Cabins gone to ruin. Don't know what happened to everyone."

"I'm sorry."

"I'd appreciate if you could watch him a little while longer, till I get a house built and land cleared. I'll pay you, once I get a crop sold."

"No need for that. I'm glad to have him."

"Charley, do you want to come back to Daybreak?" Charlotte said. "We need all the hands we can get. Maybe you and Mr. Flynn here could share housekeeping on one of the empty places."

"Yes, ma'am, I hope to come back," Charley said. "But I don't think I care to share quarters no more. Believe I might set up in Mr. Webb's old house."

"Well, that's fine," Charlotte said.

They parted then, each to their own direction. Marie returned home, where Angus was beginning to stir from his nap; she looked down at him as he rustled in his bed. So she would have him after all, at least for a while, and even when Flynn finished his house he would only be across the river. She smiled. So what if she wasn't really his mother? Blood wasn't the only kind of kinship in this world. The kinship of Daybreak was its own sort of blood, the commonality of people who shared ideas and aspirations. Angus was a good boy, helpful and sensitive, and she cared for him——that should count for something.

∽

Marie decided to spend the rest of the afternoon in the fields. Kathleen didn't need her help with supper. What the community needed was a good crop. This year, there might not be a cash crop, but at least they would be better nourished, and with the men returning, they could look forward to prosperity the next year, getting some livestock again, and who knows, maybe starting the rope mill. Kathleen was right. Things were on the mend.

She found a hoe in the barn and walked out to see where she could be of use. Several people were at work in the corn, so she decided to work on the potatoes. They were looking good; the community had managed to save enough potato eyes over the winter for a large field, and most had sprouted. The foliage was a deep, rich green, and so far no sign of potato bugs. They'd have to keep the children out here later in the summer, though.

Marie smiled to herself as she weeded around each hill. That Irishman and his 'I'll pay you, I'll pay you.' That was how most of the world thought, she guessed; nothing had value without a cash price. All buying and selling, getting and spending, as that poet said, whatever his name was. She was glad that she had grown up in the Icarian settlement and here in Daybreak, where at least they were making an effort to break free from those chains. Not that they were succeeding, but there was honor in the attempt. She reached the end of the row and stepped into the shade of an elm tree to cool off before working her way back.

That was when she noticed Turner walking toward her through the rows of potatoes, fast, his stride long and his face set. For a moment Marie feared that something had happened to Josephine, but Turner's expression was not anxious or frightened, just intent. He stopped about five feet in front of her.

"Run away with me," he said. His voice was hoarse. "I've been figuring it all out. We can go to California. I've got it all figured out. Run away with me."

She flung her hoe at him and ran.

Chapter 4

Turner woke early the next morning and headed out with his hoe before breakfast. He didn't feel like talking to anyone. He decided to work in the bean field farthest up the mountain, close to the forest's edge.

Work helped quiet the noise in his head, all the conflicting impulses and voices he was trying to sort out. Should he have said what he said to Marie? How could he have not? From outside it looked like madness, he knew—after all those years of war, of missing his home and family, within two weeks to declare his desire to abandon Charlotte and his sons and flee to the West with Marie. And in the waking day it felt like madness to him as well. But in the dark of night, and in his times of isolation in the fields, he felt a different sense of life, a sense that his ordinary wishes and desires were but masks of a deeper calling, one that came to him only in his visions and dreams. So Marie hadn't agreed to run away with him. Should he have expected anything different? At least she hadn't gone running to Charlotte. He'd had his say, and now she knew how he felt. Perhaps a few days, a few weeks, would change her mind. Perhaps she would think things over and see them a little differently.

Still, he wished he'd had the chance to tell her more, to tell her about *the moment*. If he had been able to tell her about *that*, she would have understood.

Strange. He could remember everything about the moment in perfect detail, except where it happened. It was in Virginia, that much he knew. Some engagement, a hill, late in the war. The main army had gone on ahead, and their job was to clean up, secure the lines, collect prisoners. And they had run across a hilltop of rebels, unexpectedly, dug in and not about to surrender.

He'd only been left with a couple of companies, and no artillery. But what had these rebs thought? That they could hold out? Or slip away when nightfall came? It was a fool's game, putting up resistance. They should have surrendered peacefully and gotten a good meal. But they didn't, and Turner had to lead his men up the hill.

It was one of those horrid Virginia brushpiles he'd come to hate, all greenbrier and rocks, steeper than any hill had a right to be in that part of the country, and no easy way up. The first fusillade from the hilltop caught several men who hadn't gotten low enough; standing up to drag them away was out of the question, so they had to let them lie, groaning in the rocks and underbrush. So it was to be a crawl.

The rebs stopped firing in unison after that first round and the rest of the afternoon passed in strange semi-silence, the grunting of men as they crept up the hill punctuated by the occasional roar of a rifle and sizzle of a Minie ball cutting the air. Turner lay on his belly behind a tree, thinking of his next move. There was a protruding rock four feet ahead; it should provide enough cover.

"Get up even with me and then hold," he called to the men beside him. "Pass it down."

He scrambled on knees and elbows to the rock. One shot flew over his head, but that was all. He heard scrambling and shots on both sides of him, and far away the thud of a ball on flesh. Twigs crackled overhead as his men returned the fire.

They were just going to have to stand up and make a climb of it, there was no option. He waited a few minutes behind his rock, his cheek pressed to the ground, while he waited for everyone to get into place.

"Fix bayonets," he said quietly to left and right.

As he waited, the moment came to him. His gaze, which had been fixed on nothing in particular as he lay there, suddenly came into clear focus. He felt as if he could see every leaf on every tree, every twig and branch, every flicker of sunlight. The smells of earth and gunpowder were sharp in his nostrils. A few inches away from his nose was a bloodroot flower. How could he not have noticed it before? It was still and perfect in the dappled shade, each white petal cupped in a soft green leaf like a sheltering hand. How could anything so luminous and holy exist in this place of murder?

It came to him that this was what passed through a man's mind when he was about to die—the sharpening of the senses, the awareness of the world's perfection and his own insignificance. So here it was, the moment of his death. And in that moment, the face that appeared before him was not that of Charlotte, or Newton, but of Marie Mercadier.

And in the next moment, a rock the size of a human head flew down from the hilltop and landed on the back of his left calf. The Goddamned graybacks were throwing rocks.

He loosed a cry, which he had meant to be a call to charge, but came out only as a throaty, wordless roar. He rose to his feet, rushing forward as well as he could up the slope, and felt more than saw that the rest of his men had done the same, charging in a fast-closing circle on the rebel breastworks. Rocks flew past his head; one hit him on the shoulder. He stopped long enough to fire and reload.

Turner supposed he should have realized the rebs weren't holding their fire but had simply run out of ammunition. Well, if they wanted to die here, he would oblige. The defenders were crafty, though, staying hidden behind their earthworks so his men had little to aim at.

When Turner's men reached the top, the Confederates leaped out of their works and down the hill with bayonets and swords and armloads of rocks, hoping to break through the cordon. There were surprisingly few of them. Directly in front of Turner, a man with a thick beard dashed out with a sword, yelling something unintelligible. For an instant they screamed their own mad wails as they closed, then Turner fired his rifle from his hip. It knocked the man backward, flailing the air with his sword; he slammed against a tree trunk and fell toward him with a look of wild hatred on his face. He landed on top of Turner, three-quarters dead, and they rolled down the hill in a tangle of wood, iron, wool, and blood. The back of Turner's head struck something, and for a minute he lost consciousness.

When he awoke he opened his eyes but could see nothing. His head was pointing downhill, and there seemed to be a weight that pushed him into the earth. He felt himself becoming part of the earth itself. A moment later, his consciousness returned further, and he realized the weight was that of the dead enemy lying atop him, still face to face, his beard scratching Turner's forehead and eyes. He gathered his strength and rolled over, sliding the dead soldier a few more feet downhill, and got to his hands and knees.

It was twilight. He could hear men crashing through the woods, although the gunfire had stopped.

"Down here!" he called.

"What side?" a voice above him shouted.

"Union," he said. "And there's a body."

Two men scrambled down the slope, and he could see that they were his. "It's the captain," one shouted. "Hey, boys, the captain's down here! You all right, sir?"

"I think so," Turner said. He rose to his knees. "I'll have some bruises."

"You ever seen anything like that?" said the man. "Chunking rocks and whatnot. I never seen anything like that."

"How'd we do?"

"Lost three, I think. Maybe more. Got ten bodies up here and yours makes eleven. Dozen or so prisoners and a bunch that got away."

They regrouped at the top of the hill and laid out the bodies, his men on one side and the rebels on the other. Turner put the men to work collecting names of the dead and setting up camp. The day seemed like a long, vivid dream, an early morning dream from which he was about to wake with a startled gasp of realization that it was not real after all, but just a sequence of strange, powerful images that would haunt him—the white flower, the ground pressed against his face, the man's expression, the sight of rocks flying out at them from the hilltop, and above all the vision of Marie Mercadier's face. He couldn't get it out of his mind. And as he collapsed into sleep that night he decided: he would return to Daybreak, return and claim Marie somehow, although how he would do it he had no idea. This day was a sign. He was meant to have her.

Turner had gotten so lost in remembering that moment—daydreaming, a watcher might have thought—that he was halfway down the row of beans before he came to himself again. He stopped and looked back to make sure he hadn't accidentally hoed up the beans themselves, but no, they were perfectly done, not a weed to be seen. And in the row behind him was another man, bent over, no hoe, but pulling weeds with swift efficiency.

He was a black man, and all Turner could see was the top of his tight-curled hair as he worked his way around each plant, stooped, dropping to one knee from time to time. Even on the warm May morning, he wore a heavy canvas coat that hung well over his wrists.

The man glanced up as he became aware of Turner watching him, then returned to his work as if nothing was odd.

"I can't pay you," Turner said. "I don't have any money to pay you."

The man worked on.

"I really mean that. I can't pay you."

The man shrugged.

Turner returned to his row, and for several minutes they worked in silence.

Finally the man said, "Never did care for a hoe. Always liked to be down where I could see."

"That right?"

The man shrugged and moved to the next plant. "Guess you must have been a field hand before the war, then," Turner said.

"Yessir. Still am one, I reckon," the man said.

"What's your name, then?"

The man cast a quick look at Turner, then looked away. "People call me Dathan," he said.

"Dathan, eh? Dathan what?"

"Just Dathan."

"Where'd you come from?"

With a flick of his eyes, Dathan looked east.

"That way? Bootheel? Tennessee? Maybe you had an owner down there, and that's your last name."

The answer came quickly. "Nosir. That ain't it. If I got a name, that ain't it, I know for sure. Just Dathan is all I need."

"Very well. My name is Turner." He extended his hand to shake, but Dathan displayed two handfuls of weeds and went back to his work.

They worked in silence for a few hours, until Turner grew thirsty. "Let's go to the spring," he said to Dathan, who wordlessly followed him to the springhouse. They sat on the cool rock slabs inside the building, Turner sipping from the gourd, while Dathan cupped his hands and drank directly from the pool.

"You're quite a worker," Turner said. "I'll make sure you get a good meal before you go. Where are you heading?"

Dathan looked at Turner and for the first time did not look away. His eyes were luminous, and his skin so dark it seemed to have a cast of purple beneath the brown. For the first time, Turner noticed that the man had a scar running across the width of his forehead. "Ain't headed nowhere in particular," he said. "Wherever the Lord sees fit to place me, I guess."

His gaze was disconcerting. Turner felt an eerie sense of recognition come over him. "Do I know you?" he said. "Have we met somewhere?"

"Now, that don't make no sense," Dathan said.

But Turner's feeling was getting stronger. "I think we have," he said. "I think we have." He looked into Dathan's eyes, hoping for insight. "But where?"

Dathan stood up and started for the springhouse door. "We got weeds to pull," he said.

A wild idea came to Turner's mind. "Did you ever try to run away with a man up this direction?" he asked. "A white man, kind of a crazy fellow? Seven years ago, maybe eight?"

"I ain't got no idea what you're talking about," Dathan said. "I ain't known no crazy white man."

"Yes," Turner said. The idea was becoming fixed in his mind. "And there were slave-catchers who followed, caught up with them ten miles or so south of here. They killed the abolitionist and took you back."

"I ain't got no idea," Dathan said.

"It's all right. I was there, that man was a friend of mine, or at least I knew him. I remember now."

"Maybe you got me mixed up."

Just then, the springhouse door opened, and Charley Pettibone walked in, mopping his brow with a bandana. His hair was dripping sweat off the ends. He stopped and blinked to clear his vision in the darkness of the springhouse.

"What the hell?" he exclaimed, catching sight of first Dathan and then Turner. Pettibone looked from one man to the other. "Who the hell is this?"

"Charley, this is Dathan," Turner said. "He's been up in the bean field with me this morning."

Pettibone's face clouded. "I ain't working with no nigger, Mr. Turner," he said. "I don't know what you're about here, but I ain't working, nor eating, nor living with one, either. I ain't in for that in no way, and that's that." He took the gourd from Turner's hand and looked suspiciously at it, as if it were part of a conspiracy as well.

Dathan had sidled his way to the door without speaking and was about to leave, but Pettibone held his arm. "Slave or free, you're still a nigger, and don't forget it," he said.

"Charley, this man just showed up and started working, and did a fine job of it, too," Turner said. Pettibone wordlessly filled the gourd from the spring and drank, ignoring him. Turner thought about pressing the matter but decided against it; of course Charley's feelings would still be raw. Dathan was right; there were beans to hoe. He could change the world another day. When he turned to leave, Dathan had disappeared.

Turner found him back in the fields, working on the next row. "Sorry about that," he muttered.

"Ain't nothing," Dathan said.

"Charley is a good man, and this is a good place," he said. "He's just—he fought on the other side in the war, and I guess he carries that around. It'll take us all a while to get over it."

"Yessir," Dathan said, without looking up. He said nothing else; his voice was flat and bland, and in that simple phrase, Turner felt as if he could hear the opening of a vast gulf, a gap the size of an ocean and just as unnavigable. Wasn't this what they had hoped to eradicate, this inequality of man and man? And here it was as strong and fierce as ever.

"We have empty houses," Turner said, not quite knowing what he was going to say next. "A lot of our boys didn't come back from the war, so three houses up on the north side of the village are sitting empty. Maybe you can stay a while."

Dathan kept working in silence. Turner wondered if he had crossed a line. They reached the end of their rows and stopped to straighten. In the woods across the river they could see leaves shaking and hear the *chok* of an axe; that man Flynn was clearing ground in the forty acres that the community had sold him.

"You own them houses?" Dathan said.

"Not exactly," said Turner. "We all do."

"Thought so."

From the Temple, Mrs. Wickman stepped out with a wooden spoon in her hand and walked to a sheet of tin they had recovered from a burned-out house down the valley. She banged on the tin, sending a clanging roll of sound through the village.

"Let's eat," Turner said. "Then two more rows and we're done." He laid his hoe aside and began to walk down the hill.

"I'll just find me a shady spot, I think," Dathan said. "Have me some more of that good spring water."

Before they got to the village, Dathan veered off the path and headed for the river. "I'll be over here," he said.

Inside the hall, Turner filled a heaping plate of beans and cornbread. Seeing Charlotte's questioning look, he stepped to the side of the room with her.

"There's a man outside. He's worked with me all morning." He could not hide the excitement in his voice. "I think it's the man Lysander Smith was trying to escape with."

"Did he tell you this?"

"No. He's being very guarded. But I recognize him."

"Are you sure?"

Turner paused. "Yes. I'm sure of it."

"Why did he come here?"

"I don't know. Like I said, he holds his thoughts close." Turner thought for a moment longer, then decided to let it out. "Charlotte, I want this man to stay here for a while. I feel like I owe him something. I want him to stay in one of the empty houses."

She looked out at the group of people eating their meal in the Temple, then back at Turner. Then she took the plate from his hand. "Let's go meet this man. What's his name?"

"Dathan."

Charlotte squinted. "Odd choice."

Together they walked down the center street of Daybreak. "He's around here somewhere," Turner said. And sure enough, there was Dathan, sitting by the river in the grove of cottonwood trees just south of the old hemp mill, watching the water flow by. The old mill was nothing but a wooden frame now. All the metal parts had been scavenged, except for the wheel in the river, idly turning in its frame. Charlotte handed him the plate as he scrambled to his feet.

"Sit down, sit down," she said. "I hear you've been working hard this morning."

"I do my best, ma'am," Dathan said. He didn't sit down again, but ate standing.

"Dathan, eh? How'd you ever get that name?"

"Don't know, ma'am. Just come with me, I guess."

"Back in the slave days? Master give it to you?"

"Can't say as I know anything about that, ma'am."

"My husband here thinks he might have seen you before, some years ago."

"I told him, ma'am, don't think he remembers too good."

"It's not a crime, you know, running away. Not anymore. That whole life is over and done with."

"Yes, ma'am." But he said no more.

Charlotte sized him up. "So, you're a good hand in the fields?"

"Oh, yes, ma'am. Real steady, is what they say. Ain't fast. Real steady."

"Well, we're short, as you can probably tell. Here's what. You stay and get us through the season, there's a roof over your head and food, and we all share in what's brought in at the end. How's that sound?"

Dathan had finished his last spoonful of beans and was mopping up the juice with the cornbread. "Sounds fine, ma'am."

"All right, then. Bring your things this evening and we'll pick out an empty house." She took the empty plate from his hand and turned to go. "James, I suppose we need to get you a meal, too."

As they returned to the Temple, Turner said eagerly, "You will not regret this. I am sure of it."

She gave him a sidelong look, and in that glance Turner imagined that she was thinking of the many times when he had rushed into things, and the regrets that had come of them. But he said nothing. Of course she was right. She was always right. And that was what tired him out so, sometimes. Yes, he acted impulsively, and yes, perhaps this man was not the beaten slave he had glimpsed so long ago. And yes, only this morning he had been daydreaming of Marie, and thinking to act impulsively again, to fly the roost entirely. So he was wrong, wrong, wrong. He was the wrong man for them all, no leader, not even a proper soldier, hardly the man whose judgment could be trusted in even the small things. He had led them all to this place, he had led men to their deaths, he would probably lead them all astray again if given the chance. The hell with it. Responsibility was for those who craved it, and he no longer did.

Charlotte seemed to sense his changing mood. She took his hand before they went inside. "Regrets or no, I'm glad to be here with you."

But it was too late. He didn't care if she was glad or not.

Chapter 5

The twentieth stroke was the final one. Michael Flynn put his foot against the trunk and pushed hard, and the tree began to topple—slow, uncertain, then sure as death once the weight of its branches began to pull it down. He looked around as it fell; where was Angus? Just like the boy to put himself in its path, daydreaming, and then no doubt everyone would point their fingers, the madman Flynn, pinned his own son beneath a tree. But the boy was off the other direction. Good.

This one was too small to use for building, maybe one log out of the main trunk, maybe not even that. Had to be cleared anyway. This was going to be the garden plot, good level ground, well watered, although right now it was covered in briars and clumps of grass. The soil was sandy but could be improved.

He had it all in his mind. The spot where his tent was pitched—that was where the cabin would go. It was shady, set back a little from the river, but close enough to fetch water. Between the cabin and the river, the garden. He would fence in the house and garden, and then downstream he would build a barn and a hog lot.

Damn hard way to make any money. So be it. If the Irish colony had lasted through the war, he would have had friends to help him and men to spend time with. And he would have had Aideen. But what point was there to looking backward? It just opened the door to tears and mourning, and what use of that? Bemoaning fate was for fools.

His mother had been a great believer in fate, the poor girl, or God's will as she called it. Same thing, all meek acceptance and praying for the strength to take the kicks. She would have stayed in Ireland to starve, their lives whittled down a little smaller every year, until famine or the landlord's man finally took them all.

His father was the one who had gotten them out and to America, with him as just a boy no good for anything, not even as old as Angus there, and his brothers yet to be born, in the grimy hold of a ship bound for Wilmington, and the only good thing about the darkness of the ship was that it kept them from knowing just how filthy their conditions were. His father's notion of God's will included the prospect that God might will a man to take himself in hand and make a better life by his own sweat, and from Wilmington to Pittsburgh to St. Louis they did just that. Not a better life that one could tell from outward appearances but in tiny ways, always through hard labor and thrift, and when his father had died under a collapse of railroad iron in 1855, Flynn had imagined that he might have died happy, knowing he had left behind a houseful of sons to care for his widow and the prospect of grandchildren to carry his name into the next century.

The idea had been for Michael, the oldest, to travel to Father Hogan's colony, claim the land, clear it, then bring Aideen, then his mother, then the brothers one by one. Landowners. Who would have imagined them landowners? But then the diphtheria took his mother, the war scattered the boys, and Aideen was lost to something, the letter didn't say what. Starvation from the raiders, that's what he figured. He'd done it himself in the march to the sea, taken the last bag of cornmeal from a family and turned them out to root. Was it any wonder how much hate they all felt?

The next tree was a good big one, some kind of big-leafed thing. He wasn't about to pretend to forest knowledge; a tree was a tree. Flynn's Army blues were soaked with sweat, top and bottom, but he hefted his axe to swing. He paused.

"Angus!"

He hated the harsh sound of his voice, like the sound of a barrel being dragged over rocks. But, by God, that boy was a trial. Always off piddling at something, tossing sticks in the river.

"Angus!"

"Here I am." Walking up with a snakeskin in his hand. Enough to make a man sick, handling snakes.

Steve Wiegenstein

"Jesus is Lord, boy, where did you get that thing?"

"Found it."

"Found it I know, but where?"

"Down by the water."

"Well, throw it away. It ain't clean."

"It's just a little old skin. Probably a garter snake."

"I told you once."

The boy laid the snakeskin carefully in the grass. Flynn knew he would be coming back for it when his back was turned.

"Come on. I have work for you."

He pulled a hatchet from the pile of tools he kept in the clearing and led Angus to the fallen tree. "Chop off these limbs and drag them over there. Make a pile." The hatchet was too big for the boy's hand, so Flynn showed him how to hold it with both. "Stand across the tree from the limb so you don't glance off and cut off your leg," he said. Seeing Angus's frightened look, he quickly added, "Just a joke, lad. You're not going to cut anything off. I'll be right here."

He returned to felling his big tree while Angus started on the limbs of the small one, too smart to grumble but moving slowly. All right, the boy was small and hungry, but he couldn't expect to sit in the tent or wander the woods all afternoon. Flynn let him cross the river to his precious schoolhouse in the mornings, but after noon, by God, there was work aplenty—not just clearing the trees, but building, gathering rocks, turning soil. At that age he had been picking rags off the streets of Pittsburgh and selling the bundles to the neighborhood ragman, bringing the pennies home to the family. No room for loafers.

The more he thought about the work ahead, the harder he swung the axe. He felt as if the tree itself was his enemy. Bring it down fast and hard, no holding back, no stopping for thought. By God, old Sherman had been like that. It had been a pleasure to serve under Sherman. Swing the axe, never slack. And the next thing you knew, the tree was down and you were moving to the next one. Hit hard, then harder, then harder yet.

But this tree was hollow, and the weight of its limbs began to pull it down before Flynn was ready. He called out to Angus, who scampered away as the trunk splintered about five feet up and fell toward the river, opposite to where he wanted it to fall.

"Damnation!" Flynn spat out. No logs for the cabin out of this mess, just more dead wood to be cleared away. What the hell.

Perhaps the crash of the tree had obscured the sound of his approach, or perhaps the man was just exceptionally quiet, but suddenly Flynn became aware of a man on horseback who had appeared in his clearing. He was a small man, slender with thin black whiskers, and he seemed to have come from the north, working his way through the brush alongside the river. Tied to his saddlehorn was a rope; the other end of the rope looped in several secure knots around the neck and shoulders of a thin sow.

"Afternoon," said the man. Flynn nodded.

The man looked around. "Didn't know you all had expanded across the river."

"If you mean that colony of characters over there, they didn't," Flynn said. "I'm on my own hook here, bought forty from 'em."

"I see," the man said. Flynn could tell that he was eyeing his Army uniform. "This was Harp Webb's land, before he died."

"I wouldn't know about that," Flynn said.

The man rested in his saddle and gazed across the river. "I expect you wouldn't. You don't sound like you're from around here." Flynn didn't reply. "I'll sell you this pig," the man said at last.

"You come by it honest?"

"It was wandering in my woods, and it ain't got no notch in the ear, so I figure it's mine," he said. "I was going to take it to my cousin's, but I'd just as soon not make the trip."

Flynn walked back to look at the sow. It was a young one, two or three, he guessed, and seemed healthy. "Maybe," he said.

"Five dollars," the man said.

"Five dollars!"

"Hogs has gone up." The man continued to gaze across the river, paying no attention to Flynn.

"Maybe they have, but it don't matter to me if I ain't got five dollars. Three."

"Make it four, then."

"All right. Hold on." Flynn walked to his tent and crawled inside. His knapsack was at the far end, rolled up in blankets; he unwrapped it and removed four greenbacks. No need to count the rest of the roll; he knew there wasn't much left.

"You ain't got any gold certificates?" the man said. Flynn shook his head. "Well, I guess I'll take it. Don't trust this paper money, though. You people won the war, you get to make the money."

"You fought on the other side, then."

He shrugged, and as if in sympathy his horse shook its shoulders as well. "I did indeed. All up and down this part of the state. Arkansas, too. I was a major by the time it was all over."

"Not regular Army, then." The man didn't answer. Should have figured him for a guerrilla, Flynn thought. "Well, past is past. I'll buy your hog." He untied the ropes around the hog, which immediately dashed off into the underbrush as soon as it was free. "Well, shit."

"I wouldn't worry about that too much," the man said. "Just put out some corn and it'll come back to you."

"You keep looking over at the colony," Flynn said. "Ain't you going over there?"

"Don't know," the man said. "I've got history with them. Like you say, the past is past, but I don't care to open things up if I don't have to."

"So what's your history?"

"They tried to kill me, I tried to kill them, that sort of thing." The man looked down at Flynn, and his gaze was cold. "Funny thing. A year ago I would have killed you by now."

"Or vice versa," Flynn said.

The man shrugged. "Something like that. Anyway, I don't look behind me. But I don't like to stir things up, either. Maybe I'll just ride down to the riverbank and take a look." He twitched the horse forward over the scattered branches. Flynn, axe in hand, wondered whether to follow or to return to his work; he decided to follow. He would need to cross the river and borrow a bucket of corn anyway. The rider paid him no mind.

On the riverbank, the man sat still on his horse behind a clump of bushes, gazing impassively across the quiet water. Flynn could hear the voices of children.

"Angus," Flynn said, quietly, for he knew the boy was near. Angus appeared at his elbow.

"Go up to the ford, cross over, and borrow a bucket of corn from Mr. Turner. Careful when you cross back. Keep it dry."

"Turner made it through, eh?" the man said, not looking around. "Still in charge?"

"He made it through. Made captain, too, or some such, I'm told. But I wouldn't say he's in charge. I don't think he came through with a whole mind.

He just tends his crops nowadays. If anyone's in charge, I'd say it's the missus."

The man squinted appreciatively. "Wouldn't surprise me. That lady has more gumption than most of the men I've known. Well, enough of this."

With an imperceptible touch of the reins, the man urged his horse south along the riverbank.

"Ain't no trail down that way," Flynn said.

"I know. But there's a way through." He stopped and looked back at Flynn. "That Daybreak colony is good people, even if they have funny ideas," he said. "Get to know them. And tell them Sam Hildebrand said hello."

"So you're Hildebrand the raider?"

The man turned his horse and faced Flynn squarely. "I am."

"I have a question for you, then."

"All right."

Flynn noticed that the axe in his hands felt strangely heavy all of a sudden. "Did you raid that Irish colony south of here, forty, fifty miles? Out past Doniphan?"

Hildebrand's face was still. A squirrel rattled leaves somewhere nearby. "No," he said.

They faced each other. Hildebrand finally broke the silence.

"How many men you figure you killed in the war, Irish?" he said.

"I have no idea. I march, I shoot, I sleep. I put a bayonet in a few, so them I guess I know. The rest, who knows? Half the time, your rifle don't even go off when you've got a man in your sights. I don't know."

"That's for the best, I suppose," Hildebrand said. "A man doesn't need to know that kind of thing. Me, it's eighty-six. Eighty-six. Most of them with my own hand. Rifle, pistol, rope. Knife. So I guess when I go to Hell, I'll have eighty-six devils ready for me." He turned his horse to the south again. "Good luck with your acreage."

Flynn measured the distance between them and knew that if he tried to take Hildebrand off his horse with the axe, he would be dead with twenty feet still to go; the man was bound to be armed, even if he couldn't see the weapon. But he could smell out this rebel's lies as sure as sunset. He didn't raid the Irish colony? In a pig's eye. For all Flynn knew, he had just bought a hog from the murderer of his own Aideen.

A blindness passed over him for a moment, and he felt he was dashing toward the retreating horse, leaping over its tail with the ferocity of those eighty-six devils, cleaving the man's head from his shoulders in a mighty swing.

His eyes rolled toward the sky and he heard himself breathe. But when he looked around again, he was standing in the same spot, the axe still heavy and unbloodied in his hands, and Hildebrand was gone.

He turned and strode back to the fallen tree.

By evening he had felled five more trees and cut them up, with half a dozen new logs to go to the cabin and a great mass of limbs to use for fencing and firewood. As he cleared, he had come across a big cedar tree, and beneath the cedar tree a mound of earth and a wooden gravemarker, painted with a man's name in black ink. Cunningham. So he had not only bought a farm, but a graveyard as well. So be it.

Chapter 6

First came a spring wagon drawn by a pathetic-looking livery stable mare, with a servant driving it, a slender, silly-looking young man in a striped shirt and suspenders. His face was badly pocked, but Charlotte couldn't tell if it was from disease or just bad pimples.

"Are you the innkeeper in these parts, madam?" the young man said, tipping his hat only the slightest fraction. "My name is Cowling. The children at that intersection seemed to think you were the person I should speak to."

"There are no inns in these parts," Charlotte said. "I believe those children were having some fun with you."

The young man looked stricken. "Oh, my," he said. "Oh my. This will not do. This is not good at all. Mrs. Smith is a half day behind me, or less. And her entire company as well. How far to the next hotel?"

Charlotte smiled at him. "A hundred and fifty miles, more or less."

"Oh, my," Cowling repeated.

"Don't worry," Charlotte said. "We can put you up for the night."

"You don't understand, madam. I serve a woman of the most exacting tastes. Mrs. Smith is accustomed to life's finer things, God bless her, and our travels of the last few weeks have not been easy. I knew we wouldn't find a Girard House out here in the woods, but surely someplace decent—a good meal, a clean bed—" He sighed extravagantly.

At the man's mention of the Girard House, Charlotte felt an eerie chill. "Where is your Mrs. Smith from, exactly?" she said.

"Philadelphia," said the servant. "The Smiths of Philadelphia are well known. Perhaps even in these regions."

"And your Mrs. Smith is related to Lysander Smith, who came out here some years ago?"

Now it was the servant's turn to cast an uncertain look. "She is his mother."

"Then she is welcome here for as long as she cares to stay," Charlotte said. "Lysander Smith lived here for the last several months of his life. He is buried up there." She pointed to the graveyard on the hill.

"Then this is the town of Daybreak?"

Charlotte nodded. "We have reached our end, then," Cowling said. "Mrs. Smith will be pleased."

Charlotte set about showing him the empty cabins on the north end of the village; Cowling shuddered and groaned as they walked from house to house, the log cabins empty and dark, their chinking grown loose as the logs shrunk dry. But all the while she was thinking of Smith, the doomed, foolish young man who had disrupted their lives before the war with his play-party abolitionism and his idle arrogance that masked his deeper secrets. Charlotte wondered how much this man Cowling knew of Lysander's end——his roaming into the cities and towns in search of unholy liaisons, the savage beating and lynching at the hands of a gang of slave-catchers, more for his sexual misdeeds than his political ones. All too much, she suspected. Cowling's pomposity was that of a servant who fancied himself the superior of his superiors.

"Just how many people are coming with your mistress, all told?" Charlotte said.

"Let's see," Cowling said, pursing his lips. "There's Jenny, the little Irish girl. She tends to Mrs. Smith's person. Mrs. Orr, the cook. Sally Ann, her helper. The boy Jimmy who runs errands for me. And on this trip we have Mr. Wilkinson along."

Charlotte was about to ask who Mr. Wilkinson was, but the arrival of the stranger had attracted attention in the village; the children had spread the news, and now adults were drifting over, trying not to appear too nosy, but drifting near nonetheless. Only Emile Mercadier, whose age gave him the freedom to be bold, walked directly toward them, guided by the sound of their voices, Charlotte guessed.

"I hear we have someone among us," he said, peering in Cowling's direction. "Welcome to Daybreak, sir. I am Emile Mercadier, one of the originals." He extended his hand.

Cowling shook his hand. "Thank you. My name is Cowling, sir."

"Have you come to write about us, then?"

"I don't know what you mean."

Mercadier's face fell. "You are not from the *Evening Post*? Mr. Nordhoff from the *Evening Post* has been corresponding with me."

"I am here in service of Mrs. Francis Smith, of Philadelphia, whose arrival is impending. Mrs. Smith is the mother of Lysander Smith. Perhaps that name is known to you."

"Ah! Lysander." Mercadier sighed. "Poor lad. Bad end, there. Something of a rake, yes, but still, there's no deserving that kind of end. His mother, you say?"

"Yes," Cowling said stiffly. "And I must ask you to consider her sensibilities when you speak of his end, please."

"Of course, of course," Mercadier said. "Fine violin the boy played. I am sorry for my error. I thought you might be the correspondent from the *Evening Post* or the *Tribune*. I have been writing to them quite regularly, you know."

"I didn't know that," Charlotte said.

"Oh, yes! Quite often. The story of Daybreak, you see. It's very significant, I think."

Mercadier appeared ready to go into a great deal more detail about his theories of the community, but Marie appeared around the corner of the cabin. "There you are! You worry me so, wandering off like this." She paused and nodded to the group. "Excuse me. I was seeking for my father."

Cowling swept his hat off his head, bowing from the waist with such an exaggerated show of politeness that Charlotte had to cover her mouth. "No interruption, no interruption at all, miss. Your father was just explaining to us—just telling us—"

"This is Miss Mercadier," Charlotte said. "Marie, this is Mr. Cowling."

Charlotte's amusement left her as Cowling bowed again, even lower, and a bitter taste filled her mouth. Trust the pretty girl to get all the notice. This Mr. Cowling might not be so attentive after little Josephine came strolling up, as she so often did, quiet as mice and just as alert. The little bastard child would put a stop to his gallantry, or turn it in another direction, perhaps—

No sooner had the thought passed through her mind than she regretted it bitterly. The child was not to blame for her parentage; Charlotte had always vowed never to bring up the accident of her birth, or even give it thought. But here she was, pouncing on it like a village biddy, and for what reason? Because a serving man made a swooping bow? The history of the great Daybreak indeed, and its beneficent influence on human nature. More like how human nature persisted in its worn, wicked paths despite all their efforts.

"Mr. Cowling is here in preparation for a visit by Mrs. Smith, the mother of Lysander Smith," Charlotte said, recovering her composure. "You remember Lysander Smith, of course."

At the mention of Smith's name, an ill-concealed look of distaste passed over Marie's face, reminding Charlotte of what a boorish and unpleasant man Lysander Smith had been, sad end or none. They exchanged glances in silent understanding, and Marie smiled to cover her grimace and said nothing. At least she had the courtesy not to speak, Charlotte thought.

Marie's presence still bothered Charlotte. She tried to avoid her as much as she could, especially at moments like this, when it was impossible to ignore the fact that Marie was young and pretty and that men were drawn to her. She knew these feelings brought out a side of her she did not like—the judgmental, snappish side, the side that made the villagers in Daybreak duck away from her when it emerged. It wasn't that she was hard on purpose; inside, the idealistic young woman who had thrown in with James and founded a community in the wilderness was still there. But James's fall, and Adam's death, and most of all the war had pushed that woman below the surface. Her hide had grown tough. But beneath that hide, she knew the old Charlotte still remained—hopeful, tender, and all too vulnerable. She wondered if the new, hard world, all sharp edges and cruelty, would ever allow that woman to reemerge.

Charlotte was about to say something to try to relieve the silence when the distant sound of a trumpet broke through the air. It pierced the quiet of the afternoon with a series of random, unconnected notes.

"That will be Jimmy," Cowling said. "He can't keep himself away from that thing."

They looked across the river to where the road from town descended the hill on the opposite side, and they could see two wagons making the slow passage. Even from this distance, Charlotte could tell they were heavily laden, the first wagon a big landau with the back roof folded down, and the second one smaller, a trap, with trunks and parcels tied onto the sides as well as piled in among the passengers.

"I must ride back with the news," Cowling said. "Ladies." He tipped his hat again and rushed off to fetch his horse.

The women watched him dash away, while Emile stood quiet, listening.

"Lysander Smith," Marie said thoughtfully, as if reciting a name she was uncertain how to pronounce.

"Bad end, that boy," repeated Emile.

By now, the word had spread through the village. Townspeople gathered in the street in knots of two and three, craning their necks to see as the wagons made their way into view.

Again a banished thought washed over Charlotte—she wished Adam Cabot were still alive and here today. Most of the time she kept thoughts of him from her mind, since thoughts of the impossible, the never-was, and the never-would-be, only brought pain. Why poke a wound that had mostly healed? Lost people, lost possibilities. But Adam would know how to greet this society lady, what to say to her about her lost son. They had always been able to count on Adam.

She shook off the chill that passed through her and turned away, unwilling to let anyone—especially Marie—see the look of exhaustion and sadness she knew shadowed her face. If she was going to have a silly moment of woe come from out of nowhere, she would have it in private.

The wagons crossed the ford and came into the village. In the first one was a woman in a black dress and bonnet, propped up in the back on an elaborate arrangement of pillows and supports, facing backward. She was enormous, her face wide and jowly, spreading into an even thicker neck that likewise spread downward into a wide, monstrous body that seemed to fill the entire wagon bed. Her face wore a mask of deep disdain, and from the wagon there came a strange mélange of aromas, herbal and bitter and musky all at once. In the second wagon, an older woman rode beside the driver, and in the back sat two young women and a boy—the trumpet-blowing Jimmy, no doubt, Charlotte thought. An older man with a gray face and a sour expression rode horseback behind them all.

The wagons pulled into the open area in front of the Temple and stopped. The people drew closer, but no one spoke.

"Well?" the woman boomed. "Is this how you greet your guests?"

For once, Charlotte could not find anything to say.

"Mrs. Smith," came a voice.

It was Turner, pushing his way from the back of the crowd. He had managed to get to their house and put on his frock coat, and he even seemed to have put a shine on his hat somehow. He reached the wagon and removed his hat, placing it over his heart. "Please forgive me. I was in the farthest field when news of your arrival reached me."

Turner bowed to the old woman. "I am James Turner," he said, and Charlotte could hear the old strain of oratory in his voice, the voice of that lyceum lecturer who had captivated thousands. "Perhaps Mr. Foltz of Quincy has mentioned my name to you. Lysander spoke of you endlessly, and I am honored to have you among us. I am the man who brought Lysander to this valley, and I am the man who saw him meet his end." He lowered his head and appeared to meditate. "And with every day that I rise, I wish by all that is holy that I would have been able to return him to you healthy and whole. And I regret with all my being that I did not."

He held out his hand. "May I help you down?"

But Mrs. Smith did not take his hand immediately; she covered her face with her handkerchief and held it there, still, and for a long silent moment they all waited. Then the old woman lowered the handkerchief to reach out her hand to Turner's, and when she did her cheeks were wet, her eyes fixed on Turner.

There was someone, after all, who would know just what to say, and Charlotte felt ashamed for not remembering. It was her James, her own foolish, flawed, beloved Mr. Turner returning to himself for a moment, with so many of his own best parts buried or lost, and when Charlotte herself turned away, it was not to shield Mrs. Smith's tears from her prying gaze, but to hide her own.

Chapter 7

Marie Mercadier stood in the doorway of her cabin in the early morning, trying to decide what to do first. The mornings had begun to turn cool; the leaves on the elm tree that overhung the cabin had already yellowed. Josephine was still asleep inside, and Papa, to whom day and night no longer differed much, had gotten up an hour ago, groping his familiar path to the barn to start work.

Cowling, the manservant to Mrs. Smith, emerged from the front door of the cabin next to her, his waistcoat unbuttoned and his long hair flying in several directions from beneath his hat. He smiled and bowed, but Marie ignored him; no one put on airs like a servant, and she had no intention of encouraging them. Cowling stepped around the corner of his house, and within seconds Marie was treated to the sound of him pissing against his cabin wall. Apparently modesty had not yet come to Philadelphia. A minute later, Cowling reappeared and went back inside. Marie looked in the opposite direction.

The Philadelphia group had taken the last two empty cabins at the north of the village, Mrs. Smith in the northernmost with her maid Jenny sleeping in the front room, and everyone else in the other, men in the front, women in the back. So as summer moved into fall, Marie found herself with a strange new set of neighbors on both sides—the silent Dathan in the cabin just to the south of her, appearing and disappearing like a foxfire with no words beyond the occasional remark on the weather, and Mrs. Smith's retinue to the north.

Marie paid little attention in either direction. Between her father, the school, and her work for the colony, she had enough to do. But she was aware of them all the time, the coming and going, and she liked the activity. Like the humming of a beehive, it reassured her, made her feel as if life was getting back to normal, as if the war hadn't changed everything and everyone. It was an illusion, of course; she knew that. But it was nice to imagine in the mornings that Daybreak was back to the way it was, all optimism and hope, thoughts of the common good, everyone's effort turned toward making the colony prosper.

Turner's mad declaration had stunned her, but thankfully he had not repeated it. But his return made her uncomfortable for another reason—it reminded her of older days, the days before exposure, and shame, and Josephine. She would never admit it to the townsfolk, but she missed the touch of a man. She rarely allowed herself to remember those times—alone with Turner, hiding in an outbuilding or stealing moments in the print shed, or on the rare trips to town, talking, kissing, letting his hands rove over her body. Those were memories too painfully precious to be let out willy-nilly. But she had not forgotten what she was missing. And now that silent figure out in the fields, more the ghost of James Turner than the actual Turner himself—had she really loved that man? Of course she had, or the man he had been.

Not that she was pining for him. Marie wondered if she should have gone straight to Charlotte after his awkward overture and let the two of them sort themselves out, but what good would that have done? Just more turmoil, perhaps Turner doing something else irrational, and pain all around, especially for the children. No, better to hold that knowledge to herself.

And there was Charley Pettibone hanging around, trying to be funny. Charley was a well-favored young man, in years barely more than a boy, really, although anyone who had been to the war for four years could hardly be called a boy. Once she could have imagined letting Charley charm her; but now there were times when she could hardly stand to look at him. He was a rebel and a traitor, a man who had crossed a solemn line, and as far as she was concerned that step once taken could not be undone. Everyone could talk about general amnesties and oaths of loyalty, but she could no more let him spark her than Jefferson Davis.

So there it was. Men all around, but none of them right. At twenty-seven, she was still marriageable, but barely. Perhaps it was not her fate to marry. Perhaps her task in life was to care for these children that chance had placed into her care—Josephine, and orphaned Angus, and the schoolchildren, Newton and Adam, the Wickman girls, and the rest. If it was, so be it. The life of man and woman would have to remain a foreign country to her, one that she had visited briefly but now could only see from the coast of her own, through fog.

Cowling appeared out of his cabin again, combed and properly dressed, smiling unctuously, and came toward her. No choice but to acknowledge him now. She nodded in his direction, wishing that she had put a kettle on the stove, or anything else to provide an easy escape.

"It's a beautiful morning, miss," he said.

"I suppose so."

"What, you doubt it?"

"The day has just begun. I'm not calling it beautiful until I've seen more of it."

"Ah, you're a hard case. No romance in that pretty head of yours?"

Cowling's flirting annoyed her. She turned to go inside, but he caught her arm. "Actually, I'm supposed to give you a message from my mistress. She instructed me to deliver it last night, but I couldn't find you."

Marie turned back to him. "Very well. What is it?"

"How about if you tell me where I can find you at night in case I need to deliver more messages?" he simpered. Marie did not respond. "I'll tell you this, little missy. The Smiths are one of the first families of Philadelphia, so take my advice. Say the right things to Mrs. Smith, and you'll go far."

"So what is the message?"

"She wants to talk to you today. You and Mrs. Turner. She wants you both to come see her at teatime."

"Teatime?"

"Tea and tonic, if you know what I mean." Cowling made a face and leaned toward her. "Mrs. Smith always has her tonic, morning, noon, teatime, and bedtime." He mimicked the tipping of a bottle.

"What does she want to see us about?"

"That's for her to say. But you'll do well to let me guide you on the right things to say."

"I need to get my firewood," Marie said, brushing past Cowling and walking around the side of her cabin. "Thank you for the message."

But Cowling followed her behind the cabin, and once they were out of sight of the village he grabbed her around the waist. "How about a little kiss, little missy?" He pressed his face against hers. "I hear the girls out here are a wild lot."

Marie pushed against him, but he held tight. "Come on, little missy, just one," he said. His breath was hot and sour against her cheek.

There was a sharp crack, and Cowling sprung away from her, looking around wildly. Dathan was standing behind his cabin, twenty feet away, with a long branch of wood, perhaps two inches thick, in his hands. He had one end wedged in the fork of a tree and was breaking the branch into smaller pieces.

"Go away, you," Cowling said. "We're busy here."

Dathan inserted the branch into the tree fork and broke off another piece.

"I said go away!"

Dathan looked over at them calmly and broke the branch in two another time. He tossed one of the pieces onto his woodpile but kept the other one in his hand.

"That your house?" he said to Cowling.

Marie took the opportunity to walk past Cowling to the front of her own house. "Good morning, Dathan," she said.

"Morning, ma'am. Nice day ahead."

"I believe so, Dathan." She stepped inside her cabin and shut the door. She counted three seconds and went to the window; Cowling was nowhere to be seen, and Dathan had returned to breaking up his firewood. He glanced in her direction; she gave a tentative wave from the window, but if he saw, he gave no sign.

Marie went about the rest of her day trying to keep the morning's unpleasant scene out of her mind. It wasn't hard; she spent the morning in the Temple with the children, teaching arithmetic and penmanship, and the early afternoon in the cornfields. Work was always there to keep her mind elsewhere. Then as the sun was declining, she saw Charlotte approaching through the rows of corn and knew that the time for their visiting Mrs. Smith had come. She stopped work and wiped her face as Charlotte drew near.

"So," Charlotte said.

"So."

"Any idea?" Marie shook her head. "Well, let's go see, then."

The two of them left the field and walked toward the village. "Just a minute," Marie said as they reached the road. She stopped at the pump and wet a handkerchief to wipe her face. "There," she said. "Even bumpkins can be clean."

They knocked at the cabin door, where Jenny, Mrs. Smith's maid, let them in, ushered them into the back room, and then retired. She was a timid girl of seventeen who never met their eyes, skinny with pale skin and straight black hair that she tied into a tight knot in back. She wore a wrinkled housedress with a faint calico print, probably a hand-down from someone in Mrs. Smith's family. A pretty girl if she would tend to herself, Marie imagined, although she seemed determined not to tend to herself.

Mrs. Smith was propped up on her bed in the back room, an array of tables and pillows surrounding her. Despite the stale air of the closed room, she was encased in dresses and a bonnet, and partly covered with a blanket. With a tired flick of her hand, she waved them to two chairs at the foot of the bed. Mr. Wilkinson, the dour, gray man who had not spoken to anyone as far as Marie knew, stood at the head. A platter of crackers and two cups of tea sat on a table between the chairs.

Charlotte and Marie sat down. The room was silent for a minute.

"Well, here you are," Mrs. Smith finally said. Marie had decided to let Charlotte take the lead, so when Charlotte did not answer she kept still as well. "You have met Mr. Wilkinson, I suppose." Wilkinson removed his hat and nodded to them. "You have probably been wondering why we traveled all the way to this place."

"Your son's grave is here," Charlotte said. "It's quite understandable."

With the mention of her son, Mrs. Smith gave another feeble wave of her hand. "You have no idea," she said. "No idea what a burden I carry." She groped on the table beside her. "Jenny!"

Jenny dashed through the door with a drinking glass half filled with water. She took a bottle labeled "Parker's Tonic" from the table and stirred some into the water.

"No idea," Mrs. Smith repeated, drinking a gulp of the tonic. "No one has any idea." She drank another swallow. "But I must be strong. I have come here for a purpose, not merely to sit at the graveside and mourn." She gestured at Wilkinson. "Mr. Wilkinson here is the foremost practitioner of the embalming arts in Philadelphia and even the entire country, I daresay. Wouldn't you say so, Mr. Wilkinson?"

Wilkinson bowed. "You are too kind, madam."

"Wilkinson has had entirely too much chance to perfect his trade lately, with this horrid war," she went on. "But I am going to use his knowledge for my own purposes. I am going to have Mr. Wilkinson exhume the body of my son and embalm it for travel, and return him to Philadelphia for a proper burial in our family cemetery."

Marie sneaked a glance at Charlotte, whose expression was utterly composed. "I see," Charlotte said. "You are aware, of course, that your son met his death almost eight years ago."

"I am," Mrs. Smith said, a bulldog look crossing her face.

Charlotte turned her gaze to Wilkinson. "And you have been aware of this fact as well."

Wilkinson lifted his chin. "The advances in our understanding brought about by this war have been remarkable, ma'am. I make no guarantees, but I am hopeful that some amount of restoration may be possible to allow the dignified return of Mr. Smith's remains to his home cemetery."

"Then we would not stand in your way," Charlotte said. "Mrs. Smith is willing to spend her money, and you're willing to take it. You'll get no interference from the people of Daybreak."

Wilkinson gave an offended puff through pursed lips, and Charlotte stood up to leave, but Mrs. Smith waved her back to her chair. "We have some woman talk to do," she said. "Mr. Wilkinson, please give us the room." Wilkinson backed to the door, giving Charlotte an ugly glance as he did. "Jenny," Mrs. Smith called. "See Mr. Wilkinson to his house."

Mrs. Smith paused until she heard the closing of the outside door. "They listen at the keyhole," she said. "All of them do. They think I don't know." She raised herself to a sitting position on the edge of her bed, swinging her slippered feet to the floor. With a grunt she pushed herself to her feet and tottered to the door. She swung it open abruptly, as if to catch an eavesdropper behind it, but no one was there. With an "mmph" of satisfaction, she returned to the bed and climbed back in.

"Now," she said, stirring more tonic into her water glass. "I must speak to you, mother to mother." She scanned their faces.

Marie had sat quietly through everything, watching and listening. She had wondered why she had been invited in the first place, having no part in the governing of the colony.

Mrs. Smith cleared her throat in a monstrous rolling growl. "Lysander was my only child," she said. "Perhaps you were not aware of that fact."

"No, ma'am," Marie said, surprised to hear the sound of her own voice. "I did not know that."

Mrs. Smith looked directly at her for the first time. "I am not surprised," she said. "Lysander kept his own counsel on many things, despite his reputation as a talker." She smoothed the blankets over her legs. "In fact, I know very little of his time here in your community. His letters were rare and uninformative."

Neither Marie nor Charlotte spoke. Mrs. Smith cleared her throat again.

"This is not an easy thing to come to," she said. "But I must. The thing is, Lysander was my only child, yes, as I have said, and thus my husband and I are the last of our line."

"Yes," Charlotte said.

"Unless, that is, unless something happened here. Lysander was a man of considerable appetites, I am told. And thus we come to the matter." She swung her feet out and sat perched on the edge of the bed. With a shaking hand, she poured more tea into their cups. "Mrs. Turner, I am told you come from a good family, and I mean no disrespect. But if your younger son—what is his name?—your younger son were to turn out to be a Smith, then a bright future would await him. Schooling, a place in the world, everything that goes with life at my level. A house in town, a country house out on the Main Line, a future as a gentleman and a hand in the making of the new America that we—the victors—will create."

"His name is Adam," Charlotte said quietly. "Adam Turner. And his father would not appreciate renaming him Smith, I should imagine."

"Come now, Mrs. Turner. Odd things happen in the course of our lives. It could be understood if a man of Lysander's finish might have drawn your eye, being an Eastern girl yourself. Your husband's pride is involved, but we women spend all our lives navigating around the pride of men. Think of the boy. What would be better for him—to grow up with a smooth path to prominence and achievement, or to spend his days out here scratching up the dirt?"

Charlotte stood up. "Thank you for the tea, Mrs. Smith," she said. "I believe I've had enough conversation."

"What about you, then?" Mrs. Smith said, turning to Marie. "Mrs. Turner here is concerned about her reputation, I'd say. She imagines that acknowledging Lysander as the boy's father would put her to scorn. What do you think, Miss Mercadier?" Marie thought she heard extra emphasis on the *miss*. "Mrs. Turner may have all the power around here because of her fine reputation. But you and I, we know that reputation will only take a person so far. Once discarded, reputation shrinks to a speck very quickly. It loses all importance compared to the things that truly matter—like the welfare of one's child." Mrs. Smith gripped the mattress and leaned forward. "What's your opinion, Miss Mercadier? Perhaps you are the one I should have been speaking to all along. You're a comely young woman. Did you and my son find your way out to the barn now and then? I had fancied that I would find a grandson out here, but perhaps I was wrong. Your daughter would do worse than to be brought up in Philadelphia society."

"Miss Mercadier's story is well enough—" Charlotte began, but Mrs. Smith cut her off.

"Let her speak." Her voice was a hissing growl. "You are fond of speaking for everyone. But I want to hear Miss Mercadier speak for herself. Think about it, young lady. Think about the society she would enter, the match she would make, if I were to bring her back from the West. My lost granddaughter, the story of her parentage obscure and slowly forgotten. You have nothing comparable to offer her."

Marie felt herself rise to her feet. "You are right," she said. Her breath seemed to have failed her, and the words came out in a soft croak. "My reputation is nothing to prize. But you see, I am a selfish woman. I love my daughter and will keep her with me regardless. And I would sooner die than give her to an old witch like you!"

And with that she was out the door, pushing her way past Jenny seated on the doorstep and Wilkinson standing in the shade nearby. He tipped his hat. "Go dig your bones, you old monster," she said.

Charlotte caught up with her as she reached her front door. "Well done," Charlotte said. "For a moment I thought—"

"I don't care what you think," Marie snapped. She shut the door behind herself.

The next morning found her in the same place, home, her father off to the barn, waiting till sunrise to rouse Josephine for her chores. She had spent the evening inside, unwilling to risk an encounter with all the people who had made the day so unpleasant, but this morning she stepped out into the cool air with a fresh mind. This was her community, not Mrs. Smith's, or Cowling's, or Wilkinson's, or even Dathan's. She would live in it as she pleased and not waste her time avoiding these accidental newcomers.

The sun had barely broken the horizon, but the air was already moist. Another cool morning, but it was going to be a warm day. The children in school would be hard to manage.

Marie heard the sound of something splashing across the river behind her and went around her house to look. She saw Michael Flynn climbing the bank, his son on his shoulders. She had always wondered how Angus managed to get to school with dry clothes.

Flynn carried the boy through the field stubble and put him down in the road, sending him in the direction of the Temple with something between a pat and a shove. His curly black hair was sloppily cut short, something he'd done himself with a razor and comb, obviously. He had tied his brogans together by the laces and draped them around his neck to keep them dry while he forded the river. Now he sat on a stump to put them back on. Something caught his eye; she must have moved a little. For he stood up abruptly, a shoe on one foot and the other in his hand, and took off his hat. "Good morning," he said.

"Good morning."

"Thought I'd ride the boy across the river today."

She nodded. "I didn't mean to spy," she said. "Please—"

Flynn sat back down and put his other shoe on, then stood up again, his hat still in hand.

"I've been meaning—" he began, but stopped. "I never thanked you properly for your care of Angus while I was away. I embarrass myself, should have thanked you right months ago."

"It's all right," Marie said. "You were just back from the war. Everything was strange."

"Still. And I hear the school is going well, too. All the boy wants to talk about is school, school."

"I'm glad to hear that."

There was a pause. Flynn stayed in the road. He sucked in his breath and looked her in the eye.

"I'm no beauty, but I'm a full grown man," he blurted. "And a Catholic, if that matters. I have a temper, it is true, but I try not to let it out. And you'll never find a harder working man on the face of the earth. I have a house nearly built, and fence in fine progress, and next will come a barn. I don't sit on my trousers and wait for luck. I'd ask permission of you to come sit of an evening from time to time."

They stood facing each other for a while.

"All right," she said at last. "Come over whenever you like."

Chapter 8

Charley Pettibone stepped out of Durand's tavern into the brisk air of an October Saturday night. He liked Durand's. The old man was friendly, and it was an easy walk from Daybreak to French Mills, just a couple of hours—which meant he didn't always have to wait till Saturday night to pay a visit. He avoided making a habit out of weekday trips. They were a bad practice and made his work the next day slow and miserable. But occasionally he would step over; as long as he made it back by midnight or so, he could get enough sleep to make the next day bearable.

He lit a cigar, another practice he had picked up. Charley supposed it was the war that had introduced him to drink and cigars, although he couldn't exactly recall when these habits had begun. Old McKinney from the regiment had taken him out drinking a few times, and whoring, too, although they had rarely had enough money for that pleasure. The whores wouldn't take scrip, that was for certain.

Charley knew it was insane, but in a strange way he missed the war. The days of rapid movement and sense of urgency, the comradeship, the laughter and joking in idle times. He had drifted south from Daybreak when the fighting broke out, compelled for reasons he couldn't quite explain to join an Arkansas regiment. He was not especially loyal to Arkansas, but it was his state, and a man had to be loyal to something. He had joined Hindman's Legion in Helena, lying about his age although the recruiters hadn't been too particular anyway. After that came years of marching and fighting that stretched across the middle South, Shiloh to Richmond to Chattanooga to Atlanta, ending up in the Carolinas at the Surrender.

He should not have come back to Daybreak, he knew that now. Back when old man Webb was alive, the place felt like home. Even after Webb died, there was a common feeling about the place, a hopefulness. But now it was full of Yankee strangers, and even the old-timers lacked much sense of purpose. They held the Thursday night meetings as before, but there was little enthusiasm in them.

He wondered whether those boys he had ridden in with had really gone to find Jo Shelby in Mexico and continue the struggle, or whether they had done like him and washed up onto the first sandbar that had a feeling of home. Continue the struggle? What struggle? The notion seemed even more foolish than staying in Daybreak. If he was going to be a defeated outsider, he might as well be it in a country where he knew the language. Now Oklahoma or the Western territories, that might be a possibility. But where? He didn't know anybody out there. At least the Daybreak people had names, even if the war clouded the air between them like smoke from a funeral pyre. The worst were the widows, like Mrs. Prentice, and the near-widows, like the widow Shepherson, who had agreed to wait for Jesse Wilson, only to have Wilson vanish into oblivion, leaving her without so much as a pension. The women tried to be gracious to him, but in their eyes he could always see the obvious point: he was alive and their men weren't.

As Charley stood on Durand's porch, a man rode up from the south. His gear and tack were remarkably quiet; if it hadn't been for the hoofbeats of the horse, he wouldn't have been heard at all. He swung off—a slim man who moved with deliberation, his hat pulled low—and knocked on Durand's front window with little more than a glance in Charley's direction. When Durand came to the window, he passed a jug through. "Fill me up, would you, friend?" he said in a soft voice.

Charley recognized him in the window light. "You gonna drink that whole jug, Mr. Hildebrand?" he said.

The man turned to face him. It was Sam Hildebrand, all right. "Do I know you, friend?" he said.

"Probably not. You held a gun on me when I was twelve years old, but that's been a long time."

"Can't say that I remember," Hildebrand said. "I would hope you're not the type to hold a grudge."

"I guess I am, but not for that," Charley said. "I was a mouthy little brat and no doubt deserved it."

"Well, you're still alive."

"That I am. At least you didn't pull the trigger."

"I suppose we've all had our share of guns pointed at us since then."

"Oh, yeah. My people up in Daybreak have all kinds of stories about you."

"You're one of that bunch, are you?"

Charley extended his hand. "Charley Pettibone." They shook.

"Union man, then," Hildebrand said.

"No. Second Arkansas. Joined up in sixty-one, stuck it out to the end."

A hint of a smile crossed Hildebrand's face. "That must make things in Daybreak a little odd for you."

"A little odd? I should say so. Irish and niggers, and now a whole deputation from Philadelphia. I hardly know the place."

"It's a strange world."

"That's God's truth."

Durand came back to the window with the jug. Hildebrand handed him some coins, checked the cork, and unhitched his horse. "No, I ain't going to drink this alone," he said. "There's a few like-minded boys down the road a little, and they're going to drink it with me, talk over old times. You walk on down a mile or two, you'll find us."

"I just might do that."

Hildebrand mounted his horse and disappeared into the night. Charley listened as the sound of the horse vanished. He'd heard all about Hildebrand, the bushwhacker. Who hadn't? Strange, he didn't seem like such a fearsome man at all. Just a skinny fellow. Of course, put a gun in a man's hand and it didn't matter how tall he was. The story was that Hildebrand might have gone into banditry, but who could know if there was truth to that, either? It wasn't the sort of thing you'd advertise.

Charley knew he was going to walk down the road and drink with the men, but he stood on the porch a while longer, waiting. Didn't want to seem too eager. Let them have their jug for a while.

The air was getting colder and the sky was clear; there would be hard frost tonight. Charley felt the need to get into motion. He felt exhilarated, the way he used to when he knew there was a big scrape coming up. The approach of a battle affected men differently; some grew melancholic, some prayed. And some were like him—they became excited, almost giddy. There was fear, of course. He had wet himself at Rowlett's Station, their first real fight. But after that he learned to overcome his fear and let it add to his excitement. There was no more beautiful sound in the world than that of a rifle ball flying past, missing him. It was the sound of life itself.

He strolled south down the dirt road, alert to the sounds and smells of the night air. He stuck to the middle of the road. Best not to surprise a man like Hildebrand in the darkness.

After a mile he could see a fire ahead, off in a hollow to the side, flickering through the trees. He stopped in the road when he reached it.

"Hey," he called out, just loud enough to be heard.

"That you, Pettibone?" came a voice.

"It is."

"Come on in."

Hildebrand and three other men were seated on saddles and rocks in a close circle. Charley could hear the snuffing of horses a few feet farther into the woods.

"This is the fellow I was telling you about," Hildebrand said. "Charley Pettibone. This here's Green Pratt, Lewis Dowd, and Horace Landsome. They rode with me from time to time." The men nodded to each other. Pratt was a big, puffy man with a black beard that covered his entire mouth, and a slouch hat with the brim tilted straight up in front, as if he were facing a strong wind. Dowd and Landsome were smaller, each wearing a buff leather overcoat.

"They's rocks over there," Pratt said, pointing to a vine-covered pile a few feet away. "Grab one, we'll scoot." Charley brushed the dirt off one and placed it in the circle.

"Now who do you suppose piled up all them rocks?" he said. "That's the work of many a day right there." The men shrugged.

"These boys don't like to speculate about such matters," Hildebrand said. "They're creatures of the here and now, ain't you, boys?" To their silence, he went on, "Now me, I like that question. That's the kind of thing I could chew on for a week or more. What's your opinion, Pettibone?"

Charley studied Hildebrand's face for a moment to see if he was being spoofed. "I don't know," he said carefully. "Could be a flood come down this valley sometime, piled 'em up. Could have been a farm here at some point, farmer piled 'em up out of his field."

"You're a logical man, Pettibone," Hildebrand said. "I like that. But let me ask you. You ever see a flood make a pile of rocks like this?"

Charley shrugged.

"Pass the jug," Landsome said. Lewis Dowd handed it down.

"Me, neither," Hildebrand said. "Not ruling it out. And we know a flood will carry things a long way. But it ain't likely." The jug came to Charley. He took a short swallow. It was better than some he'd had, good corn whiskey, watered down a bit but not too much. He took another.

"Now a farmer," Hildebrand continued, "that's a high likelihood. Only problem is, I don't see no other evidence of a farm. No old cabin, no rails, no sheds. Not even a foundation."

"Could have burned," Charley said.

At that, Green Pratt laughed, a harsh, knowing laugh, and reached for the jug. Charley passed it on. "Could have burned," Pratt repeated.

"That is the truth," Hildebrand said. "Green here has helped me burn a farmstead or two. But even our best job never completely destroyed everything. We might have burnt a house, but we never bothered to burn the chicken coops or hog pens. So I am not convinced."

"So what do you think done it, then, Sam?" said Dowd.

"Indians," said Hildebrand. "We know the Indians run up and down this river valley for centuries before we got here. I think this pile of rocks is a sign of some sort, maybe like a milepost, or maybe a grave."

The five men looked over their shoulders at the rockpile.

"I don't care if it's a gravestone or not," Pratt said after a minute. "I ain't getting up off it."

The jug went around again.

"Sam tells us you're an Arkansas boy," Pratt said. "What unit?"

"Second infantry," Charley said.

"We never got no number up here," Pratt said. "We just rode around and fought wherever we found a fight."

"I expect that wasn't too hard," Charley said.

"You'd be surprised," said Pratt. "Most of them Yankee boys didn't like to see us coming."

They shared a laugh at this and passed the jug around again.

"That was Hindman's bunch, wasn't it?" Hildebrand asked. "I hear he's in Mexico now."

Charley nodded. "Him and Shelby's whole army. Never surrendered."

"Did you surrender?"

"Greensboro, North Carolina. What was left of us. We were in the Army of Tennessee by then."

Pratt grated out his harsh laugh again. "We ain't surrendered."

"Not entirely true," Hildebrand said. "I turned in all your names at Jacksonport, remember? We got our parole."

"Ain't the same as surrendering," Pratt said. "We didn't give up our guns."

"I ain't done fighting, either," said Dowd.

"That's fine for you boys, but I have a wife and children," Hildebrand said. "I can't go running off to Mexico."

"I didn't say anything about Mexico," said Pratt. "My idea is, we know this country better than anybody. There ain't a Federal officer in St. Louis could find us down here. We take the run of the place, live off the fat of the land just like always, and any Yankee tries to stop us gets a nighttime surprise. What do you say to that, Hildebrand?"

Pratt passed the jug to Hildebrand, but he handed it on. "I'm getting too old for sleeping on the ground," he said.

"What, you're going to live the quiet life? You think they're going to let you live the quiet life after all we done?"

Hildebrand glanced to where the horses were tied up. "Probably not. Not around here, anyway." He reached behind himself and lifted his rifle out of its scabbard. "See these notches? Every one of 'em is a man, and a lot of them have family around here. I'd be lying to myself if I didn't know there was ten dozen people who'd like to be the man who killed Hildebrand."

"Some of Quantrill's boys are still on the ride over west of here, and nobody bothers them," Pratt said. "Afraid to."

Hildebrand stood up and brushed the dirt off his pants. "Is that what I want? Everybody afraid of me? I don't know." He walked toward the horses. "You boys keep the jug, I'm riding north. Any luck I'll see my wife tomorrow."

"How about you, Pettibone?" Pratt said. "War over for you?"

"Maybe," Charley said. "I ain't got a whole lot of quarrels."

"Ain't got a whole lot of money, either, I'll bet," Pratt said. "And Sam tells me that town of yours is getting overrun."

Charley sat silent. He didn't think he was cut out to be an outlaw, but at the same time he knew Pratt was right. He'd seen that man Flynn crossing the river in the evening to sit at Marie Mercadier's house two or three nights a week, the son of a bitch. Just swagger in and start courting the only local girl worth having. And those crazy people from the North, and the nigger. He was the worst, waltzing around like he owned the place. The world had turned upside down.

"I ain't stealing anything," he said. "I ain't a thief. But if you're talking about protecting our way of life, maybe running off some carpetbaggers, then I might be your man."

At the edge of the firelight a possum trotted by, veering neither to left nor right, heading to its destination as intently as a trainman with a pocket watch.

"Watch this," Pratt said. He took a short square-handled knife from his boot, hefted it by the point, and in a swift overhand motion threw it at the possum. The knife missed by a foot as the possum continued into the darkness and the men chuckled.

"Well, shit," Pratt muttered. "Can't get no aim from a sitting position." With his foot, he nudged Dowd, who was sitting on a higher pile of rocks. "Bring me that knife and I'll show you better."

"I didn't throw that knife," Dowd said.

Pratt nudged him again. "Yeah, but you're half standing already and I'm down here. Fetch me that knife."

"Ain't my knife."

Pratt kicked him a third time, hard enough to knock him off his seat and onto the ground, and the chuckling stopped. This time his voice was low. "You never know," he said. "Maybe I'll give you that knife."

Dowd rose to his feet and brushed off his hands from where he had caught himself on the ground. Everybody waited.

But Dowd did not turn to face Pratt, who was still sitting on the ground. He turned away and walked to the weeds at the edge of the fire where the knife had flown, cursing under his breath. Charley could hear him kicking in the brush as he disappeared into the dark.

Hildebrand mounted his horse and reined it toward the road. "Your aims are good, boys, and I'll help you where I can," he said. "But for now, I'm home-ward bound. I may try to start over somewhere people don't know me, maybe Kentucky or Illinois. We'll see." He called to Dowd. "It should be right there where you're looking, Lewis. Maybe a little farther. Them things always slide."

"Good luck to you, Major," Pratt said, standing up, a little wobbly, to shake his hand. Landsome and Charley followed suit. "If you change your mind, we're meeting on Rockpile two Sundays from now to talk things over. Noontime." Hildebrand waved his hand and rode off.

"How about you, Pettibone?" Pratt said, turning to him. "You know Rock-pile Mountain, across the river?"

Charley shrugged. "Sure. Ain't no road up it though."

"Follow Trace Creek a couple of miles up from the river, and you'll see a track. If the farmer stops you, tell him you heard there was going to be a preaching up on the mountaintop. Don't come armed."

"All right. I'll come if I can." The men sat down to their jug again, but Charley had tired of the talk. He waved them goodbye and headed up the road to French Mills, following the silvery fragments of light cast through the tree limbs by the sinking moon. The dark, silent village made him feel mournful; it seemed deserted, although a blanket of wood smoke hovered over it in the crisp air.

He awoke the next morning, his house cold, with a pounding head and a cottony mouth. Maybe that corn of Durand's wasn't so good after all, or maybe he had needed to pass the jug more often.

Although it was a Sunday morning, the *thock-thock-thock* of someone chopping wood rang in his head in time with the thumping of his temples. It wasn't far off, either—a few cabins up the road, from the sound of it.

Charley snapped his galluses over his undershirt, threw on his overcoat and a pair of boots, and stepped outside. He paused to decide whether to fetch some firewood for his own house or find out who was making the racket. The racket won. Breath frosting the air, he set out up the road.

He should have guessed. The goddam Irishman, pants wet to the knees from having waded the river, was chopping logs behind the Mercadiers' house. Anything for attention. Charley walked behind the house and stood, watching.

"Ain't you ever heard of the day of rest?" he said.

Flynn looked up but did not stop. "Didn't get it done yesterday. Got busy digging out a stump."

"You could at least wait until a decent hour."

This time Flynn paused. "Sun's up. Decent enough." He finished the chunk and scooted the log farther onto the rick.

"Sunday's the day for worship. You're disturbing people."

Flynn swung into the log and let the axe stay. "I'm disturbing you is what you mean. Go put your pillow over your head, then, before you start disturbing me and I have to kick the slats out from under you."

Charley laughed. "Now there's a yarn."

"You think so, Johnny Reb?" Flynn straightened and faced him across the log-rick. "I'll tell you a yarn if it suits me."

"You're a big man with an axe in your hand," Charley said. "Typical. I seen that in the war, all you Mick brigades. Wait till everybody else done the hard fighting before you stuck your noses out."

Flynn laid his hand on the axe handle; took it off again, his face scarlet; then stepped away from the logpile into the open yard. Charley squared to face him. Then a curious scratching sound stopped them both.

It was Emile Mercadier, feeling his way along the wall of the house with a stick.

"Boys, you make such noise," he said. "Working at such an hour? Good lads, good lads. But I'm an old man, I need my sleep. Come back later. Michael Flynn, I hear your voice, but who's that you brought with you? Charley, is that you I hear?"

"Yessir," Charley said. "But—"

"Go wash up, you boys, and then come back in a couple of hours. Marie, she makes you breakfast, and then you chop wood, and I get my sleep."

Everyone knew the old man didn't sleep any more than a house sparrow, but the men didn't contradict him. Charley withdrew, and a couple of hours later, his head still pounding, he found himself with a belly full of biscuits and pork, his coat off and steam rising from his sweaty body in the cold air, grimly chopping wood with Flynn while Emile sat on a bench and sawed his fiddle. His ear was still good, but he couldn't make his fingers obey, and the tunes were painfully slow.

"What do you want to hear, boys?" Emile said. "Least I could do is entertain you."

"Play 'Marching Through Georgia,'" Flynn said.

"No, never learned that one."

"Play 'Dixie,'" Charley said, not missing a swing.

"'Dixie,' I can do 'Dixie,' I think."

"Not that one," said Flynn. "I can't stand that tune." He glared at Charley across the pile of wood.

"You're going to have to let me pick, then," Emile said. And in the cold sun, he scratched at one string and another for a while, until he finally found a key he could play in, and the sounds of "The Girl I Left Behind Me" crept out into morning.

Chapter 9

Turner did not overlook Marie's new beau, wading the river two or three evenings a week to sit in the Mercadiers' front room. He knew he had no claim on Marie, but still it galled him. He sat in the Temple at dinner in the evening, watching her out of the corner of his eye, wondering guiltily how far the son of a bitch had gotten. Flynn never came to dinner at the Temple; only Daybreak people could do that. But as Marie sat with her father and Kathleen, he imagined her thinking of Flynn. He could almost read her thoughts. And a bitter trickle of jealousy dripped constantly on his mind.

He had given up publishing *The Eagle*; there seemed no sense to it any more. He had run out of ideas, and even if he had any ideas he wasn't sure if he would want to share them. What had the world ever done for him? So he went out in the morning in silence, worked in the fields in silence, came home in the evening, ate dinner, and went to bed in silence as well. And on Thursdays, when the community met in the Temple, he attended or did not attend as the mood struck him, but never spoke or voted. He listened to Charlotte until the listening tired him, then left. It all seemed pointless.

Turner and Dathan often worked side by side, harvesting, woodchopping, tending the horses. Neither of them cared to speak, so they labored silently across the valley. They spoke only of their tools, the crop, whether they could make another round before the rain hit.

On the first day of November they found themselves in the field below the cemetery, where Wilkinson was walking in circles among the gravestones.

He called out to them. "You boys live here, don't you?"

"We do," Turner said.

"Come up here, then. I want to ask you something."

Turner and Dathan looked at each other a moment, then walked up the hill. Wilkinson was gazing at the ground.

"So this is Lysander Smith's grave," he said.

"Yes," Turner said.

"You're sure of that?"

"I helped lower him down myself."

"Hm." Wilkinson walked to the other end of the cemetery, up one side, down the other. He seemed lost in thought. Finally he returned to the two men and looked down at the grave again. Then he stared at Turner and Dathan. "You boys seem like a trustworthy pair."

They said nothing.

"How about it? Can I trust you? There's work to be had here for a man who won't tell tales."

Dathan showed no interest in speaking, so Turner took the lead. "Why don't you tell us what you want, and we'll go from there."

Wilkinson eyed him suspiciously. "All right. But if any of this gets back to the old lady, I'm calling you a bald-faced liar, just so you know. So tell me—who's the last man buried in this place?" He took in the cemetery with a sweep of his arm.

Turner returned the suspicious gaze. "Buried a whole bunch in October sixty-one down there," he said. "Federal troops, rebels, some of our people. And I believe I see what you're thinking, and I don't like it, sir."

"Oh? Sharp fellow, are you? Mind reader? Well, maybe you know what I'm thinking, and maybe you don't. I'll tell you what, friend. That old lady wants a body, and she's going to get a body."

"She wants her son's body."

"You think she would tell the difference after eight years in the ground? You think she'll even look? Hell, I couldn't even tell a white man from a Chinaman after that amount of time, and I'm a damn professional. I am going to give that lady what she wants—a body of some sort with some skin on its face, hopefully, and a veil and some salts to cover the smell."

"I ain't digging no bodies," Dathan said unexpectedly. The sound of his voice startled them both.

"What did you say, son?" Wilkinson said.

"You heard me. I ain't digging no bodies. The body after death belongs to the Lord, and it ain't for me or you to interfere with."

"By God, you'll dig if your boss here tells you to dig."

"He ain't my boss. Neither are you."

Wilkinson looked incredulously at Turner. "What the hell kind of place is this?"

"Mr. Dathan here is correct," Turner said. "He is as independently employed as you or I. We fought a war over this business, in case you've forgotten."

"Well, I'm damned," Wilkinson said. "I thought Philadelphia had the most insolent niggers in the country, but they don't hold a candle to you boys. All right, I'll dig my own goddam graves. Sixty-one, you say?" He looked at the corner of the cemetery. "Not much better than fifty-nine."

"You'll dig Lysander Smith's body and no others," Turner said. He felt a sudden fury rise in him; he could feel his face getting hot, and his hands trembled. It was a sensation he hadn't felt since the last time he'd gone into battle, the strange taste of iron in his mouth. Wilkinson seemed to sense it and backed away.

"All right, all right," he said. "Didn't come here to make trouble. Just want to make my living and go home. Didn't mean any disrespect." He retreated further, wiping his hands on his black frock coat.

Turner spun on his heel and walked down the hill toward the village. He felt that if he looked behind him, he might run back there and start beating the man. He thought of Adam Cabot, buried in that corner of the graveyard, and the Federal soldiers, and the others. To imagine Harp Webb ending up buried in Lysander Smith's family tomb! The irony was so thick that he didn't know whether to smile or curse.

"The boys in that cemetery didn't die just so this body snatcher could come along and carry them off," he said, not looking in Dathan's direction. "It's not right." Dathan was silent.

At dinner that night, he thought about mentioning the incident to Charlotte but held his tongue. He didn't quite know why. It was just another of the many things that he preferred to keep to himself these days.

They were eating pork again, pork as always. Turner was heartily sick of pork, boiled, fried, stewed, or baked in a pie. It was still pork. He knew they needed the eggs, and everyone had voted not to kill any chickens for a while, but still. Another month and it would be hog-killing time again, and more pork. Pork stretching out to meet the horizon.

"What?" Charlotte said. Turner raised his head, startled.

"What?" he said in return.

"You were saying something, something about hogs."

He tried to cover his confusion. "I'm sorry, my dear, I must have been thinking aloud. I was thinking about pork, and the many ways we eat pork, and I was just thinking—thinking about a chicken, or a fine steak, how good a juicy steak would taste nowadays. Not that I don't understand the necessity—the necessity—in the war, we dined on mule more than once—"

He stopped. He had run out of words. And in the silence, he became aware of the stares of his wife and children: Charlotte weary and guarded, Newton red-faced with anger. And Adam? Tears were streaming down his face, though he sat still with his hands in his lap.

"Papa, have you become a madman?" Adam asked in soft voice.

"Shut up!" Newton cried, but Turner put a restraining hand on his shoulder and turned to his younger son.

"Why do you ask, son?" he said as gently as he could. But his voice trembled.

"The boys say—the boys say you are. They say you've become a lunatic, a harmless lunatic who wanders the woods and fields all day. You lost your mind in the war, and—" He turned away.

"And you idle away the days with some old slave from who knows where, and pay no mind to your family or the common good," Newton said, his eyes burning. "That's what they say."

"Boys, I don't know what to tell you," Turner said. He stared at his plate. "There's justice in the things these people say, I'll grant. But I'm no lunatic. Perhaps I lost myself a touch in the war, but I'm as sound a man as any. Just give me time, and I'll find a purpose to it all. I have an idea! Let's all take another lecture tour. You boys have never been farther than Fredericktown. It'll be good for you to see the cities. We'll raise money for Daybreak and see the world." The sudden inspiration made perfect sense to him; he had been seeking a purpose, something to do with himself that would mean something, and here it was. He would do what he had always done best, talk. Why hadn't he thought of it earlier? He lifted his eyes to see their reaction.

But Charlotte had left the table.

That night they lay in bed together, awake but not speaking. "You heard what I was thinking," he finally said.

"Yes." Her voice was soft in the dark.

"Well?"

She sighed. "What makes you think you can lecture? You hardly speak two words to me in a day."

He felt the sting of truth in what she said. "I can't explain it," he said. "I hadn't even thought about it before. But when I said it, I knew it was right. Charlotte, I have to find something to do, something bigger than myself. I need a big thing."

"Will I get my old James Turner back if you do this?" Her voice was plaintive.

"I don't know if that man is still alive," he said into the night. "But if he is, you can have him."

"All right, then," she whispered. "But only with a vote," she added hastily. "The community must approve."

The vote was easily passed the next Thursday night; Turner wondered if many of the people in Daybreak weren't secretly glad to see him leave. But as Turner and Charlotte wrote for halls and plotted the schedule, Newton declared he had no interest in making the trip.

"I want to stay in Daybreak," he said. "Ain't no need to ride around on trains."

"Isn't any," his mother corrected. But he met her glare with a fierce look of his own.

Charlotte tried to command, then persuade, Newton to change his mind for a few days, but softened as it became clear that Turner wasn't going to force the boy to travel. "We'll go to Washington, see the Capitol," she told him. "Won't that be a fine thing, to see the Capitol?"

"It'll still be there later on," he said mulishly.

Adam, by contrast, could barely contain his excitement. He sat on Charlotte's lap in the evenings as she studied the rail tables and wrote to lyceums, tracing their predicted course as it developed, and though he could not read, he traced his finger over the map. They settled on February as a start date, when the worst of winter would be over but it was still too early for planting: St. Louis to Chicago by way of Springfield and Bloomington, then across to Detroit and Toledo, Cleveland, Buffalo, Albany to Boston, then back by way of the East Coast cities to Washington, then home on the B & O to Cincinnati, Vincennes, and wherever else they could produce a crowd by then.

Turner felt like Adam, transformed by excitement at the prospect of a new tour. But what would he have to say? He could hardly lecture on the same subjects as before, but what else did he know about? River valley farming? Hemp growing?

"Lecture on the war," Charlotte said. "Or the foreign situation."

"If I knew what the foreign situation was, I'd try it. And I think the only thing I want to say about the war is let's not have another."

"Suit yourself. But we need to have handbills printed by January. Perhaps—"

"Perhaps what?"

"Never mind." Turner saw it in her look, though.

"Ah. The woman question."

And there the issue hung for several weeks while Turner thought it over. To draw a crowd he would need to take a stance that put him apart from everyone else, and that meant only one thing. But could he plead the women's case in good conscience?

As the days grew colder he retreated to the old print shed behind their house, closed since he had left for the war. He cleaned out the stovepipe, dusted the chair and desk, pulled down the grimy curtains, laid in a supply of paper and ink.

Through the window he could see everyone going about their business—the men with tools and loads of wood, the women with baskets of laundry, steaming in the winter air, to be thrown onto the line. Yes, the women in Daybreak had the franchise but were they really less subjugated than the men? Or than their voteless sisters in the country at large? Was their toil any less, or their freedom any greater? It was hard to see it.

But Charlotte was right; it was a fine lecture topic, one to bring in the crowds now that the slave had been freed and talk of the Negro franchise was in the air. Greeley himself would probably turn up when they got to New York. Turner put another stick of wood into his stove and tried to think of what to say.

By week's end, he had little to show. On Saturday evening, restless, he got up from the table where the boys were playing dominoes and put on his coat. "I need to talk to Emile Mercadier," he said to Charlotte and was out the door before anything could be asked.

Kathleen answered his knock. "Emile's over sitting with Marie and the girl," she said with a glance to the side. "He feels the need to chaperone or something, I suppose. I don't mind, I can do my mending in peace."

"Could you ask him—ask them—if I might come in?" Turner said. "I hate to intrude."

"Of course." She disappeared out the back and across the dogtrot. Within a moment Marie came out of her front door and called to him.

"Come in, come in," she said. "Certainly you are welcome."

Emile sat in a straight chair at the table, his fiddle in his hands, Josephine and Angus across from him playing cat's cradle. Marie and Flynn were on the sofa. Flynn, sitting stiffly with his hands in his lap, gave him an edgy glance as he entered and pulled out another straight chair beside Emile. The old man's hand was extended in his direction; Turner took it.

"You are kind to visit us on a cold night such as this," Emile said.

"I need your advice," Turner said.

Emile laughed. "Now there's an honor," he said. "A dotard like me, asked for advice." He fingered the strings, playing a tune only his left hand heard.

"No one has a longer history with our cause than you, Emile. You were a citizen of Daybreak before Daybreak even existed."

Mercadier nodded. "Fourier, Proudhon, Cabet, I have read them all. I knew Cabet, you know. I wrote this all in my letters to the man at the *Evening Post*. I shouldn't be surprised to get a visit from him any day now," he said with a satisfied smile. Marie and Flynn said nothing; Turner got the feeling that this subject was all too familiar.

"Yes," he said. "But it's Daybreak I want to ask you about. You've heard I am planning another lecture tour, I suppose."

"Fine work if you can get it," Flynn said.

"Mr. Turner's lectures have brought good money to the colony several times before," Marie replied. Flynn sniffed but kept silent.

"How can I help you, my boy?" Mercadier said. He patted Turner's hand. "I don't know where you should go. I'm a silly shoemaker. You know that."

"Emile, I don't know what to say," Turner said softly. "I don't know if it's all been worth it. I don't know if there's any sense to what we are doing anymore. We work, we share, we hold our goods in common, but have we improved anyone's life?"

Mercadier's sightless eyes glittered toward Turner. "I don't know, my boy," he said. "What do you think?"

Turner had nothing to say. He felt empty. "Perhaps," he said. "I'd like to think so."

The room was silent for a moment, filled with Turner's gloom, with only the quiet chanting of Josephine's string game to break the stillness.

"You're expecting something from me better than 'perhaps'?" Mercadier said. "What is there in our lives that is guaranteed? I tell you this, I have liked my life and I do not regret it. Would my life be better as a shopkeeper back in France instead of an old socialist here in this valley? How should I know? I'll take this life, it's mine and I'm satisfied with it."

Turner spoke to Marie. "I may speak on the question of the vote for women. You remember when we reprinted the Seneca Falls letter in *the Eagle*."

Marie blushed and turned her head. How could either of them not remember? It was that moment—reading the great words, the declaration of women as a powerful people, deserving of all the rights that men so smugly hoarded as their own—when Marie had felt her own power and declared her own passion, and from that moment all their lives had changed.

"Vote for women?" Flynn said. "Now I've heard it all."

"Women have voted on matters here in Daybreak for years," Turner said, a little defensive even though he was not sure of the issue himself. "You don't see us growing scales or horns as a result."

Flynn sniffed again. "The women rule us enough as it is."

Something in Flynn's dismissal aroused Turner's old debating instincts, and he began to make his case, but Flynn waved him off. "You're the good man with words, I know that already. Heard it many times before. I ain't going to try to argue with you. I just know what I know. Angus, time to go home." He stood to leave.

"I need to go home, too," Turner said, standing also. "Emile, you've been a help. Thank you." He shook the old man's hand and took his hat off its peg.

"Mr. Turner," Marie said. "Thank you for coming by. And if you'd care to know it—" She paused. "I have liked my life, too, and do not regret it."

Turner stammered a few words and let himself out the door. He was a few steps down the dark road when he felt a strong grip on his bicep; Flynn's face pressed close to his.

"You stay away from her," Flynn whispered in a voice full of hate. "I see your game." Then he disappeared in the other direction, pulling Angus behind him as they made their way to the ford.

Turner watched the man's shape vanish in the moonlight. Behind the curtains of Marie Mercadier's house, shapes were moving, silhouetted by the lamps. Everything else was dark.

Yes, he would lecture, and the woman question would do just fine. He would talk. He would talk and talk.

Chapter 10

Michael Flynn did not like being as angry as he was most of the time, but when he looked around there was plenty to be angry about. Loafers like James Turner, wandering around his side of the river valley, flouting all the rules of normal society and getting rewarded for it. And his wife, Mrs. High and Mighty, with all her "let's vote on it" talk. As long as things went her way, of course. Angus, the little snot, sneaking around trying to get out of chores. Or whatever it was that he did; Angus was a mystery to him more often than not, a silent little daydreamer, but a smart lad, he'd give him credit for that. Came from his mother's side.

Even Marie made him angry sometimes. She had that schoolmarm quality about her, always wanting to improve everyone, and he didn't much care to be improved. He was who he was, and people would just have to take that. And she rarely let him walk her out to a quiet place where he could grab a kiss or a cuddle, which God knows he wanted more of all the time. It had been too long, much too long. And she still wouldn't say yes to him or set a date. Just sit on the sofa and talk, holding hands once in a while. She of all people should know that a man needed more than that; it made him feel as if she were waiting for someone better to come along or staying faithful in some crazy way to that bastard Turner.

And then there were all the Goddamn rebs walking around, unrepentant and proud as Lucifer. The way they acted, a man would think they had won the war. Pettibone, that pup, not the worst of them but bad enough. He'd heard the talk of them forming some sort of vigilance league; it sounded more like a Sunday afternoon drinking society to him. Let them do what they want. He had no objection to their keeping the niggers in line, but, by God if they tried to interfere with him, he'd remind them who could fight the best.

He'd show them all. All the doubters, the Irish-hating bastards, the goddam Army officers worst among them, carrying on about the lazy Micks while they sat in their tents and drank tea all day. The man had not yet been born who could outwork Michael Flynn, and if everyone wanted to underestimate the Irish, well, bully for them. He'd come into this piece of property by a fine bit of luck, and in a few years, he'd have the whole valley cleared, barns raised, and a herd of cattle on the ground. He'd already picked out the breed, Devonshire, only decent thing ever to come out of England. Beef cattle for him; more profit in it. The hell with these mongrel cattle and the roaming hogs. He wanted his own herd, cattle he could mark. He could pay off much of the debt to the Daybreak people with the first slaughter. And when it was all his, free and clear, he'd build his house. He'd pictured it in his mind since he was a child. It would be a house that people would come from miles around to see. He had talked of it to Marie, a little embarrassed by the grandness of his plans—an octagon, three stories, framed all the way to the top, with a little walk-around space on the roof to see out over the fields. By God it would be fine.

But tonight was no time for thoughts of work. He'd persuaded Marie to leave the children with Kathleen and her father and ride with him to Oak Grove. There was a Christmas dance at the schoolhouse; he had brushed down the horse and cleaned out the wagon, bought a little jar of whiskey from Durand, and if they ended up taking the long way home, who knew what might happen? If nothing else, he could press her for an answer; if she wouldn't marry him, he wanted to move on. All these nights perched on her sofa had to amount to something pretty soon.

He picked her up at sunset, fording the river carefully to keep from splashing water onto her skirts. "That's a fine dress," he said as they climbed the hill.

She seemed lost in thought. "Thank you," she said after a moment.

"You make it?"

"Yes."

"That's a fine skill, dressmaking."

"I don't pretend to be an expert at it. Before the war we used to make clothes for Grindstaff's store in town, but he quit buying."

Now that they were away from the scrutiny of the old man and the ever-present ears of the children, he had nothing to say. They followed the ridge in silence. A man would think that the lady could help him out a bit, surely, but she just rode along, wrapped in her heavy coat. He gathered the reins into one hand so he could reach into the clasp of her hands and take one in his grip. She let him.

"You cold? I have whiskey in my pocket," he said after a time.

"No. I'm fine."

He tried to think of conversation topics. Of course, everyone was talking these days about the Turners and their upcoming travels, but he didn't care to speak of that.

"Working hard lately?" he ventured.

To his surprise, she jerked her hands away and covered her face. Her muffled sobs sounded to him like the snorting of a hog, a comparison he immediately regretted and tried to banish from his mind. He let her cry for a while, the horse at a slow walk.

"Of course I'm not good enough for you," he said once she had settled down. "I'm sorry. You're a pretty thing, and smart. You made a mistake, with the child and all, but God almighty, who hasn't made mistakes? I'm a brute who never went to school a day in his life. It's all right if you can't stand me. I'm all right. I'll turn the wagon around."

She looked at him, and there was a smile through the tears. "I wasn't crying over you," she said. "I was thinking about my father."

Then it all poured out, how the old man was losing his hold, his memory failing, his eyesight gone, his body giving out. How the new wife was kindhearted but sharp-tongued, and how she didn't feel right to speak but felt pained to hear her scolding. How little Josephine was so silent and watchful all the time, never letting her know what she was thinking, and she feared that the child was feeling the shame of her parentage, judging her, scorning her own mother. He took her hand again as the torrent of words emerged.

"Aye," he said. "The new Mrs. Mercadier, when she was Mrs. Flanagan, she was quite the article even then. You should have seen old Flanagan. He lived in fear, he did. We'd be at the barn, and she'd get the notion we were dodging some piece of work, and oh, he'd tremble to see her come out of the house. She'd eat the head off him." They laughed together at the tale, and he chucked the horse's reins. Then melancholy swept over him again. "He didn't run from the bushwhackers, though. He stood up and took his shot." She squeezed his hand. And then unexpectedly she leaned in and kissed him, the first time she had ever done such a thing, and his surprise and elation was so great he nearly lost his hat into the back of the wagon.

He fetched the whiskey jar from his coat pocket and took a swallow. "There's a fine thing for the cold," he said. He handed the jar to Marie. She took a tiny sip, made a face, and handed it back.

The dance was another fine thing. There was a fiddler and a banjo player, and a strong-voiced caller for the squares. Marie partnered with him in all the round dances, and when she needed to sit out a dance, Flynn stepped outside with another Irishman, a livery stableman named Cavanaugh, and took a few more pulls from the jar. He was determined not to drink too much for any possible romance on the ride home, but the whiskey was good and warmed him.

"Big money ahead," Cavanaugh said.

"Oh? And where is that big money?"

"Now that the war's over, they're sending the railroad on down into Arkansas. Two, three hundred miles of track before they're done. Dollar a day plus meals, is what I hear."

Flynn didn't answer. It was something to think about, though. He could clear ground and build fence on Sundays and during the long summer nights, and earn money to pay off the land during the week. It would be hard. But he could do it.

Some of the local boys came out and stood on the schoolhouse steps above them. Drunkards and rebels, the sons of bitches. There were three of them, lean as coonhounds, laughing and talking in their ignorant-sounding drawl, one of them still in a tattered Confederate uniform coat. Cavanaugh got quiet and headed inside, but Flynn stayed where he was. He wasn't about to let some traitorous parcel of local boys make him come or go.

"Hey, Charley," said one. Flynn, startled at the name, stared at the men in the dim light.

No, it wasn't that bastard Pettibone, but he wouldn't have been surprised.

"What, partner?" said another, loud, trying to be heard.

"You know what the difference is between a nigger and an Irishman?"

"No. What's the difference?"

There was a curious kind of pace you adopted when you assaulted a fixed position. It was a run, a fast run, but controlled, not so fast that you risked a stumble. You had to cover the ground as quickly as possible, because the bullets and cannon shot were coming at you hard and furious. The less time spent in the open ground, the better. You held your musket in front of your breast, tight gripped, and shouted with whatever wordless cry you needed to get the fear out of your lungs. There was no slowing down and no stopping to think, because a thousand men were a step behind you, dashing at the same hard pace, and it was better to take a Minie ball in the chest than to be trampled underfoot by your own boys. If you were lucky enough to get within thirty feet of the enemy line, you dropped the rifle to horizontal and got off your shot. From there on out it was bayonet to bayonet, strike at whatever moved, and God help the slow or indecisive.

When Flynn awoke he was in the back of the wagon. Stars were bouncing from side to side above him. His face felt numb, but a throbbing pain was centered between his shoulderblades.

He blinked a few times to clear his vision. He seemed to still have both eyes. Good. He clenched and unclenched his hands, which were painful and bloody.

As his vision cleared he could see Marie Mercadier's back, above him on the wagon seat. Ah. She was driving, so they must be headed home. His hat had been folded into something of a pillow beneath his head.

Flynn opened his mouth to see if he could talk.

"I'm awake," he said.

She glanced behind her. "That's good." The wagon hit a rut, throwing him to the side in a rolling wash of pain; he must have groaned, for she said, "Sorry."

After a moment his head cleared. "I must have embarrassed you." He would have liked to sit up, but didn't feel capable.

She thought it over. "No. I'm not embarrassed. You're a strange man, but I'm not embarrassed."

"How'd I do?"

She glanced back again. "Well, you didn't kill anyone, although you certainly seemed to be trying."

He closed his eyes and felt the rocking of the wagon. Then they took a sharp dip; he slid forward in the wagon, hitting his head on the front of the bed.

"Where are we?"

"Crossing the river."

"All right. You hop down, and I'll drive myself home."

"You'll do nothing of the sort. I can make you a pallet in the front room."

Now that they were in the river, the rattling of the wheels softened to a gurgling whisper. He opened his eyes again to see the moonlight streaming down the back of Marie's coat; her dark hair glistened.

"Marry me. Marry me, Miss Marie," he said.

Chapter 11

The Turners left for their speaking tour on the first of February. With Charlotte gone, the Wickmans were appointed to lead the community, but neither of them had the inclination; they were keeping Newton, which was enough of a handful for them. At the funereal Mr. Wilkinson's request, Wickman was building an oversized coffin, dovetailing the corner joints and sealing the inside with tar; he had built a little tar kiln on the side of the mountain and fed it every few days with slivers of pine and birch. The idea was that they would raise Lysander's coffin one cold day and set it directly into Wickman's construction. The coffin was a fine piece of work; Wickman had brought down some walnut lumber he had been drying in the barn rafters for two years, and he would allow no help in the labor. So everyone began following their own desires at work.

That was all right with Charley. He liked to work on his own anyway. It was too early to plow, the harness mending was all done, and the occasional birth of a colt was all that broke the monotony of late winter. It was a good time of year for picking rocks off the fields. And on Sunday afternoons, no one questioned him when he disappeared to meet with the Law and Order League.

The trail up Rockpile Mountain was a damn hard climb from the creek, so Charley found a way to come in from the north. He crossed the river, passed Flynn's place, and climbed the hill to the old Indian camp; from there he could follow a ridge south almost all the way, and then it wasn't much of a climb to the top of Rockpile. Their bunch had evolved into a regular group of twenty or so, mostly old fighters for the Confederacy, with Green Pratt acting as leader. There was always a jug, and some brave talk, and vague plans.

As Charley passed by today, Flynn was out splitting rails with a maul and a couple of wedges. He'd started working for the railroad during the week, doing his farm work at nights and on Sundays; in the nights they could see his lantern out in the river bottom and hear the heavy thud of his maul. He had three courses of rails laid out already, enclosing a good twenty acres.

"Couple more levels of rails and you'll be able to keep the groundhogs in," Charley said.

"Talk all you want," Flynn said. "Your trip's in vain anyway. Tavern's closed on Sunday."

"Oh, a man can find a jug if he wants one."

"Wouldn't know."

"That's not what I hear, Irish."

"Go to hell." Flynn resumed his work.

"What's the point of fencing in all this ground anyway?"

"Ah," Flynn said. "Now there's a subject for a man." He straightened up and looked around the valley. "You build the enclosure so you can keep cattle. Not these rangy beasts you see around here, but a real breed. Beef cattle for market. Once the railroad is finished, you can drive them five miles, load them on the railcars, and sell them anywhere you want. And once you have built the cattle business—" he gave Charley a significant look—"you can marry."

Charley turned away. He didn't care to discuss Michael Flynn's marriage plans. He knew he'd been bested there and couldn't figure why, but the hell with it. They could have each other. The world was large.

He was ready to start up the hill to the Indian camp, but the sound of a descending wagon made him pause. There was always time to check out a visitor.

They were soon in sight, an old couple on a narrow spring wagon pulled by a single horse. The wagon appeared to be empty, but its boards made a tremendous rattle as they came down the slope. They pulled up beside Charley.

"Maybe you boys can help us," said the man.

"All right," Flynn said.

The old woman leaned toward them. "We are looking for the grave of our son," she said. "We got a letter from a Mrs. Turner." She produced a tightly folded letter from a coat pocket.

Charley and Flynn exchanged glances. "Cemetery's on the hillside across the river," Charley said.

"No," said the woman. "The letter says he's over on this side, under a big cedar tree." She looked at them expectantly. "His name is Cunningham, Matthew Cunningham."

"We had a stone cut," the man said, gesturing to the back of the wagon. Charley peered over the side; it was a long slab of limestone with "A True Son of the South" carved in an arch above the man's name and dates.

"That must have set you back," Charley said.

"I suppose it did," said the man.

Flynn wiped his face with the palm of his hand. "I think I know where you mean. I had that spot all picked out for a hog lot, too."

"We could fence it off for you," the man said.

"Let's not worry about that right now," Flynn said. He opened up a row of rails. "Drive on in here, I'll show you the place." As the wagon lurched past, he looked over the side at the grave marker. "You won't be able to get that thing to stand up. You can't just stick 'em in the ground, you know."

"I figured we'd lay it flat," said the man.

"It'll weather."

The old couple's faces looked so unhappy that Charley wanted to assure them that everything would be fine, that he would personally dig a base for their son's tombstone and set it into a ring of stones so that nothing could harm it, not weather nor time, but knowing how false that would sound, he did not speak.

"Just show us the place," the man said. He drove past, Flynn following, and Charley resumed his walk up the hill. Enough of parents and their children's graves. But when he reached the Indian camp, another surprise awaited him: a gray curl coming out of the smokehole of one of the huts, and Dathan of all people standing in the doorway, a pipe in his mouth. They regarded each other for a moment.

"You want something to eat?" Dathan said. "Got cornbread."

Charley shook his head, still trying to figure out what Dathan was doing in what he had always thought was an abandoned village. There was movement inside the hut. A woman's face, brown and leathery, peeked out from behind Dathan. Some kind of Indian, obviously, although she was dressed in white people's clothes.

"This is Persimmon," he said.

Charley waved awkwardly. He had never liked Dathan, and not just because of his color; his long silences made Charley feel uncomfortable working around him. Charley liked to chat while he worked to make the day go faster, and Dathan's insistent quiet seemed gloomy and vaguely ominous to him. Put him together with Turner, and it was like working with Death and Misery themselves.

"You living here now?" Charley ventured.

Dathan shook his head. "Not all the time."

"Well." Charley didn't know what else to say. "Got yourself a squaw, eh?"

Dathan regarded him with a steady gaze. "The word is 'wife,' young man. Persimmon and I are married proper. Her real name is Cedeh, but that means 'persimmon,' so that's what I call her." At the sound of her name, the woman bobbed her head and smiled.

"Well," Charley said again. What Dathan had said sounded a lot like a rebuke, and he had never been rebuked by a colored man. He didn't know what to make of it. "You know their language, then."

"Indian languages ain't hard to learn if you listen close. Some of the sounds are kind of funny."

"All right. Well, better keep going." Charley felt as if he was sounding like an idiot. But he didn't want to be introduced to Sadie, or whoever that was. He thought the Indians had all cleared out years ago, but leave it to this wandering ex-slave to turn one up. Next thing he knew, they'd be setting up house down in Daybreak—and everybody would think it was just fine. So this was what living in Mr. Lincoln's world was like.

By the time he reached the gathering place, it was past midafternoon. There were fifteen men, lounging on the rocks on the southeastern slope of the hill like lizards. By their relaxed postures, Charley guessed that most of them had been there for a couple of hours.

"Well, Pettibone," said Green Pratt as he approached. "You gotta quit coming in from the backside. Somebody's liable to shoot you one of these days."

"From the looks of this bunch, I'd say more likely that somebody'd miss me. Or shoot his foot off," Charley said.

"You got that right," said Pratt with a laugh. "We're better shots when we're sober, but we ain't as bloody-minded." Then all the levity disappeared from his voice. "How about it, Pettibone? You feeling bloody-minded these days?"

Charley shrugged. "Maybe. What do you have in mind?"

Pratt straightened up and addressed the group. "Here's the thing," he said loudly. "If we're going to be a Law and Order League, it's time to stop talking and start enforcing. Saturday night, we go on a ride. And yes, I am feeling bloody-minded."

The men shifted nervously, but there were a few murmurs of agreement.

"This Goddamned radical constitution has got us shut out from everything a man holds dear," Pratt went on. "Can't vote, can't hold office, can't teach school. Hell, I couldn't even legally preach if I had a mind to."

"That'd be a sight," said one of the men with a laugh, but Pratt silenced him with an evil look.

"I've preached in my day, and I may preach again," he said. "But not until more of this world's business is taken care of. We meet under the Stout's Creek bridge east of Ironton, two hours after sundown," Pratt went on. "I've got our first people all picked out. There's an uppity nigger lives in Pilot Knob, walks around all day with a bowler hat. Needs to be taken down a notch. Then we ride down Marble Creek and visit old McHaffie. You boys know McHaffie, don't you?"

"That old bastard," one man said. "Short-weights you at his mill, short-weights you at his store."

"And all the time talking about the Union," said another. "Makes you sick."

Pratt nodded. "From there we'll ride up to Roselle. There is a known horse thief up there, and I expect you all know who I'm talking about."

Glances passed. "There'll be a fight there," someone said.

Pratt folded his arms across his barrel chest and blew through his beard. "If you ride with me on Saturday night, you should be ready to burn, hang, and shoot. If you are not ready for that, don't come. And yes, you might get shot back at. You boys ain't afraid of that, are you?"

"I'll go," Charley found himself saying. "But I'll have to borrow a horse. I ain't got one of my own."

Horace Landsome, one of the men he had met while drinking with Sam Hildebrand, spoke up. "I'll loan you one."

"That's the spirit, boys!" Pratt cried. "Tell you what, I've got a rope and a railroad bridge all picked out for that sassy boy up in Pilot Knob. Bring a kerchief to wear over your faces. Gotta keep the mystery."

"I tell you who we ought to go visit," another man said. "There's an old boy up Musco Creek, I traded hogs with him before the war, and I know half them hogs was stolen."

"Good thought, but old grievance," said Pratt. "Let's let bygones be bygones. But watch him, and if you hear anything new—" He waved his hand in the air. "How about you, Pettibone? Got any names to add to the list?"

Charley felt a flush of excitement. Maybe the first would be last, and the last first, after all. That bastard Flynn and his airs, Dathan and his race mixing, who else could he think of? But something held him back.

"No," he said. "Nobody."

Chapter 12

The window in their hotel room would not close all the way, and a sift of snow whistled in through the crack. Charlotte tried stuffing her handkerchief into the gap but it was too light; sometime in the night she rolled up a pair of Turner's trousers and wedged them against the sill, which worked as well as she could hope for. But by then she was wakeful, lying under the greasy covers with Turner fluttering his lips on one side and Adam hot and sweaty on the other.

Where were they again? Toledo. There had been a train from Chicago, and an argument with a man at the lyceum, and a walk through snowy streets to this hotel. The night's crowd had been sparse and unreceptive; there were two more nights here, then another train to Cleveland. Perhaps Cleveland would be better.

Or perhaps not. They had covered their expenses in Chicago, but nothing more. Toledo was shaping up to be a loss. Turner had tried switching his lecture, but apparently no more people wanted to hear about communal living than wanted his opinion on the woman question. Still, he had carried on admirably despite the rows of empty chairs. In fact he had seemed to relax and speak better in a half-empty hall. Despite that, he still seemed fragile and uncertain. The verve had gone out of his speaking voice, and even a simple question threw him off.

She closed her eyes. There were voices in the hallway, drunk-sounding men. She shouldn't have come on this tour. She should have stayed home with Adam, where she could have kept an eye on Newton instead of handing him off to Frances Wickman, who was surely not up to the task. Newton had become so obstinate lately, filled with a floating anger that erupted in strange moments at the wrong people. She had never been one to take a strap to a child, but by heavens she had been sorely tempted lately. At eight he should be past tantrums and settled into his work and studies.

And if she had taken Mrs. Smith up on her offer? She could see it all too well—the pampered child in his knee breeches, his whimsies indulged and his storms feared. If Newton was going to be a mess, at least he would be her mess and not someone else's.

The voices moved on. No robbers tonight, she guessed, although on second thought the robbers wouldn't announce their coming so loudly. She kept a chair wedged under their doorknob in every hotel, a move to which James and Adam gave silent assent.

Adam wormed himself closer against her, his nose pressed into her side. Now there was a surprising boy. Every night he sat on her lap offstage at his father's lectures, rapt, never moving, his eyes never leaving Turner, though surely he only understood every fifth word. It was as good an education as any, she supposed, and at least he was seeing his father in a new light. He seemed bright enough, bright as Newton, but he had a dreaminess about him, always losing himself in snatches of songs or odd phrases he picked up from Dathan or Charley.

Or Flynn. Once she awoke in the morning and started to think about her troubles, there seemed to be no end to them. He would pay back the loan for his land, she had no doubt, but she didn't like him around, cussing everything he saw. And now that he was marrying Marie—well, good luck to them both. It could only be good for Angus to have her around, but the good for her was harder to see. Perhaps Marie felt the blush of infamy more than Charlotte had realized. Angus was such a fearful little sprat, all duck and hide, his eyes always downward. Josephine was a silent one, too, but her silence was watchful, keeping track, passing judgment. In her unkinder moments Charlotte might call it scheming. Very well, she didn't like Josephine, go ahead and say it. Nobody said all little children were meant to be loved.

So. Toledo, and Cleveland, and then where? Buffalo? No, there was somewhere between. Erie. The trip was hardly begun, and she was already tired. And whose bright idea had it been to loop them up around the Great Lakes in February? Hers, she supposed.

She felt a heaviness surround her, fog drifting around her thoughts. She didn't want to sleep. There was too much to think about, too much to plan. But the fog kept drifting, and in the cloud of iridescent shapes that filled her eyelids, she lost herself.

૭૭

She awoke at first light, found the chamber pot, slid it back under the bed; but by this time the boys were up, and she stepped out into the hall to give them some time. The hall was dark and smelled of tobacco smoke and sweat.

They ate in the restaurant downstairs. Charlotte was grateful for every rush of frigid air that came in when someone entered; the stale indoor air was almost too much to bear. Afterwards they went to find the newspaper offices; Turner had wanted to spend the day talking up the editors.

"And us, Mother?" Adam asked. "What shall we do?"

"We will stay nearby while your father goes in and talks. Perhaps this city has a library."

But the streets were snowy, and no library could be found; they returned to the hotel, where Charlotte read and Adam played games on the floor.

The lecture that night was better attended, but it soon became clear that half the crowd had paid their money for the privilege of jeering. They were a rough-looking crew, greasy-haired and loud, and they spoke in an indeterminate mix of accents. Turner could hardly finish a sentence before someone would interrupt. He tried to stay ahead with wit, but Charlotte could tell he was laboring.

"You would have us give up the vote?" a man shouted from the back. "Give up what separates us from the mob?"

"I ask no one to give up a blessing," Turner called back. "The vote is a blessing, and blessings were made to be shared." He paused a beat. "As for separating you from the mob, I'd never take a man from his friends."

The roar of laughter put the crowd back into his hands. But after another minute, the man was on his feet again, his arms waving, the tendons in his neck as taut as banjo strings. "We fought a war!" he shouted. "We fought a war! And now you tell us we should change our way of life."

"I don't remember it being a war over keeping our privileges," Turner replied. But his voice was soft and weary; Charlotte could tell he had no stomach for a shouting match.

"First they want to give the vote to the niggers, and now the women!" the man shouted. "What kind of country are you trying to make? This ain't the country our grandfathers created."

"Your grandfather was sleeping in the woods so the Grand Duke's men wouldn't find him," someone said, and the crack brought a brief laugh. But the man would not be deterred. He marched down the center aisle shaking his fist.

"I fought!" he shouted. "I fought in this war, by God! I fought!"

There was a wooden chair behind the lectern. Turner sat down in it, heavily. "I fought, too," he said.

"I just bet!" the man said. "I know your type. Armchair generals. Big talkers. Idealists. Get down in the mud with me for a day, and we'll see how easy you want to give up your privileges, Mr. High and Mighty."

The stage was small; it only took Charlotte eight steps to reach the center. She planted her feet at the edge of the stage, her hands on her hips, and bent down to face the man.

"Well here I am!" she cried. "Take a good look at me! I'm your enemy."

The crowd grew quiet.

"Not too scary now, am I?" she went on. "You've seen us before. I'm a daughter, I'm a wife, I'm a mother, and yes, I am a citizen. I've got a brain and an idea of how this country should run. Some pretty good ideas, if you ask me. But you'd never ask me, would you? Because I'm the weaker sex."

"Ma'am, you should get off the stage," the man said, his tone abashed. "It ain't proper."

"I know that," Charlotte said. "But you'll go to a theatre to watch the dancers and actresses, won't you? It's only when we want to express ideas that it's not proper."

"A good hit!" someone called. The audience was murmuring restlessly, though. After all the years of leading Daybreak, Charlotte had nearly forgotten how strange it was to outsiders for a woman to take charge of a crowd.

"I'm not interested in who I hit or who I miss," she said. Out of the corner of her eye, she could see the lyceum manager talking animatedly to one of the stagehands, and she knew she only had a few more moments before they would wrestle her off. "Hit or miss is not the point. The point is, we have thoughts, we have opinions, and we deserve to be heard. We can run a home and a family. Give us a chance, and we can help you run the state and the country. And make no mistake about it, *we will be heard!*"

She hadn't meant to sound so rhetorical, but she had to admit, it was a good flourish. Now how to get off? Her mind raced. Perhaps something about Turner's service. She couldn't let that man get away with the "armchair general" remark.

In the instant she was considering, though, a voice called from the crowd, "Here's your hit!" She looked up to see an egg fly from the back of the room. It arched into the smoky darkness above the gaslights.

Instinctively she pulled out her skirt with both hands. The egg came down, lazy, almost hovering, it seemed so slow, and miraculously she caught it.

"Thank you!" Charlotte shouted to the man in back. She held up the egg to the whoops and whistles of the crowd. "My son will have this for breakfast tomorrow."

But the next egg came in lower and flatter, and she didn't see it until it was too late to duck. It caught her on the left shoulder and broke with a splat. Raw egg oozed down her sleeve.

"At least it's not rotten," she tried to say, but the spell was broken. Two more eggs flew up, and some kind of vegetable—she couldn't tell what it was, it flew past her so fast. A tomato? The manager stepped out, his arms waving, crying for order.

Then another egg hit her on top of the head, and in a rush Turner charged past her, leaped off the stage in a single bound, and knocked over his antagonist, who was still standing at the footlights.

"By God!" Turner cried. "Not my wife, you don't!"

"I didn't throw nothing!" shouted the man. By then they were rolling in the center aisle, all fists and elbows, a knot of excited men piling on, though whether to stop the fight or join in it Charlotte could not be sure.

An hour later they were back in the hotel. Charlotte had found some soap to wash her hair and sat in a chair to let it dry. Turner was lying on the bed, bruised though with no permanent damage, Adam resting against his shoulder.

"Well, there's a loss," Turner said, his gaze on the ceiling.

Charlotte did not answer. She knew what he meant: they had paid in advance for the lyceum, and their proceeds from the first two nights could hardly cover the loss of the third. She let her thoughts settle for a while.

"Not necessarily," she said after a bit.

Turner tilted his head to view her. "Think they'd let me back in for another night?" he said.

"He would if it meant a packed house. A packed house, all that food and drink he could sell. Cancel, and he gets none of that."

"All right," Turner said in a doubtful voice.

"But tomorrow night we need to plan better. When I come out and say my piece, it's not because you've been bested by a heckler. We plan the moment."

"Oh, I can't—"

"And I get offstage before they start to throw things. And for heaven's sake, don't jump into the crowd. You're lucky you didn't break a bone."

Turner didn't speak, but Charlotte could tell he was thinking. Together they sat in the lamplit room and contemplated the rest of the trip. If the spontaneous appearance of a suffrage-advocating woman socialist aroused to-night's crowd to such a frenzy, what kind of turnout could they expect if it was advertised in advance? But there would be notoriety, anger, and no doubt more eggs. Or worse. And Turner—Turner would become something else. The side act, the butt of jokes, the man who couldn't control his wife.

"Not everyone will rent to us if they know you're on the bill," he said.

"I would guess not," Charlotte said.

"We'd likely get run out of a few towns."

"Yes." They both looked at Adam. Send him home or keep him close? Hard to decide.

Turner rubbed his face. "All right," he said.

Chapter 13

Emile Mercadier's end came without warning. In January he developed a cough; in the first week of February he decided not to get out of bed one morning; and by the end of the month he was breathing fast and shallow, his heart fluttering, and his eyes vaguely focused on the wall. His mind wandered, and as Kathleen bathed his forehead he lost his sense of her, thinking back to his first wife, Josephine. Marie spelled her in the afternoons to let Kathleen have some quiet, though Kathleen never asked for it, and indeed when left to herself walked to Marie's cabin to fix dinner and watch Josephine. "I don't need crying time," she told Marie. "What with my first husband and everything else we lost in the war, I cried myself out years ago. I am plenty acquainted with grief."

Flynn had sense enough not to complain about Marie's time with her father, though she knew he was eager to marry. And why not? Surely it wasn't too vain to think of herself as something of a catch. She could cook, she had a way with children, she could do his reading for him when necessary, perhaps even teach him to read. And you couldn't fault the man for ambition, despite his evil moods and quick temper. It wasn't an impossible partnership.

She found herself alone with her father in the late afternoon of his death, Kathleen away sleeping, and a soft crackle of sleet on the roof. The room always seemed cold to her, no matter how she stoked the fire, but Emile didn't complain.

"*Cherie*," he said. His voice was scratchy. He had been lapsing into French a great deal lately, and Marie was disheartened to realize that she could no longer speak it well.

"I'm here," she said.

"J'ai peur."

Marie stood up and walked fast into the front room. No one there. She opened the door. She could see into the front room of Mrs. Smith's cabin next door, where Jenny the maid sat at her darning. There was a stick lying next to Marie's feet; she tossed it at Jenny's window, startling her out of her chair. She waved Jenny out to her door.

"Please," she called. "I need you to run down to my house and bring Mrs. Mercadier. I need her."

Something in Marie's voice made Jenny run without asking questions. Marie walked rapidly back to her father's bedside and took his hand again.

"Don't be afraid," she said. "I am here."

"If the man from the *Evening Post*…" he said. But then he seemed to lose his train of thought and gazed at the ceiling. After a minute, he repeated, *"J'ai peur."*

Marie didn't know what to say. Don't be afraid? Why not be afraid? "I'm here," she said, feeling inadequate. "Don't be afraid."

"Je n'ai peur pour moi," he said. *"Pour toi."*

She felt a sudden chill. Who was supposed to be comforting whom here? She had nothing to say and didn't want to ask why he was afraid for her and not for himself.

There was a rustle behind her; Kathleen had been found. Marie tried to stand but felt Kathleen's hand on her shoulder.

"Stay," Kathleen said. "He's been your father longer than my husband. Stay where you are."

So she sat, Kathleen standing behind her, and watched. Her father's lips moved a little but no sound came out. "Are you all right for this?" Kathleen murmured. "I think we've reached the end."

Marie didn't answer but stayed where she was. Emile either did not hear or was unable to respond; his breath continued to rasp. Marie felt a tightness in her chest and realized that she had been holding her breath for several seconds. It felt good to let it out.

Then his breathing stopped, and all was silent.

Marie felt oddly disappointed. No final blessing, no words of wisdom, just breathe, and breathe, and then stop. Was that the sum of a man? Apparently so.

The next several days were a blur of grieving, comforting, food, and decisions. With Turner away, the eulogy fell to John Wesley Wickman, who did a good job, though mild and halting. The tent Mr. Wilkinson had erected to shield his exhumation of Lysander Smith from prying eyes took up the front part of the cemetery, so Emile was buried toward the back, near the woods. Her father had always feared the forest, so it seemed wrong to have him back there. But so it was.

Afterward came the parade of condolences, all sincere enough, she supposed, although her own feelings were too numb to register them much of the time. There seemed to be an expectation that she should do something now. But what to do, and how to do it, were never mentioned. And Flynn was always close by. He had muttered some condolences to her on the day her father died and stood in the crowd during the burial, but other than that he was silent about the wound, planting and clearing instead of talking. The ways of men. But every morning her woodbox was full, without a word spoken, and she appreciated Flynn's silent attention. Nor did Dathan call on her, appropriately enough. But one evening she stepped out of her back door to fetch firewood and found a hot bowl on her chopping block, wrapped in a cloth. It was a thick stew of some sort, ground corn and squash and some sort of wild meat, and she could tell that the corn had been hand ground in a mortar, not milled between stones. It was bland and rather gamy, but filling. She had heard tales of Dathan's Indian wife but had never seen her; she washed the empty bowl the next day and set it on the chopping block, and in the morning it was gone. That night it returned, refilled.

After a month Flynn brought up the unspoken subject. "I guess you've put me off long enough," he said, whittling a stick in her yard as they said farewell for the evening. "Or ain't you going to marry me after all?"

"No," said Marie. "I'll marry you."

"All right, then. I'll go see the priest."

"Do we have to bring in the priest?"

Flynn shot her an angry look. "You may not care about the Mother Church, but I do," he said. "You should have sent for a priest back when your papa was passing. A man in his extreme moment needs all the comfort he can get."

Marie held her tongue. "All right, go talk to the priest."

A few days later he was back. "He'll marry us any time," he said. "But we have to make confession first. And I want to finish my fence. Won't take me more than another couple of days."

On a surprisingly cold April day, he fetched her in his wagon, and they took the long ride to Fredericktown. Despite the chill, the redbud was in bloom, and its splashes of lavender brightened the dull gray-brown of the hillsides where the trees had not yet come into leaf. Marie could not help remembering the times she and Turner had ridden out in the wagon together, how filled she was with passion and curiosity and wonder, wonder at their mutual audacity and at her own, amazed at herself that she could be so fearless or reckless or whatever it was, and filled with the excitement of the forbidden. This trip felt nothing like that. She felt as though she was giving in, though giving in to what she did not know. The need to be normal, perhaps. The need to have a father—a real father—for Josephine. Then, she had ridden out in the wagon with the thrill of a girl; now, she was riding out to marry with the sobriety of an adult. She glanced at Flynn from time to time; he was a decent enough man, she guessed, the hardest-working man in the county, as he liked to say. She would have to learn how to talk to him.

When they reached the rectory, Flynn stepped down and tied up the horse. "You wait," he said. "I'll tell him we're here."

He walked to the door, knocked, and went inside. In a moment he was back at the wagon. "In here," he said, helping her down from the wagon. "I'm to go first."

The church was a drafty brick building with a dim interior. Marie sat in a back pew while Flynn walked to the confessional nearest the rectory door. When she was a child in the Icarian colonies, she used to accompany her mother to confession once in a while, although her father had declared himself secular and refused to go; she had even made it through to her own first communion, and a few more, at thirteen. But after her mother's death, she had given it up. She hoped she could remember the ritual.

After several minutes Flynn emerged. He walked to her and laid his hand on her arm; Marie realized to her surprise that this was the first time he had touched her since before her father died.

"Father Tucker is his name," he said. "He's all right."

Marie found her way to the confessional and sat on the bench. "Bless me, father, for I have sinned. It has been many years since my last confession," she said. At least she remembered that much.

"How many years, my child?" The priest's voice was gentle. Through the screen she could see the outline of a round face with a mop of white hair on top.

"Many. A dozen? Fifteen, perhaps?"

"Oh, my! This may take a while. But that's all right. I have all the time we need."

She went into it, the adultery, the child out of wedlock. The lying that she had to do to accomplish the adultery. The loss of faith in God. She felt as if she would never reach the end of her sins. But eventually she did, or at least reached the end of her recollections. Then finally came the absolution, and she stepped back out into the light.

Flynn was outside, watering the horse with a bucket. "We're supposed to go into the rectory," he said. "He'll marry us there."

"Not in the church?"

He shook his head. "Ain't neither of us what you'd call faithful members here. He comes along the railroad now and then and says mass. I give him what coppers I have. But the rectory parlor is what we get."

They waited inside while the priest's housekeeper found some witnesses. "You're a child of Daybreak, then?" the priest said to her while they stood.

"Yes."

"But across the river, you'll be in my house," Flynn said vehemently. "Ain't no voting every week on everything."

Father Tucker noticed the consternation on Marie's face at the sudden force in Flynn's tone. He took her hand.

"Marriage is a solemn covenant, my dear," he said. "As Jesus is the head of the church, the husband is the head of the home. You must be prepared to accept your husband's admonitions and bear his reproofs with a cheerful heart. Can you do that?"

There seemed to be nothing for Marie to say but, "Yes, Father."

"And, my son, you must approach marriage with a loving heart. There is no room in a Christian marriage for resentment over old things. Can you look forward, and not behind, and give your wife guidance openly and lovingly?"

"Sure, Father. Sure I can."

Then the housekeeper showed up with a couple of old men in tow, and they lined up in the parlor, and within five minutes it was done.

They spoke little on the ride back. Marie's thoughts circled again and again around how she had gotten to this moment—first scandalized, then alone, and now married to man she still barely knew. Had she ever let her reason rule her? Hardly. She might claim that she was marrying Flynn for the home and for Josephine, but she didn't believe it herself. She certainly didn't feel rational.

She felt a sudden loss of confidence in her imagined adult decision and turned away from Flynn to hide the tears that were streaking her cheeks.

"No crying," Flynn said. "I'll have no weepy wife in my home. Crying women make me nervous."

"Sorry," Marie said, wiping her face with her coat sleeve.

She had sent Josephine and Angus to stay with Kathleen for the night, so the cabin was dark and silent when they arrived. Flynn dropped the rails in one section of his fence and led the wagon through. "There ain't a finer fence in the county," he said, pride in his voice. "Mule high, hog tight, and bull strong. My herd comes in next week, maybe the week after that."

"And who will tend your herd while you're off working on the railroad?"

Flynn's reply was quick and fierce. "My son and my wife, and her daughter, that's who. Unless you think you're too fine for cattle farming."

"Of course not," she said. She regretted that her question had sounded querulous. She hadn't meant to start the night on the wrong foot. "But I don't know anything about cattle, I'll warn you that."

"What's to know?" They eat grass. In the summer we make hay and in the winter we feed it to them. They drink from the river, and in the fall we drive them to a siding on this railroad I am building and sell them to whoever gives us the most."

He helped her down from the wagon and went to put the horse in the barn while Marie stepped inside.

So this was to be her home. She lit the lantern hanging inside the door. Flynn could certainly use a woman's touch. The floor needed sweeping, the makeshift window was covered with grease and cobwebs, and ashes had spilled out of the hearth, blackening the planks on its border. It was a wonder he hadn't burned the place down by now. Marie reminded herself to bring in flowers from the fields whenever they were in bloom, the place was so dark and colorless.

Marie found some cornmeal and salt pork in canisters. It was getting dark; no time to gather greens. Hoecake and salt pork would have to do for their wedding meal. She would have been glad to have some of Dathan's Indian stew right now. There were forks and plates on a shelf, not necessarily clean, but cleanish enough to use. She wiped them with a towel and set them on the table, and as she did, she saw a tin of lard on the shelf as well. *That might come in handy later on.* She scooped out a thick fingerful and wiped it into a teacup, which she placed on a table beside the bed in the other room.

It seemed like Flynn had been gone a long time. When he finally came in from the barn, his hair and skin were wet; Marie realized with a pleased start that he had bathed in the river.

They ate as they had ridden, in long swaths of silence broken by bursts of awkward conversation, the night ahead weighing on them. "That was good. Thank you," Flynn said, pushing his plate away.

"I'll do better once I've sorted out what you have," Marie said.

"I don't doubt that a bit. I ain't been much of a cook or an eater, as you can imagine. Be good for Angus to have some honest food."

They both knew it was time. Marie stacked their plates in Flynn's washing pan and went into the bedroom.

Her trunk had been placed on the floor at one end of the room. She opened it; her nightdress was on top, right where she had placed it. She put it on and lay on top of the covers. The room was cold; she reminded herself to bring in a bed warmer tomorrow night. With a quick gesture, she dipped the lard out of the teacup and inserted it into herself.

She cleared her throat. "You can come in now," she said.

Flynn entered, carrying the lantern. He looked at her as she lay on the bed. "You're a pretty thing," he said. "I ain't no beauty, I'll admit to that. But you got me, for whatever that's worth."

He took off his shirt. He was lean and strong, and his body was scarred. Marie could not stop looking at him.

"I'm a brute, ain't I?" he said. She didn't answer. "I know I ain't the kind of fine-thinking man you deserve. You wanted Horace Greeley, and you got a Irish railroad navvy."

"You're a good man," she said, her voice no more than a whisper. "You're not just a railroad navvy."

"That is the goddam truth," he said hoarsely. "I am a man, and a proud man at that. Wouldn't matter what I am, though. 'Cause you got me now, and I got you. Ain't that right?"

"Yes," she said. "That's right."

He dropped his pants and climbed on top of her. With both hands he pulled her nightdress over her head.

She wasn't ready for this, wasn't ready for him. But he was already nose to nose with her, and she was glad she had greased herself, for he was right there before she knew it, before she had a chance to say 'wait.' He gripped her shoulders.

"Don't you holler now," he said.

No, she wasn't going to holler. And maybe he was just a dumb Mick with no manners and no idea of how to treat a woman. But she had done this of her own free will, she had married Michael Flynn for better or for worse, and there was no repining. Everyone in Daybreak thought she was mad to marry this man, this illiterate oaf. Everyone in Daybreak could go to hell. Michael Flynn could go to hell, rutting her like a brindle bull in springtime. No one was going to get her tears from now on, not even herself. She would holler for no one and nothing. And as he labored above her with his eyes closed and a look of vacant concentration on his face, Marie felt a strange sense of freedom. So she had thrown her life away; she had done it her own damn self.

Chapter 14

The hiding place was good. Newton, being the oldest, had the most freedom around the colony; the old empty house south of the village, the Webb place, was off-limits to the children, but Newton found he could go up the mountain, into the woods, and then swing down behind the old barn and sheds without being seen from the kitchen windows of Daybreak. And that was how he found the cave behind the old Webb place.

A spring ran out of the cave, a muddy, sulfurous trickle that dribbled through some wooden troughs into one of the sheds. They would gather at the mouth of the cave after chores, Newton, Josephine, Angus, and the Wickman twins, Sarah and Penelope, and feel the warm air blowing out, warm now but in summer it would feel delightfully cool, and they reveled in its moist dirty odor. They moved carefully; the girls had to keep their dresses clean, and Angus kept fearfully looking down the road.

"Papa'll tan my hide if I ain't watching the cows when he comes home," Angus said.

"Those cows ain't going anywhere," Newton said scornfully. "They're in a field with grass and water. No reason to jump the fence."

"It's not the cows he'll be after. It's me."

"When's your brother coming home?" asked Penelope. She leaned against a limestone boulder, her leg braces propped beside her. Penelope's hips had never healed from their birth problems, and she walked with a wide-legged swing on the braces her father had fixed up for her, first one side, then the other, like the make-believe walking of a doll carved from a tree joint.

"Letter said this week, maybe tonight even. Depends on the trains," Newton said.

"I miss him," said Penelope.

"I don't," Newton replied. "Always following me around, asking dumb questions."

Sarah looked up from playing cat's cradle with Josephine. "That's what brothers are for."

"Well, I can do without it," Newton said. "He's a pest."

Both Sarah and Penelope had inherited their mother's amiability, but while Penelope had a gentle quality, Sarah was peppier, quick to tease. She was as active as Penelope was contemplative. "Your mama's a good teacher," she said to Josephine. "I like her."

Josephine said nothing, but smiled to herself.

"Papa's gonna tan my hide," Angus repeated.

"Your papa's cows are scary," Penelope said. "I don't like their horns."

"A cow is a cow," Newton insisted. "There is nothing to be scared of in a cow."

"They're too big," Penelope said. "Big old cows with big old horns. I don't like them."

"Suit yourself," Newton said. "Don't go around them, then."

"Lordy, I won't," she said. "They're across the river, anyway."

"Let's do something," Sarah said. "I'm tired of sitting here."

They sat silent for a moment, waiting for Newton to suggest something.

"All right," he said. "Let's go look in the old Webb house."

This was more than anyone had counted on. "Are you joking?" Angus said. "Somebody'd see us for sure."

"I think that house is haunted," Sarah said. Newton answered her with a look. "Well, I do!" she repeated.

"It's not haunted," he said. "Charley Pettibone lives in it. We won't go inside. We'll just look in the windows."

Dubious looks passed.

"Charley Pettibone was a rebel," Sarah said. "He and some old ghost would probably get along just fine."

"If anybody sees us, we're as dead as the old gray goose," Angus said. Penelope nodded agreement. Sarah shrugged but looked doubtful.

"All right, I'll go," Josephine said.

And with that, they were off, Newton and Josephine in the lead, the other three trailing. From the cave mouth they followed the wooden troughs to a dilapidated shed, where the troughs drained into a series of old tubs, now filled with silt. "I remember old Mr. Webb," Newton said over his shoulder. "He was all right. He wouldn't be a ghost. Or if he would, he'd be a good ghost."

"I remember Harp Webb," Josephine said. "He wouldn't be a good ghost."

"Harp Webb is buried up in the graveyard. If he haunts anyplace, it would be there."

They walked around the back side of the barn, out of sight of Daybreak.

"That's where we should have gone, up to the graveyard," Angus said. "We could see if that man Mr. Wilkinson is digging somebody up like he says he is. My papa says he just goes up there and drinks whiskey all day."

The group stopped at the corner of the barn. From here it was a long walk across open ground to the house. "Think anybody's watching?" Sarah said.

"Nah," said Newton. "They're all working."

Angus's gaze was turned the other direction, south down the road where his father would be coming.

"How come your daddy doesn't make you mind the cows, too?" Sarah asked Josephine.

"He's not _my_ daddy," Josephine snapped. "Mr. Turner is my daddy. I used to get letters from him."

The certain tone of her reply stopped them short. They knew there was something irregular in the whole business, something in the past that the adults didn't talk about. Newton's daddy was Josephine's daddy, too, though how that had all happened wasn't clear. There was a secret story to it that none of them quite knew. Newton had always sensed the strangeness, and of course his mother didn't like Josephine; everybody could see that. It all tied together somehow. One day he would have to ask.

"Well, your stepdaddy then," Sarah said.

"He knows I don't care if his cows walk off a cliff," Josephine said. Her hair was long and black and straight, like her mother's; she flipped it to one side with her hand, as if the flip itself was sending cows to their perdition. "I don't know why Mama married him anyway."

"Are you going to get married someday, Newton?" Penelope asked. But Newton was busy peeking around the corner, looking for grownups. He glanced over his shoulder with a sniff.

"Nope," he said. "I'm going to join the Army and go to West Point, like my grandpa," he said. "A soldier's got no time for marriage."

"Your grandpa was married," Penelope persisted. "And your daddy was a soldier."

Newton paused. "Well, maybe someday," he said. "All right, let's go. Walk brisk, don't run. You'll just draw attention."

He started at a quick walk across the yard to the corner of the old Webb house, Josephine following, Sarah and Penelope behind. But Angus was not to be seen. The children walked faster, then began to run, piling into a laughing heap once they had reached the safety of the house. But Angus?

Angus was nowhere. Then a few seconds later, there he was, off in the distance, dashing back from the shed where they had hidden, running toward the Daybreak barn, and from there presumably to the Temple, the river crossing, and his father's cattle pasture.

"Well, beat the Dutch," Newton said. "Angus has run off. Oh, well, let's get to exploring." He looked around for something to stand on to peer into the windows of the Webb house. "Story is, when old Mr. Webb died, he left ten thousand dollars in gold buried somewhere around this place. Everybody went crazy digging for it, but it was never found."

But Penelope Wickman, always perceptive to things around her, was paying no attention to Newton's story. Her eyes were fixed on the far distance, to the north, where the road from town emerged from the trees on the other side of the river. A wagon was descending the hill and had reached the ford.

"Newton," Penelope said, "I think your mama and daddy are home."

Chapter 15

As soon as they crossed the river, Adam hopped down from the back of the wagon and ran ahead to join the children. Turner watched him go with a moment of longing. When was the last time he ran to anything with such carefree pleasure? The envy of the adult for the hearts of children.

They had kept their eyes averted as they passed Michael Flynn's place—a tender subject for a constellation of reasons, but even a sidelong glance revealed much: the tall rail fence surrounding twenty acres of woods pasture; a half dozen tightly muscled, compact-looking red cows browsing under the trees; a hog lot closer to the river, built, it appeared, directly over the grave of that bushwhacker Turner had killed.

The fence was well done, the cattle good looking. Perhaps that was how they should have done it, enclosed their pasture instead of letting their cattle roam the mountain, bought a real breed like these Devon reds or some shorthorns, instead of their rangy mixed-breed milkers. But they hadn't, so what was there to say. He knew Flynn still owed them for the land, and the word was that he had borrowed heavily from someone in town for the cattle. That was the new order of business, everything on credit, every man for himself. Their old ideas of equality and common sharing, those were finished.

The lecture tour had proved that. Nobody wanted to hear about Daybreak or their ideals. Charlotte was the attraction, and it wasn't her opinions that had mattered most of the time; it was the novelty of them, the man-and-wife team, lecturing on suffrage to the scoffing crowds, more a performing act than a true lyceum talk. But the goal had been accomplished. They had brought home money, plenty of it, enough to finance the colony until the fall harvest. After that—well, they would worry about after that when after that came.

The farther east they had gone, the less they had to deal with ridicule and egg-throwers; in Boston the crowds argued more about tactics than about the rightness of the cause. Turner could tell that Charlotte liked the debate; she stayed late taking on all comers, as he had once done, talking to anyone who would talk, while he took Adam back to the hotel room, returning for her once the boy was safely in a maid's care. He knew the role made him a figure of fun. He'd seen his caricature in the *New York Herald*, with an apron over his officer's uniform, trailing the figure of his strutting wife with a basket of flowers to cast in her path. But he didn't mind. The limelight no longer gave him pleasure. The longer the tour went on, the more he dreaded those nights, standing before a hall filled with strangers, men with hostile faces and angry questions. One night in Baltimore, a man had rushed toward the stage waving his fist, incensed by something he had said, and Turner had felt as if he were back in battle, summoning every fiber of his nerve to stay in place, not run from the scene. He had found himself five feet behind the lectern, unconsciously thrown back, and had to force himself to step forward again. Charlotte could have the limelight, as far as he was concerned. And now someone was writing her, wanting her to come to Kansas, where there was a big fight shaping up over suffrage.

The first thing Turner noticed as they approached the village was the smell of camphor drifting from the graveyard. More of Wilkinson's flimflam. It was a wonder Mrs. Smith had put up with it as long as she had, wintering in Daybreak on the wagonloads of tinned food and Parker's Tonic she had shipped in from Philadelphia.

They stopped the wagon at the Wickmans' house to greet John Wesley and Mary; Adam and the other children had already disappeared. As always, Wickman greeted him warmly but formally, in his mild way. They walked to look over the fields. Evening was falling; the ride from the train depot at Pilot Knob had taken them the better part of the day.

"You are well?" Turner asked. "And the children?"

"Oh, yes. Newton was a fine help. He's a boy to make you proud."

"Perhaps before too long he'll stop by and say hello," Turner said dryly.

"Oh, he will," Wickman said. "Whatever fancies the boy may have, when he acts, he acts responsible. He does near the work of a man."

They stood at the edge of the cornfield. The ground was plowed and dragged, ready to be planted. Turner squatted and crushed a clod between his fingers. It was damp, too damp for this time of year. "Late planting this spring," he said.

Wickman grunted in agreement. They remained there, sniffing the air, unwilling to go inside.

"Dathan's taken a wife," Wickman finally said. "Indian gal from somewhere."

This news smelled like trouble. "Are they living in Daybreak?" Turner asked.

"Not that I can tell. He's in and out of that house, but I never see her. I think they're up at Creek Nation most of the time."

"How do you know he's married, then? Maybe they just jumped the broom."

"He came around and introduced her! Just like Commodore Vanderbilt on a social call. The missus didn't know what to do."

"What did she do?"

"Gave 'em some shortcake. What else would you do?"

They smiled together at the absurdity of doing anything else, knowing that for most, Mary's response would have been the absurd one. "Not going over well around the county, I would guess."

"I'm not for sure anybody else knows or cares."

"If they knew, they'd care. Freedom is one thing, mixing of the races is another."

"Minding my own business has kept me out of a great deal of trouble," Wickman said. "I recommend it to the general."

They said nothing for a while. Finally Turner said, "The trip went well. Good hard cash for the colony. It's in the wagon."

It felt comfortable to stand there with Wickman, communicating the way men do, talking about objects and processes. Turner realized that he had lost his need to retreat to the far ends of the valley; maybe his sojourn in the cities had done him some good after all.

"Glad to hear that," Wickman said. "We read a few articles about your tour. Cash is low around here right now. Grindstaff is happy to carry us, of course."

"I'm sure he will," Turner said with a grimace. "He'll carry us all the way to the poor house and even help us with the auction."

"He's a businessman, all right."

"Everyone's a businessman these days, except us."

"What, you've regained your faith in capital?"

Turner shook his head. "Just feeling a bit outmoded at the moment." He brushed off his hands. "Let's walk up and see Mr. Mercadier's grave."

As Turner and Wickman walked up the valley toward the graveyard, they saw Wilkinson emerge from his tent and walk toward them in the dim light. He met them halfway down the slope.

"Gentlemen." Wilkinson nodded gravely. "Mr. Turner, it's a pleasure. News from the world?"

"None to speak of," Turner said. "The work of reconstruction has hardly begun in some places. Mr. Johnson is no Abe Lincoln, I'm afraid."

Wilkinson sighed. "Gentlemen, speaking of reconstruction, I have failed here. I have tried everything in my powers, and Mr. Smith cannot be restored to a viewable state." He glanced at Mrs. Smith's cabin in the village. "I must tell madame."

Turner shook his hand. "Good luck with that."

Wilkinson shook Wickman's hand as well. "I've said this before, but it bears repeating. That coffin you built for me is as fine a piece of work as I've seen. You should come back to Philadelphia and work for me."

"Thank you, no," Wickman said. "I came from back East and I like it fine here."

"There's good money in this line of work. Real good money."

"I'm not interested in the money. That's the joy of this place. I don't have to be interested in the money."

Wilkinson gave the two of them a humoring smile. "You people are a mystery," he said. "If I hadn't lived among you, I'd say you were a dangerous lot of radicals."

"Maybe you should write a book," Turner said. "I hear that travels among the exotics are big sellers these days."

"Just an 'umble undertaker," Wilkinson said. "You're the great author." He walked off down the hill toward Mrs. Smith's cabin.

"She'll eat him alive," Wickman said as they continued toward the graveyard.

Wilkinson's tent had blocked their view of most of the cemetery, but as they drew closer they could see around it. Someone was standing beside a new grave near the edge of the woods—it could only be Emile's. Another step, and he recognized her: Marie.

His heart sank. He had not wanted to see her, or at least wanted the first time he saw her to be at a time when he could prepare himself and control his feelings. He stopped and turned around. This was wrong, all wrong.

Too late. She had seen him. He could see her stiffen and turn away. And now Wickman had caught on, and he didn't know what to do either, and everyone was embarrassed. But here they were, with nothing to do but press forward.

Marie kept her head turned away from him as she came down the path, seeming as she was going to walk right past them. But the path was nothing more than a wagon track. They could not simply pass.

"I'm so sorry——" he began as they drew near. But there were congratulations to offer, too. "But I understand there is happiness to balance the——" Nothing seemed right. He stopped.

"Thank you," she murmured, her face still averted. "My father was always one of your great admirers."

"Those cattle of your mister's are a fine-looking breed," Wickman observed placidly, as if there were no tension in the air.

"Yes," Marie said, moving to go around them. "He will be home soon."

And it was in her turning sidewise to pass them that Turner saw her face at last, not quite full on, but three-quarters profile in the fading light. But even that glimpse was enough to see what she was hiding: a bruise on her cheek and jaw, yellow in the center, purple around the yellow, streaks of red toward the neck, the side of her face swollen and rounded. "I must go," she said, hurrying down the hill.

Turner held himself in until they reached Mercadier's grave. It was still a fresh, raw heap of red earth, mounded over, rocks and clods spilling down the hillside.

"I don't know what to say," Wickman said apologetically. "I've seen little of the girl since she married and moved across the river. They're having a tough time of it, so it seems." He patted Turner's shoulder and gestured toward the grave. "I'm sorry you missed your chance to say goodbye to old Emile. Grand old gentleman, he was. I'm working on a marker," he said. "There was a nice piece of gray limestone I found downriver, and it shaped up real good. Need to decide what to carve on it, though."

Turner tried to reply, thankful for Wickman's effort to redirect his thoughts away from the ugly thing they had just seen and for his tact in not mentioning the past that lay between them, and he managed to get out a word or two. But then something happened. His legs refused to hold him up, and his vision went away. And before he knew what was going on, he was on the ground, wallowing and writhing like a wounded snake, and he could taste dirt on his lips and in his throat even while he could hear Wickman, his voice seeming to come from a great distance although Turner knew he was kneeling right there beside him, telling him easy son, easy, you don't really know anything, but Turner was crying out although he knew it was none of his business what went on in someone else's family, especially this family and especially him, but he was crying out and moaning anyway, saying that he was going to kill him, the dirty Mick. He was going to kill him, break his neck, chop off his head like a goddam chicken.

Chapter 16

They brought Sam Hildebrand's body by wagon from southern Illinois to Missouri for viewing with several different stories about how he had come to die. It wasn't even clear how he had ended up in Illinois. The last Charley had heard, Hildebrand was in Texas. But the story was he had moved to Illinois, he had come out of a tavern, been recognized by the town marshal, and shot dead on the spot before he could draw a weapon. Or he had been killed in a fight inside the tavern and claimed by the marshal for the reward.

Or he hadn't been killed at all.

The mood on Rockpile was glum. It had been raining steadily for a week; the creeks were swollen, forcing everyone to walk in from the high ground— Charley's route—instead of coming up from the south. The river could no longer be forded. At Daybreak, they had tied skiffs to trees for those who had to make the crossing. Even in a skiff, crossing the river was nerve-racking; the swift current brought limbs downstream at a frightening speed, and a large scour hole had opened up where the road once sloped gently into the stream. Wouldn't you know, Charley had thought as he fought his way across, right where that Irish son of a bitch could put in a ferry and charge everyone a dollar to cross. Despite the high water, though, the Law and Order League had a good turnout for its Sunday afternoon meeting.

"I tell you one thing," Horace Landsome said. "If somebody did kill him, it wasn't a fair fight. The man ain't been born that could best Sam Hildebrand in a fair fight."

Charley knew this wasn't true. Once a fight started, luck was what killed or saved a man, mostly. He'd seen it plenty of times, a seasoned man carried away by a load of grapeshot while the raw idiot standing next to him didn't even get his hat knocked off. But this was no time to start an argument.

Green Pratt took the news with his usual roars of rage. Their first raid had been a success. They had hung three men, two well-known criminals who had used the war to enrich themselves and the uppity black man Pratt had picked out, given two men severe beatings, and carried a loose woman to Marble Creek and ducked her a couple dozen times. Even better, they had made the St. Louis papers, and now the Law and Order League was the talk of the state. Pratt had been eager to make a new list and spent their meetings shouting for more names, more names, despite the Federal military patrols that now rode the countryside. Charley was ready to quit the group if he could figure out how to do it without getting his own name on the list as a traitor to the cause.

"The bastard!" Pratt cried. "The man should have been given a hero's welcome, not run out of the state to die among strangers. What's the name of that town? Pinckneyville? Let's ride to Pinckneyville and give the marshal a taste of Missouri medicine."

"I don't even know where Pinckneyville is," someone said.

"I think it's on the Ohio River somewhere," someone else said helpfully.

"God damn it!" Pratt hollered out. "Shut your traps. All right, we won't ride to Illinois. Too many damn troops between here and there anyway. Besides, plenty to do here."

"They'd spot us and hang us before we got halfway there," the Ohio River man said.

"I said shut up!" Pratt repeated. He made as if to strike the man, but changed course and hit the side of his own head instead. "We gotta go up and see Sam, that's what we gotta do. Comfort the widow and console the orphan."

"His wife died last year, is what I heard," the man said.

This time Pratt didn't hesitate. He cuffed the man above the ear, and in an instant the two of them were rolling on the rain-slick rocks, locked and punching. Men rushed to separate them. It was a brief flurry that ended with muttered apologies and a handshake, blood wiped from scraped skin.

"All right," Pratt said, huffy with embarrassment. "We'll go see Sam. He's up at the courthouse in Farmington. But here's the thing. If nobody identifies him, the marshal don't get the reward money. So even if it is Sam, we don't say a thing."

Hildebrand's body was propped against the courthouse wall in a narrow wagon bed, which Charley suspected was destined to serve as his coffin unless somebody came through with a better one. It was Sam, all right, although his head was gaping on one side from a pistol wound, and his body had begun to putrefy and swell. The group filed past a few at a time, hoping to avoid attention from the Federal troops that lounged about staring rudely at all who came.

Hildebrand's mother and brothers-in-law, the Hampton boys, stood on the lawn a few feet away, speaking with those who stopped. Charley shook the woman's hand.

"I'm sorry for your loss," he said.

She said nothing, eyeing him suspiciously, until one of the Hampton boys leaned in. "He's all right," he said. "He was in the war."

"You ride with Sam?" she said.

"No, ma'am," Charley said. "Regular army."

"Better choice anyway," said the mother. "For you, it's over. Sam's boys, they chase them like barn rats."

"Yes, ma'am." Charley didn't know what else to say, so he moved on.

Harley Willingham, the Madison County sheriff, had been squatting under a tree at a corner of the courthouse lot. He fell into step beside Charley.

"You all ain't been doing much lately," he said.

"Too wet to plant," Charley said. "Half the field's underwater."

"That ain't what I mean. You know what I mean."

Charley stopped and looked the man square in the face. "I'm sure I don't know what you mean, Mr. Provost-Marshal."

Willingham's face was impassive. "War's over, son. The quicker we all forget what we did in the war, the better off we'll be."

Charley walked on, Willingham keeping pace. He knew Willingham had a point. Green Pratt and his boys could rave and holler all they wanted, and hang a man here and there, but that didn't change the fact that the war was over and they had lost. One of these days they would be the ones being hung, a prospect Charley didn't care to contemplate.

Willingham seemed to read his thoughts. "I ain't looking to arrest you. I ain't looking to enlist you, either. Just let me know if anything too crazy is getting ready to happen, and I'll work from there. Come November, I'll be up for election again, and I'll need some new deputies. I can see you as a deputy sheriff a lot quicker than some of these damn Germans that're overrunning the county."

"OK," Charley said. "I'll think about it."

"You do that."

Charley waited for Willingham to get out of sight. He had ridden to town in Pratt's wagon and didn't want Willingham to see him join them again. For that matter, he didn't want Pratt to have seen him talking to Willingham, either. Trouble both ways.

There was a dense cloud on the southwest horizon. Sure enough, they hadn't gone a mile before the rain started again, this time with lightning.

"Well, God damn it," Pratt muttered, pulling his slicker over his head and looking back in the wagon. There was Charley, who had to get to Daybreak, and another horseless man from Fredericktown. "Pettibone, I'm dropping you at the Oak Grove turnoff, and you're on your own from there. It'll be hard night before I get home anyway."

By the time Charley started walking from the main road down to Daybreak, it was sunset, or what would have been sunset if there had been any sun to see. His rain slicker had done him little good; he was drenched and shivering, and figured that just his luck somebody would have paddled the skiff to the other side. He would have to holler until someone heard him, someone who was brave or foolish enough to cross that damn river in near darkness.

A glimpse of light and the smell of smoke from one of the huts in the Indian camp tempted him for a moment. But he was damned if he would take shelter with Dathan and his Indian bride, not half a mile from his own house. He worked his way down the bluff in the dwindling light, his lower half covered with mud from slipping on the wet rocks.

As soon as Charley reached the river bottom, he knew he would never cross tonight. He could hear the river's low roar and could smell the earthy musk of ground covered by water that shouldn't be covered by water. Out of curiosity more than anything else, he walked ahead.

Then he heard cries and shouts, and knew there was trouble. A lantern waved wildly through the trees. Charley ran toward it.

Flynn, the fool, had built his house too close to the river. He had put everything too close to the river. By the time Charley got there, the hog lot was gone, and two feet of water covered the floor of the house. Flynn, Marie, Josephine, and Angus were frantically carrying everything out of the house to a hump of ground about a hundred feet back.

"Carry it farther back!" Charley shouted as he dashed to help. "You'll have to carry it again later tonight if it keeps raining."

"Go fuck yourself!" Flynn shouted in reply, holding up the lantern to see who had arrived. "Help or don't help, suit yourself. We'll carry it again once we get it all out."

Charley waded through the chill water to the back bedroom. The mattress was gone—removed already, or perhaps lost to the water—but the bed frame was still in place. He threw it over his shoulder and fought his way to the door. The children were wading around in the front room, chasing floating papers and toys.

Charley half-floated, half-carried the bed frame to the spot of high ground, followed by the children with armloads of goods. The water was only a couple of feet from it already, and he could feel the current tugging at his ankles. He tossed it onto the highest spot, where Marie and Josephine struggled to throw a canvas over a pile of clothing.

"That ain't worth doing," he said, but helped her anyway. Flynn arrived with a trunk over his shoulder.

"God damn river," he said.

Marie put on a brave face. "Now we can start building that octagon house you are always talking about," she said. "We'll put it back here on the high ground." Flynn just shot her an angry look, and she fell silent.

Charley didn't want to get between them at this moment. He returned to their flooded house and waded in the door, feeling with his feet for anything that might be a possession. Flynn arrived with the lantern, and together they surveyed the interior.

"It'll clean up," Charley said.

"I know that. I don't need consoling," said Flynn. They walked into the back room. Nothing left to carry out but a crucifix on the wall. It was ingeniously made, with grapevines twisted into the shape of a man on a cross of two neatly mortised slats.

"I did that," Flynn said, taking it down.

"Nice work," Charley said.

"Damn straight. Now let's see if we can salvage some of my rails."

From the house to the river, Flynn's rail fence gradually disappeared into the brown water.

"River's still rising," Charley said. "Some of them rails are halfway to the state line by now."

"I put a lot of work into these rails," Flynn replied. "Don't worry, I'll pay you for your time."

"Don't insult me," Charley said. He waded into the water and started pulling rails, which was a tougher job than it looked. Flynn had fixed each length with two uprights, cross-and-rail style, and in some places he had tied the crossed uprights together. Charley had to admit as he tugged at the rails that Flynn had done a fine job of fence-building.

Finally Charley got some loose and tossed them behind him. Angus, chest-deep, scurried to fetch them.

"Push 'em into the shallows," Flynn said. "We'll collect them in a minute."

Flynn waded further into the water to pull out more rails. Charley stayed where he was, groping in the dark for the bottom ones.

Angus followed his father, who handed the lantern to him. "Here, boy," he said. "Just hold this high so I can see. I need to work with both hands."

It seemed to Charley that they were in the hog lot. He remembered that Flynn had curved his fence inward here so there was only a narrow V leading to the water. He felt his way past Flynn to where the ground dropped off, what in normal times would be the riverbank.

"You ain't getting anything past here," he called out to Flynn.

Flynn glanced up from his work and nodded.

Angus, too, came forward to see, holding the lantern high in one hand while corralling a couple of rails with the other. Charley thought to warn him not to come too far, that the ground sloped down very quickly and the current was strong, but Angus pushed forward before he could speak. He could tell that the boy was about to say something, because he opened his mouth, but then the rails slipped out of his hand into the deeper water. Charley made a grab for them; Angus made a grab for them. Charley cried out—no words, just a shout, which got Flynn's attention. He saw what was about to happen and reached for his son.

But the water slowed them down as they grabbed for Angus; the boy's expression was startled, then frightened, as he stepped in a hole. His head bobbed under the surface of the floodwater. Then the lantern went underwater as well. All was dark, and Angus was gone.

Chapter 17

They had built a rude chicken coop in the woods out of tied-together sassafras saplings and salvaged fence rails; it was enough to keep out the foxes, but that was all. Marie could only hope that a bear wouldn't come by. But eggs were down, and as Marie collected them one afternoon she could see one reason why.

A three-foot blacksnake was curled in one of the nests, its body lumpy from the eggs it had swallowed; Marie could count two, perhaps three. She gazed at it. Surely it was aware of her presence, but it did not move.

There was an egg in the nest beside it. She needed to gather it. But if she reached down for the egg, the snake would bite her.

Once she would have called for Angus. He had no fear of these creatures. He would have laughed at her dread and picked it up, carried it off to the far woods somewhere.

But now there was no Angus, and she couldn't call Michael. He would just take his almighty ax and kill it, perhaps give her a cuff for taking him away from his work, leaving her to deal with the bloody remains. She would kill it herself.

But of course she wouldn't, she no more had it in her to kill that snake than to take wings and fly. Michael was wrong about many things, but he was right about this one—she was a soft woman, soft to the core, unsuited for the strife and scrabble of a working existence. For Michael everything was war. He was at war with the railroad builders who were always wanting to work him an extra hour for no extra money. He was at war with Ferguson in town, who had loaned him the money for the cattle. He was at war with Daybreak across the river, although she doubted if they were aware of it. Marie wasn't sure if he considered her an ally in his wars or another enemy. Probably some of both.

At first this feeling had worked in their favor. He was angry, she was angry, and in the night they turned their anger into a strange sort of passion. They gripped each other's biceps, they couldn't bear to have clothing on, they pressed their faces together as if trying to push through to bone. It was animal, and it was good. Sometime in the early spring they had made a baby, although she hadn't told him yet. She wasn't that far along.

But then the rains came, and the farm flooded, and Angus was lost. There was no longer any way to turn Michael's anger into anything warm or productive. The cloud under which he labored was impenetrably dense.

The first time he had struck her, she had cried, naturally. A slap across the cheek hurts. But the look on his face—proud, belligerent—gave her to know that tears would only make things worse. So she did not cry anymore, not even the time when he had popped her shoulder out of joint. She took a perverse pride in that.

She had felt worse things than the bite of a snake.

She reached into the nest, grasped the egg, warm in her fingers. She drew out her hand.

The snake did not bite.

Marie put the egg in her apron pocket and bent her way out the makeshift door of the coop. Small victories, but she would take them however she got them.

The night Angus had drowned was a blur to her now. She remembered the chill of the water, the gritty filth of it in her shoes. She remembered Michael flinging himself into it again and again, Charley Pettibone dragging him out, a mad scramble to find poles or ropes, anything to locate Angus, and their failure, the dread realization that came over them, and Michael now in a frenzy, words and cries that made no sense, and then the fear. Charley had led them up the hill to the Indian camp, where Dathan and Cedeh wrapped them in blankets. Then unconsciousness, till morning when they descended the slippery hill again to find that Michael had gathered all their possessions and piled them on a high spot farther back, and there he lay upon them asleep, like the old tales of a dragon and its hoard.

They went for days without speaking. Men and women came by to comfort them, left food, but Michael turned them away or retreated to the woods when he saw them coming. There was no funeral because there was nothing to bury. Marie lived in dread of the moment when the waters would recede and reveal Angus, lodged in a willow grove or trapped in a root wad, for then all would be raw and fresh again and Michael's madness would return. But no Angus ever appeared as the river returned to its banks. Their grief turned to a dull, hollow pain, no less painful despite the dullness, the pain of an amputation rather than that of a wound.

Now, months later, Michael was no less mad but had grown cunning. He had built a ferry where the flood had washed out the river crossing, and sometimes in the night he deepened the hole. "Mother Nature needs our help," he would say, slipping out the door barefoot, a shovel in his hand. He worked without a lantern so the people in Daybreak wouldn't see him, although she didn't know why it mattered; they kept a wagon on their side of the river and crossed in a skiff, swimming the horses. Marie suspected it was just the thrill of getting away with something that spurred him to secrecy. Hardly two travelers a week came by, so it wasn't as though the ferry made them much money.

Marie cradled the eggs in her apron pocket. She supposed she should find Josephine and get her started in the garden. Beans were coming up and needed to be weeded. But as she emerged from the woods into the house clearing, Josephine was already out there, bent down, pulling the weeds from the roots just as she had shown her. She did not speak as Marie passed by.

Marie placed the eggs on the counter and thought about lunch. Now that it was just the two of them during the week, she sometimes forgot lunch until mid-afternoon; she felt as if she was just pushing through the days, barely able to distinguish one from another, morning from night. There were only two parts to the day, Michael-at-home and Michael-away. During Michael-away you prepared, you anticipated, you waited; and during Michael-at-home you stayed alert and ready for whatever might happen. But it was never possible to be alert and ready enough.

Her thoughts of lunch were interrupted by the ringing of the bell for the ferry. Just her luck, somebody needing to cross and Michael not here to do it. She would have to haul it across herself.

Marie walked to the river crossing. Cowling, Mrs. Smith's man, stood on the other bank.

"Tell your husband we need his boat," he said, a little grouchy.

"Right now?"

He shook his head. "After lunch. We are removing."

"How many wagons?"

"Two."

Marie considered. Two heavily loaded wagons meant two trips across, plus another for the people. Whatever else one might say about Michael, he was a good man with a device. He had braided a heavy rope around a cottonwood tree on their side of the river, then paddled across and done the same on the Daybreak side. With ropes attached to the corners of the ferry and looped over the crossing line, it no longer took much strength to pull the ferry across; even Marie could walk it over, advancing each rope a foot or two at a time. Michael would be happy at the money from three crossings in a single day.

"All right," she said. "I'll watch for you."

"Husband not at home?"

"Mind your own business."

As they stood across the river from each other, a boy came into view downstream, poling his way toward them from the rear of a twelve-foot johnboat. He worked slowly and steadily and gave no sign he noticed them until he was almost even. He looked about fourteen or fifteen, in a coarse cotton shirt and a wide-brimmed hat that had to have been someone else's originally. He tipped it to her as he poled toward her bank.

"This the Daybreak landing, ma'am?" the boy said.

"It is."

He steered the boat straight in, and as soon as the bow touched land he skipped lightly over the cross-members, the pole horizontal in his hands, and hopped ashore with dry feet. He dragged the johnboat farther onto the bank.

"Glad to hear it," he said. "I been standing at the tail end of this thing for three days. Be good to walk on my own two feet for a while."

Across the river, Cowling waved and turned away. Marie ignored him.

"They told me I wouldn't be able to pole any farther than the Daybreak landing," the boy said. "That right?"

"Probably so," Marie said. "The shut-ins start just around the next bend. You could never get a boat through there. Three days, you say?"

"Yes, ma'am. Been walking for two days before that. I'm from Paragould, Arkansas, but I found this boat up in Missouri."

"Found it tied to somebody's dock, you mean?"

The boy grinned. "Shame on you, ma'am, for thinking ill of a man. Fact is, I'm headed north to look for work. Know anything going on?"

"There's a railroad crew just south of here. You probably paddled right past them."

"This is a pole, ma'am, not a paddle, and yes I did, or at least I could hear their hammers a ways off. I ain't the hammering kind of fellow." With his pole, he plucked a cloth bag from the middle thwart and flipped it into his hands.

"No work in Arkansas?"

The boy puckered his face. "I'm tired of flat land. If I'm going to live on the flat, I'd like to have people in it."

"Well, there's work across the river if you want it. Hundred acres under cultivation and not enough men to manage it."

His face puckered again. "I never fancied myself a field hand. But what's it pay?"

"Room and board, and your share at harvest time."

The boy snorted. "No thank you very much," he said. "Working on shares is not my play. What's in it for me, that's my question."

That was everybody's question nowadays, Marie supposed, the brash new generation bowing before the cold new realities of cash only, please, and payment on demand, and every man for himself.

"Well, I'm off," the boy said, interrupting her thoughts. "Mind watching my boat for me? I'll be back to get it."

"What's in it for me?" Marie retorted.

He laughed. "Point well made, ma'am. Tell you what, if I ain't back in a month, you can sell it or claim it, and no harm done. How's that?"

"Fine," Marie said.

The boy slung his bag over his shoulder and marched up the road toward Fredericktown. "Hey, by the way," he called over his shoulder. "Know what I heard in Greenville? I heard some of Quantrill's old bunch are headed down this way. They robbed the bank up in Liberty a couple of months ago, and they're going to Kentucky or Tennessee or somewhere."

"Just hope that wasn't their boat you took," Marie called after him.

"Them boys don't ride boats. They never even get off their horses," the boy said as he disappeared up the hill.

"You should have made him pay you to watch his boat," said a voice behind her. Marie jumped. It was Josephine, of course, creeping up as she always did. She stepped out from behind a bush. "He had money in that bag."

"Now how do you know that?" Marie said.

"I heard it. He had it wrapped, but I could hear it plain as day."

"I don't doubt you." Marie put her arm over Josephine's shoulder and they walked to the house. Marie never knew what to make of the girl, daughter though she was. She had to credit Michael—for all his humors, he had never unreasonably raised his hand to the child. Or was it that Josephine knew how to manage his moods so that his wrath was always directed elsewhere? No matter. Josephine was not paying the price for her unwise marriage, and that was what counted.

"Mr. Flynn will be pleased at the ferry earnings today," Josephine said, as if reading her mind. Never called him 'Papa' or anything endearing. But Marie didn't remonstrate; the girl had a father, after all.

After lunch the ferry bell rang, and the two of them walked to the riverbank. Josephine was not tall enough to reach the rope and pull the ferry across, but she could help the passengers load and unload, which she always did without being told.

It looked as though the entire Daybreak community was on the other side, gathered with Mrs. Smith and her retinue at the landing. Marie pulled the ferry across while Cowling began to swim the horses over, two at a time.

"I'll need two of those to pull your wagons onto the ferry," Marie said to him midstream.

"I know that," Cowling said, grouchy.

The oversized wooden casket Wickman had built to hold Lysander Smith's coffin took up one entire wagon, wedged in place by crates and boxes. Wilkinson, the undertaker, appeared to be in charge of that one. He eyed her suspiciously.

"Do you know what you're doing, young lady?" he said.

"About as much as you do."

Ignoring his growl, she led the horses onto the ferry, tied down the brake, blocked the wheels, and unhitched the team. Horses on a ferryboat were trouble; you didn't need to be a teamster to know that.

Once the horses were safely on the bank again, she pulled the boarding planks up and began the tedious process of pulling the ferry across, hand over hand. At first Wilkinson held onto the wagon as the ferry embarked, tilting into the current, but finally politeness got the better of him.

"Let me help," he said, reaching for the back corner rope.

"It won't save you anything on the fee," Marie said.

"Dear girl! I had no thought of that. I just want to cross this stream as fast as possible."

"All right, then. When I get the lead rope set, then you pull yours ahead. Don't pull yours until mine is firm."

They worked their way across the river. As they approached, Cowling stepped forward, holding the bridles of the two horses he had swum across. He backed them onto the ferry, and the men hitched them up.

"This is a heavy son of a bitch for a skeleton," Cowling muttered as he urged the horses off the ferry and up the bank.

"Not the skeleton, it's the zinc lining and the camphor," Wilkinson said. Now that the two were out of Mrs. Smith's earshot, they talked more freely. "Believe me, you wouldn't want to sit on this wagon without them." Wilkinson nodded to Marie. "Your friend Wickman back there is a fine woodworker." Marie noticed that all the joints and screw holes on the casket had been sealed with wax.

"I'm going to stop on the flat ground up ahead and add another horse," Cowling said. "I don't like that hill."

"A word before I go back across," Marie said. She drew the two men to her and told them what she had heard about the former Quantrill men.

"But Quantrill's dead," Cowling said. "They killed him last year."

"Don't these boys know the war's over?" said Wilkinson.

"Ours is, but theirs isn't," Marie told them. "Might never be. Anyway, if you're stopped, give them whatever they want and don't tell them you're from the North. These men are used to killing, and don't think that the women in your group will save you."

"Oh, we read all about this gang during the war," Wilkinson said. "But Mrs. Smith will never stoop to lying to them. She makes a grand point of her principles."

"We'll not let her do the talking," said Cowling. "Mrs. Mercadier can talk to them. She can talk to anyone."

"Mrs. Mercadier?" asked Marie. "You mean—?"

It was true, as Marie learned on her next trip over. Jenny, the serving girl, had decided to join the colony, and Marie's father's widow, the former Mrs. Flanagan, was taking her place. Mrs. Smith, perching backward in the wagon in her velvet armchair, feigned disappointment at Jenny's ingratitude, but she was plainly pleased at the trade.

"And with a name like Mercadier, everyone will think I have gotten myself a French maid, unless she opens her mouth, which a woman of her years will have the sense not to do," Mrs. Smith said. Mrs. Mercadier, although she was standing beside the wagon, didn't appear to mind being spoken of in the third person.

Mrs. Smith refused to get down from her chair, even though the wagon swayed alarmingly as they pulled it onto the ferry. "You'll cross me over, I have no doubt," she said. "You're too tough a little vixen to let me fall."

Kathleen avoided Marie's eye and shrugged in response to her whispered question. "Why not?" she said. "There are plenty of Irish in Philadelphia. I'll feel at home there. With your father gone, and now Angus gone, I have no reason to stay here." She gave Marie a searching look. "You should think about that offer Mrs. Smith made you, and yes, I heard about that offer. Sometimes hanging onto a child is not the best thing you can do for it. Just think about it. Mrs. Turner has our address."

They embraced after Marie had gotten the ferry safely to the other side, but Marie's heart felt cold. True, she had no family connection to Kathleen, but was it really that easy for her to leave Daybreak? She remembered when Kathleen had led the group of women and children up the road after their disaster in the wilderness. Hadn't Daybreak meant something to her then?

Kathleen seemed to sense her thoughts. She squeezed Marie's hand as she climbed into the wagon. "Things never last," she whispered. "Keep looking ahead. That's what got me through all my years. Two husbands, three boys, three homes lost. Take what life gives you, but do not try to hold onto it. You'll just bring yourself pain."

Marie squeezed her hand in return but said nothing. She could not agree. There had to be something to hold onto in this world, something, anything. One couldn't just keep letting go.

Marie roped the ferry across the river one more time with Josephine aboard, although it was clear that everyone who wanted to cross had already done so. She didn't want to be by herself as the visitors departed.

The Daybreak residents drifted away to their work one by one, and by the time Marie had reached the bank, only Charlotte Turner and the new girl, Jenny, were left. Marie stepped ashore and tied the ferry to a stump. She greeted Charlotte with a nod and took Jenny's hands.

"So you're staying behind," she said.

Jenny's knee bobbed in a half-curtsey, a reflex movement that she was clearly trying to stop. "Yes, ma'am," she said.

"Well, you follow the lead of this woman here," Marie said. "Watch her and you won't go wrong." Jenny cast a sidelong glance at Charlotte, who blushed with pleasure. "Marie, you're too kind."

Marie turned to her and took her by one hand, and for a moment they stood as if in a ring-a-rosy, the three women in the afternoon sunshine. "How old are you, Jenny?" Marie said.

"Seventeen, ma'am," and Marie was taken aback at her youth.

"And you've been in service with Mrs. Smith for how long?"

"Since I was twelve, ma'am."

Marie looked more closely at her. She was young, it was true. But her face did not have the softness of youth. "It's not an easy life out here, but I suppose you've seen enough of that to judge for yourself."

"Yes, ma'am. House service with Mrs. Smith is not as easy as it might have looked from the outside, neither, and I'm inclined to try life on my own shake for a while."

Marie remembered herself at Jenny's age, a girl in years but already a woman in experience of the shocks of life, her mother gone from the cholera and her father raising her as best he could, their settlement dissolving in strife. The rosy accounts of Daybreak they had read made it seem like paradise, light work and weighty conversation, and while they knew it could not be as ideal as portrayed, still the dream had carried them along. She had been about the same age when she first arrived, and likely no wiser. And was this the place where a single young woman could make a life on her own? No worse than the rest of the country, that was for sure.

The three of them watched as the wagons disappeared up the hill. Kathleen did not turn around or look back. Take what life gives you, eh? Hardly a philosophy, but perhaps a way to cope. Marie watched the road for a moment, then turned toward home. She could see Josephine waiting on the ferry, invisible through stillness, observant as always. The sun was dropping low. Two more hours, maybe three, before Michael would be home.

And here came John Wesley Wickman, up from the village at a fast walk, an ill-concealed look of agitation on his face. He reached the three of them and stood uncertainly, clearing his throat and scratching his head.

"Mr. Wickman?" Charlotte finally said.

"After all this fuss with Mrs. Smith and her retinue, I decided to go fishing," he said.

The women waited.

"Down river, under those sycamore trees, where the channel takes a bend to the left." He scuffed his feet in the dirt of the riverbank, and they waited. Wickman turned to Marie.

"And I found your Angus."

Arms reached for her as she fell.

Chapter 18

Turner sat up in bed in the dark, his eyes open. It had been the death of Newton Carr again, one of the many deaths that visited him in the night. Strange, which ones came back over and over. Colonel Carr. The rebel on the hilltop. And the one-armed man he had killed so many years ago, buried across the river in what was now Michael Flynn's hog lot.

They didn't haunt him, exactly, and he didn't know why out of the thousands of men he had seen die and dozens of men he had killed, these were the ones who inhabited his dreams. There was no particular fear or emotion, although afterward he felt an overwhelming sadness, a sadness that burdened him for days. The dreams were the same: he returned to the moments of their deaths and saw them die.

He looked to the window. No sign of any light from the sky. Might as well try to sleep, although probably futile.

It had been the boy who had stirred this all up again, no doubt. Wickman's fishhook had caught the boy's shoelaces—a remarkable coincidence, to be sure—and when he saw what he had dragged up, he had the sense to leave the boy in the shallows rather than try to pull him all the way out. He ran to find help, and when Turner and the other men arrived, they knew immediately to keep the women away, for the water had done its work and Angus's clothing was the only thing keeping his body together.

Turner sent Wickman to the barn for a horse blanket. When he returned, they waded in on each side of the boy's body, stretching the blanket between them. They lowered the blanket into the river, and once it became soaked they held it to the bottom on the downstream side of the body.

"Just grip it tight," Turner said, and inch by inch they slid the blanket up beneath the boy until the moment when the current caught him and he drifted into it, and a man cut the fishing line and Wickman and Turner folded up the blanket with the boy inside, slowly, letting the water drain out, and carried him to the bank. Someone stepped up for a closer look, but Turner kept the corners tight in his hands. "Nobody needs to see," he said. "John Wesley, bring your harness kit."

They sewed the blanket shut and stood in silence. Then Wickman quietly recited the 23rd Psalm, a few others joined in, and that moment set them in motion again.

Everyone assumed that Michael Flynn would go mad when they brought the body back, so by unspoken agreement four of the men walked south to meet him when he came home from his railroad work, in case things went bad. But he took the news in silence and walked past them.

"We can help you bury him," Turner said.

Flynn glanced over his shoulder. "Won't need it."

By the time they returned to Daybreak, the women had gathered up the body in its blanket and placed it on the ferry. Marie, revived with a splash of river water, rested her hand on it as Flynn silently pushed off from the shore and looped the ferry across on its heavy rope. Josephine squatted at the far end, gazing into the woods.

Since then they had seen little of them, though the children recounted from Josephine that Flynn had wrapped his son in another blanket that night and carried it, still dripping, into the far fields of his property, burying him alone and in darkness, and from that time had alternated between terrifying rages and equally terrifying bouts of silence. When pressed as to whether his rages had crossed into violence, Josephine was, as always, evasive. Turner's dreams returned, always of those who had gone before, their faces, their voices, the strange angles of their bodies.

What came back to him about Colonel Carr's death was that he had been looking straight at Turner when it happened. He was giving morning orders, and said, "Tell Williams—" when the Minie ball hit him in the eye. They always buzzed as they flew, a horrible whining buzz like an insanely powerful bee, so you knew one was coming an instant before it arrived. That one had a lower, spent sound; it had traveled a long way and was at the end of its arc. So for the smallest of moments, Carr must have heard his death arriving, maybe even seen it as it fell toward him. Too fast to react, and inevitable anyway. No dodging a bullet. Turner had been splashed with Carr's brains and blood, but then the fighting started, and he had had no time to clean himself off for two days. And people wondered why he didn't care to talk about the war.

Charlotte laid her hand on his back. "Is it morning?"

"No." He had never told her about that day. He should have told her before now. Some sort of protective urge, he guessed. Not that Charlotte had ever shown a need to be protected from the truth. "Your father," he said.

"Yes?"

"I was there when he died. I've told you that."

She sat up, too. "Yes, you have." She waited.

"There was nothing especially heroic about it. We were astride our horses, he was giving me instructions, and a rifle ball came out of the sky, and smack he was dead. Just like that. We never knew where it came from, a sniper, a lucky shot, maybe even an accidental discharge."

She continued to rub his back. "Did he say anything?"

"No. Just fell off his horse."

"So he didn't suffer."

Turner thought. Did he suffer? How was he to know? Did the sight of a rifle ball flying toward one's head at unimaginable speed cause suffering, even if only for the merest of moments? Did the soul, the mind, continue in some state of existence, suffering, after the body had been struck down? But he knew this was mere philosophizing, and not what Charlotte was asking. "No. He was alive one moment, dead the next."

She sat up beside him. "Don't continue to mourn. He died doing his duty. No matter if he wasn't waving a sword, leading a charge. He wasn't the sword waver, anyway. You know that."

He nodded and rested his head against hers. "I'm not mourning, exactly. I just can't stop the thoughts from running. They run over and over." He stopped, not wanting to sound too watery, but then continued. "I think of all the times I have been splashed with blood. Too many times."

Turner felt that if he continued in this vein of thought much longer he would start to cry, but he didn't really care. Charlotte had seen him manly, and she had seen him unmanly.

To his surprise she gripped the back of his neck, a little hard. "Don't indulge yourself," she said, her voice intent. "I'll not have the man I love become one of those blubbering old veterans who gather on the courthouse lawn every Fourth of July. I saw too many of those when I was a little girl. They'd come up to the Point on the anniversary of their battles, tracing out their charges and fortifications like Uncle Toby, and goading the young ones into following their example with all their talk of honor and glory. Mourn as you have need, but don't you forget that we have work to be done. My father led troops in Mexico, and he came here and built a barn. Both deeds did him honor."

Then she stopped herself. "I'm sorry. I didn't mean to sound harsh. But I grew so tired of the old warriors rehashing their old wars, and I don't want us to become like them. This war is like a fever in our veins, and until we purge that fever, we won't be well." She paused and her grip became a caress. "I've been covered in blood plenty of times myself. Births and healings, mainly. But blood is blood. So we're both marked."

Turner was about to reply when he noticed the light of dawn flickering through the bedroom window. But it wasn't right, there had been no dawn only a few moments ago, and this light was not the soft gradual brightening it should have been. In an instant he was out of bed, into his trousers, pulling on his boots while he threw off his nightshirt.

"Something's on fire," he said.

Charlotte was right behind him as he dashed out the back door. They ran north through the village to where the firelight was flickering through the trees. But as they got closer, Turner slowed down, and he gestured for Charlotte to slow down as well.

The firelight came from no burning house, but from torches carried by a dozen horsemen. They wore homemade masks made from flour sacks with grimacing faces painted on them, and they had arranged themselves in two lines, in front of and behind the cabin where Dathan and Cedeh sometimes stayed.

"So this is the famous Law and Order League," Charlotte said in a disgusted tone.

A big man on the front center horse seemed to be their leader. He waved a revolver, a torch in the other hand. The other men were armed as well but kept their weapons low. Turner pulled Charlotte into the shadow of the empty Mercadier house next door to listen for a moment.

"Come out, nigger!" the man shouted.

There was no reply from the dark house, no sound, no sign of movement. The men stirred in their saddles.

"Don't make us have to come in there!" the man shouted again. "It'll go easier on you if you come out on your own. If we come in there's somebody's going to get hung!"

Turner thought of Lysander Smith, and stepped into the ring of light.

"Gentlemen," he said.

The leader wheeled in his saddle, revolver leveled at Turner. Turner walked toward him steadily but slowly until he was standing between him and the front door of the house.

"You want to share this man's fate, that's your business," the leader snarled. "But I'd advise you to get out of the way."

"I'm not accustomed to talking to a grown man with a funny face on," Turner said. "Makes me feel like Halloween came early this year."

"Oh, a comedian," the leader said. "We'll see who's laughing when I horse-whip you down the road a ways. Right after I hang this nigger and his Indian bride. You hear that in there?" he shouted to the house again. "You're going to hang by sunup. But come out now and I'll spare the woman."

There was no answer from inside.

"You'll have some problem with that," Turner said calmly. "There's nobody in that house. The man you're looking for doesn't live here."

The leader's head snapped toward a rider at the end of the line. "You said this was the house," he said. "Is this the house?"

The man shrugged. Something about the rider's build and posture seemed familiar to Turner.

"Well?" the leader asked again.

"Thought so," the rider said. Even though the man's voice was muffled by his mask, Turner could tell it was Charley Pettibone.

"God damn it!" shouted the leader. "What kind of ignorant shit is this? Either it's the right house or it ain't."

Charley shifted uncomfortably in his saddle and shrugged again.

"I'll show you," Turner said. "Come inside with me."

The leader pointed his revolver at Charley. "You go," he said. "If anybody's going to get a shotgun greeting, you're the deserving one."

Charley clambered down from his horse and walked slowly toward Turner, torch in hand. Feeling the revolver at his back, Turner led him toward the door of the house, hoping that he had been right and that no Dathan awaited them with a cocked shotgun. He lifted the latch. It opened easily.

The light from Charley's torch threw shifting shapes on the bare walls as they stepped inside. There were some pans on the floor, and the head of a hoe, but otherwise the room was empty.

"You can take your mask off if you want, Charley," Turner muttered. "I know it's you."

Charley's head jerked toward Turner, but he said nothing. Nor did he remove the mask, which had a pair of red rings painted around the eye-holes and a jagged red mouth, meant to look terrifying, but in the torchlit room it merely looked silly.

"Let's look in the back," he said.

They walked to the back room of the cabin and stood in the still darkness.

"You need to get away from these people," Turner said.

"That's kind of complicated."

"I know. But you need to figure it out. This is not going to end well for you down the road."

"Ain't much ever has."

"You don't belong with those people. You belong with us."

"Only thing I ever belonged to was the Confederate Army, and that ain't a going thing anymore. It's just my own self I belong to now."

"You're wrong there, Charley. Even if you don't think you belong, you still do. Be careful what you belong to. For that's what you become."

A laugh came from inside the mask. "You were always a good man with the words, Mr. Turner. Take more than words to help us now. Those boys outside are primed up to kill somebody, and if they don't get the one they want, they'll just pick the next man. Could be you, could be me."

He turned on his heel and walked to the front door. "He's right," he called, stepping into the yard. "It's empty."

"Did you check the rafters?"

"Of course I checked the rafters. First place you look. Ashes in the fireplace were cold, too."

"You weren't in there long."

"How long does it take to check two goddam rooms?"

The leader raised himself in his saddle. "Come out of there, you!"

Turner stood in the doorway. "I'm right here. Believe me now?" In the light of the torches he could see that some of the citizens of Daybreak had gathered and were watching.

The man snorted. "I wouldn't believe you if you told me my pants was on fire. Now where's that nigger?"

"I already told you I don't know, so you can either believe it or not."

The man lowered his revolver toward Turner and pulled back the hammer.

"What, you think that's going to make knowledge pop into my head?" He was about to speak further, but Charley stepped in front of him.

"I think I know where we can find him," he said. "I think they stay in them old huts on the ridge."

"We rode right past them huts, you idiot!"

"Didn't think about 'em then."

The leader released the hammer on his pistol and tucked it into his belt. "All right." He turned to his men. "But first, burn this house."

He stood in his stirrups and threw his torch on the roof. "It is not proper for niggers and whites to live side by side!" he shouted. "People take notice!" He pointed at Turner. "If this happens again, you're the responsible party. Keep that in mind."

Two other men threw torches into the windows of the house, then the gang rode into the street and turned north toward the river crossing. Charley mounted his horse to follow.

"Remember what I told you," Turner said.

Charley didn't speak, but nodded briefly, then yanked his horse's reins and spurred it to catch up with the rest.

As soon as the horsemen were out of sight, everyone rushed wordlessly to their homes to fetch buckets and pans. Wickman had a ladder against the side of the house in an instant; Turner guessed he had slipped away as soon as he saw the first torch fly and had been waiting in the shadows with it.

The riders' hasty efforts to burn the house were extinguished within a half hour, leaving nothing but scorch marks on the floor and roof. The commotion had awakened the community's children, who dashed from place to place in ineffectual excitement—except for Adam, who took his hand and led him to the steps of the Temple of Community, where they sat down together. Turner suddenly realized that he was weak in the knees.

"Was this what the war was like?" Adam said.

"Not really," said Turner. "Men with guns, yes. But lots more of them, not as organized. You didn't see people face to face very often."

"Scarier than this?"

"No. This was plenty scary."

"I was scared."

Turner put his arm around his son. "Anybody not scared would have to be plumb crazy," he said. "But you do what you need to, scared or not."

"Are they going to hurt Mr. Dathan?"

Turner held the boy close. "I'm guessing that Dathan figured out what was happening when they rode by the first time and made sure they wouldn't find him when they rode back. But when sunrise comes we'll go up and see."

Charlotte joined them on the steps, a smudge of ash across her face.

"Where's Newton?" Turner asked.

She nodded toward the cabin. "Inspecting the work. Making sure we doused everything sufficiently."

They exchanged smiles in the breaking dawn.

"Let's go to bed," she said.

Chapter 19

Charley Pettibone ran through his options as he forded the river with the Law and Order League. None, really. He'd been a damn fool for joining this bunch, and a damn fool for sticking with them this long, and a greater fool for calling out Dathan's name at the last meeting. Now there was blood to be shed. Dathan's, if indeed he was bonehead enough not to have sensed the danger and melted off into the night when they had first ridden by, or more likely his own.

His own fault. But this was no time to kick himself for past deeds. He could drop his torch in the river, feign a loose cinch when they reached the bank, then disappear into the darkness when they rode on. Fat chance, now that Pratt had called him out. His horse, a chestnut gelding borrowed from Landsome, seemed a good mount. Perhaps he could bolt past them, make a dash to town. And then what? Spend his life fearing an ambush? Not damn likely, not for a man who had fought at Chickamauga. If there was to be a fight, then he'd fight. He took his revolver from its holster and held it under his coat.

The men regrouped on the bank as the last ones clambered up. Pratt turned his horse to face the rest. "Well, that was a goddam mess," he said, speaking directly to Charley. "Don't you tell us something if you don't know it's true. We lost a half hour of darkness down there, and if we don't get moving we'll have to ride home in daylight. And that's how the law gets on you."

"I thought we were going to be the law around here," Charley answered.

"Wasn't that the plan?"

"Sometimes plans don't go as fast as you'd like, smart boy," Pratt said. "You just better hope Old Zip Coon is up where you said he'd be this time."

"Sometimes people don't sleep where they're supposed to sleep," Charley retorted. "I'm starting to see why you never joined the regular army." Charley backed his horse up a little.

"What's that supposed to mean, Arkansas?" Pratt said. All the other riders shifted in their saddles but did not speak.

"You ain't got the head for it," Charley said. "In the real war, you'd have been shot for insubordination or busted for incompetence in a month's time."

"That right? We'll just see who gets shot for insubordination!" Pratt shouted. He went for his revolver, but Charley already had his out and cocked. He raised and fired, knocking Pratt off his horse, then threw down his torch, jammed his revolver in his belt, and spurred to a sudden gallop past them all. In five seconds he had disappeared into the darkness.

Charley flung off his hood as he raced through the flat ground alongside Michael Flynn's farm and reached the spot where the road climbed out of the river valley. He figured the surprise had given him a minute's head start, at most, and riding without a torch another couple of minutes. The others would keep their torches and pick their way up the hill, but he knew the terrain well enough to ride it by moonlight. He could make the ridgetop, pass the Indian camp, and reach the plum thicket at the end of the long lane before the road turned toward town. There he could loose the horse and give it slap down the road, push his way into the thicket and wait. Charley guessed that no more than one or two of them cared enough for Green Pratt to risk their lives chasing him into the woods, and if they did, well, they'd all discover who was the best fighter of the bunch.

He longed to look behind to see what sort of pursuit he was getting, but couldn't spare the time. He could hear hoofbeats, though, and urged on the gelding despite its labored breathing. There'd be plenty of time for it to rest once he turned it loose.

Charley pressed his cheek to the horse's neck and hissed into its ear. "You can do it, honey," he whispered. "This ain't no hill. You've climbed worse." The horse stumbled and then righted itself. "Hay barn up ahead, with sweet clover." He gripped the cheekpieces of the bridle. "Sweet clover and a bucket of oats, and cool spring water, and I'll brush you down myself, honey pie."

At last, the roadbed leveled off, and Charley could hear the smooth sound of dirt beneath the horse's hooves rather than the sharp clatter of horseshoes on rocks. All was darkness ahead.

Another hundred yards and he could ease up. He sensed he was passing the cluster of huts. Although he could not see them, he could feel their silence. Next the long lane of overhanging oaks and hickories, and then the thicket. He made up his mind not to shoot first unless pressed. They could take the horse and go in peace, and that would be a sign.

Unexpectedly his horse reared and snorted. Charley had to seize the saddle horn to keep from falling.

"What the hell—" he gritted.

Then there was an answering snort from another horse, not behind, but ahead. A match was struck, and in its glimmer Charley could see riders—fifteen, maybe twenty—lined across the road ahead of him. They closed around him, carbines and pistols drawn, and all in Federal uniforms except for the man holding the match.

Harley Willingham.

The sheriff leaned in and removed the pistol from his belt.

"Charley Pettibone, you're under arrest," he said.

Charley raised his hands. From the distance behind him came the flicker of torches as his pursuers topped the hill.

"Don't you make no noise," Willingham said. He blew out the match.

Chapter 20

I t wasn't the sound of the horses riding past that woke Michael Flynn from his sleep. Nor was it the light from the torches as the Law and Order League surrounded Dathan's house in Daybreak. He was sleeping too deeply for those things to stir him; after his day on the railroad, he had returned as usual on the flatcar back to town, jumping off as it passed the river valley and walking the last three miles. Then after dinner he had stopped by Angus's grave for a minute and then cleared trees until dark, too dark really, to where he couldn't see what he was cutting, just whaling away at trunks till something fell. He would clean them all up another day.

What awoke Michael Flynn an hour before dawn was the bawling of a calf.

There was no reason for a calf to be bawling at that hour of the morning unless it couldn't find its mother. And no reason for it not to find its mother unless—what? Unless the mother had wandered off. But where? Or a bear had gotten her. Or wolves had scattered the herd. But they would go for the calf, not the mother.

Or somebody had stolen her.

By now Flynn was fully awake and angry. The woman was sleeping, or pretending to sleep, so he slid out of bed and dressed quietly. He found his boots, took his shotgun from its pegs, and stepped into the night.

Instantly he was aware that things were not right. He could see flames flickering though the trees across the river; someone's house was on fire, one of the cabins at the north end of the village. Then he saw the torches and heard the splash of several horses swimming the river, and knew that more was going on than a simple chimney fire.

Flynn stepped into the shadows of the bushes at the edge of his house and edged closer to the ford. He counted the torches as they crossed: a dozen or more, and some men weren't carrying torches. Too many for him to confront. And no cattle. Whoever these people were, they were no band of ordinary thieves.

As they climbed the riverbank, he saw the hoods over their heads. So it was that gang of old rebels, out to make trouble. No surprise that they would raid Daybreak. He felt an urge to knock one out of his saddle, let them know what it felt like to get ambushed, but held back. Another day.

He watched in silence as the men argued, and recognized the voice of one of them as that bastard Pettibone. They were too far away to be intelligible, but he could tell the tone. Then to his surprise, a pistol materialized in Pettibone's hand, the other man was blown off his horse, and Pettibone disappeared into the night. The son of a bitch was more dangerous than he had imagined.

There was a moment of stunned silence among the other raiders. Then two men jumped from their horses to tend to the fallen one, while three others raced after Pettibone. The others stirred nervously.

"He's alive," called one of the men kneeling over the wounded leader. "You're alive, friend," he said more softly. He took the hood off the man's head, revealing in the torchlight a mass of matted black hair, a thick black beard, and a face contorted in pain.

"Set him up," someone said.

Flynn hunkered deeper into the shadows of the bushes as the two riders dragged the injured one out of the road. They set him against a tree a dozen feet away. Flynn was torn between his desire to see better and his need to stay hidden. He could hear the man gasp.

"You'll be all right, Green," one of the hooded men said. "I don't hear no air running in and out. He missed your lungs."

"Bring that little fucker to me," came the rasping reply. "I want to cut his nuts off before I shoot him."

"Hold me that torch closer," said the man who was tending his wounds. One of the others dismounted and lowered his torch, while the others stirred nervously on their horses.

"This ain't a good place to be standing around," one of them said.

"You shut your muzzle," said the kneeling one. "They'll catch up to

Pettibone soon enough, and then we'll parley and decide." The reproof shamed them all into silence for a while.

Then as if in answer, the sound of shots came from up the hill. "There you go," one rider said.

But then came a full volley of shots, more than could be accounted for by four men on a dark road, and some of them were the sharp cracks of carbines. Then the sound of galloping horses.

"That bastard Willingham is up there with a troop of Federals," a man cried, reining in his horse in the middle of the road. "McDonald is down. Not sure about Jasper."

"We've been sold!" another shouted. "That son of a bitch Pettibone has sold us!"

"Don't worry about that now," said a third. "Douse your torches and scatter. We'll meet at the Rockpile."

"I say we stand and fight," the first one said. "We can take this bunch." But half the men had already thrown their torches into the river and ridden into the woods. A dwindling handful stayed where they were. "What about him?" he said, nodding toward the tree where their leader was propped.

"Lewis, you watch after him," said the rider who had been tending him. "There's a farmhouse around here somewhere."

"First place they'll look. Hide in the bushes by the river."

By then the hoofbeats of more horses could be heard, a lot more, approaching fast. The rest of the men jumped Flynn's fence into his pasture and rode away, firing a few ineffectual shots behind them as they fled. Willingham and the soldiers arrived, their horses blowing. They formed a line at the fence and fired a quick ragged volley into the field.

"Come on, boys," shouted one of the soldiers. "They ain't far off." But no one advanced.

"I don't know," Willingham drawled. "You boys know this countryside in the dark?"

For a moment Flynn considered stepping out and volunteering to guide them, but he stayed put. This wasn't his fight.

"All right," said the soldier. "We got two of them, anyway."

The soldiers stirred in their saddles, a little uneasy that the fight had ended so quickly. But Willingham seemed content. "Three," he corrected the soldier. "Two killed and one captured."

"Captured is as good as killed as far as I'm concerned," the soldier said.

"Oh, you let me deal with that boy," Willingham said. "He'll have his uses. Let's get a little sleep and finish up here when we can see what we're doing."

"My men don't answer to you, sheriff," said the soldier. "They answer to me." He paused. "Very well, we'll bivouac up in those shelters at the top of the hill and then I'll decide what to do next."

Typical, thought Flynn. Officers were the same the world over.

Squatting in the shadows, Flynn felt a strange feeling come over him. It took him a moment before he realized he was enjoying himself. It felt good to be sitting in darkness, a gun in his hand, ready to fight. His senses were filled with the sounds and smells of the night, the creaking tack, the rustle of leaves, the sweat of the horses. He imagined he could hear the breathing of the wounded vigilante, dragged to the riverbank by his companion, as they waited in silence, hoping the soldiers would leave. He smiled to himself. How did those boys imagine they would make their way to safety, with one of them bearing a pistol wound in the chest? The son of a bitch was a dead man already. He thought about hunting them down himself after the soldiers left, but it didn't seem worth the bother.

As the sheriff and the troops started up the hill, Flynn's thoughts returned to the sound that had awakened him in the first place—the bawling of the calf. It had continued like the drone string on a banjo throughout the events of the night, the voices, the shots, the rumble of horses, and now it stood alone again. He listened. The calf was somewhere south of him, but more toward the woods than the river. He listened further. That rider and his pal were somewhere down to his right, armed, but he couldn't hear any stirring. He could skirt through the field, avoiding them, and find the calf. Maybe some of the other riders would come back, but he doubted it—once a man started running, he didn't turn around unless forced. Flynn cocked his shotgun just in case.

He eased to his feet and stepped into the open. There was enough daylight now to see better; he could make out the house and sheds, could see the fence rails where they snaked into the undergrowth. He held the shotgun at hip level, stepping quietly around the edge of the dewy pasture.

Every few steps, Flynn stopped and looked around. He wished for a couple of revolvers like the ones those vigilance boys had carried; there would be no time to reload the shotgun if it came to a fight. He would have to take his shot and then rush the body, grab whatever weapon he could. If he missed—throw down the gun and run for the river, hope whoever he met didn't care for water.

He was getting close to the calf but still could not see it. He was in the thicket of brush and treetops where he had been clearing yesterday, a tangle of sprouts and limbs felled in every direction, dropped to be trimmed into firewood lengths on a later day. He pushed his way through the brush, wet cobwebs draping his face.

There was something hiding the calf from his sight, a big mound of earth or something, a big lump that looked like—

That looked like the dead body of its mother.

The calf pressed against its mother's flank, vainly seeking an udder. Flynn laid his hand on the animal's side; it was barely warm, dead for a couple of hours at least. He felt along its neck and face for wounds or blood. Nothing. But how could a healthy cow, not three years old, simply die?

He straightened. Ahead he saw another lump among the brush, and another, and another. He pushed his way past the calf to the next—another of his cattle. And in the growing light he saw that his entire herd was dead. Dead without a mark on them, or a grain storehouse for them to get into and bloat themselves, or a lightning storm to kill them. What had happened? Poison? The hand of an enemy? What could have killed them all so fast and so invisibly? He sank to his knees and rested the shotgun against the side of the dead animal.

He was ruined. It would have taken him five years to pay off the loan on the cattle, even assuming steady prices and healthy calves every year. But with no breeding stock, he could never repay it. He could work on the railroad the rest of his life and never put back enough to repay Ferguson in town. And getting clear on the cattle was to be the first step toward getting clear on the land. Now—

Now there was no way to get clear on anything, ever. He would lose the land. Ferguson would take him to law, and if he didn't get the farm, he'd force the Daybreak people to sell it and get his money that way.

Flynn leaned back into the side of the dead cow and laid his head against its flank. He had the shotgun. He should just kill himself now and be done with it.

He'd be damned if he would.

Better to kill Ferguson instead. There would be prison, sure, but after prison a return. No. He was not thinking right. He should take the woman and leave these debts behind, go to California or Oregon, let Ferguson and Mrs. Turner fight over the corpses of these cattle. Modern though the world may be, there was still room out West for a man to get lost.

There would be time to plan all this, but for now he had a couple of old rebels hiding somewhere nearby and a calf to try to keep alive. He glanced toward his cabin. A lantern was moving in the near-dawn. The woman had no doubt come out to see what had happened with all the shooting.

"Michael?" Her voice softly carried through the darkness. He didn't answer.

The lantern moved toward the ferry landing, away from him. Just as well. She would only get in the way. There was a roaring in his ears as Flynn tried to organize his thoughts.

"Ma'am?" a voice came from the riverbank. "Ma'am, we need help. There's a man hurt."

The damn vigilantes. Well, first things first. Flynn strode back to his house, his shotgun cradled and cocked.

Marie stood at the edge of the slope, lantern high. The vigilante was at the water's edge, a tall man with a wild scruff of hair and a long coat. Flynn stepped into the lantern light and lowered the shotgun toward him.

"Find the road," he said.

"I've got a man over here who's hurt," the man said.

"I know you do. He's likely dead by now, or soon will be. Same as you if you don't find the road in another ten seconds."

The man shifted his feet and glanced at Marie. She better not peep, Flynn thought, or else there would be more hell after he put a hole in this rebel boy.

She did not speak. Sensible gal.

"Start moving," Flynn said. "But first open your coat and toss me your pistol."

The man did as he was told and then trudged up the slope.

"You know the way to town," Flynn said. "We'll bury your friend for you."

"We'll be back," the man said over his shoulder. "We didn't have no quarrel with you, but now we do."

"More the fool."

"We'll see about that."

"You ought to be thanking me for not sending you to join your friend, and here you are still trying my patience."

The man did not answer as he disappeared up the road. Flynn watched until he had disappeared into the dimness. For a moment he thought about firing after him—to wound, kill, or frighten, didn't really matter—but by then the man was gone. What the hell, let them come.

Marie turned toward the house.

"Where are you going?" Flynn said. "I may need your lantern. I want to see if that son of a bitch is dead yet."

She reached it toward him, eyes averted. "I'll have your breakfast ready."

The little bitch. Always judging, judging, judging. The roaring in his ears nearly deafened him. He should kill her now and get it over with.

The wounded vigilante was lying under an overhang of the bank about twenty feet down from the ferry landing, still breathing, eyes open.

"What's your name?" Flynn said, bending down.

The man licked his lips and managed to croak out, "Green Pratt."

"I'll tell them to put that on your marker."

Pratt did not respond. Flynn flipped open the man's coat; the wound was low in the torso. Too bad; a few inches higher and he would have been spared some misery. He took the pistol from Pratt's waistband and tucked it into his own.

"Bring me some water," Pratt whispered.

"All right." Flynn straightened and looked around. Nothing to carry water nearby, and he'd be damned if he was going to spoil his hat by using it as a vessel. He stepped to the water's edge and cupped his hands. Only a small trickle was left by the time he made it up the bank again, but it would have to do. He tipped the water into Pratt's open mouth.

"Thank you," he said, dropping his head against the earth.

"You got any word you need passed along?" Pratt closed his eyes in answer. "You ain't going to see nightfall. I expect you know that. Maybe not even full sunup."

"My pal make it out?" he finally said.

"Yeah. I sent him on his way."

Pratt said no more. Flynn turned to leave. "I'll bring you some more water later, in a proper cup."

Now to more pressing matters. The sun would soon rise on a pasture full of dead cattle, and word would find its way to town. That bastard Scotsman would be down within the week, wanting his money. Better to make a run.

Inside the house the woman had ham and hoecakes in the pan. He rested the shotgun against the table and sat to eat, not bothering to hang up his hat. The girl was standing in the corner, eyeing him as always, the little snipe. No doubt the woman had fed her the best bits already.

"How much milk have we?" he muttered as she set the plate before him.

Her glance was darting and suspicious. "A couple of gallons, I guess."

"I'm going to need it all. There's a calf has lost its mother." He gave a look to Josephine, who was studying a crack in the floorboard. "You'll be drinking water from now on, missy."

"What happened to the mother?" said Marie.

"She's dead," said Flynn. "They're all dead. And you have to get started. We are packing up the wagon and moving on today."

"We're doing what?"

"Packing up. Are you deaf?"

"No, I just—"

"Then shut up and get to it. We'll cross the river here and go west on the back roads. I want to keep the calf alive until I find someone to sell it to. With any luck that will be enough for train tickets. If not, well, it's a long ride."

He stood up from the table and took the shotgun. Just his luck, one of those Law and Order bastards would wander in.

"But wait!" Marie said. "All dead? How could this happen? Was it all this shooting?" She plucked at his coat as he walked to the door. "Has someone shot our cattle? We should fetch the sheriff!"

"We'll do as I say!"

The anger boiled over at last and he swung the barrel of the shotgun hard, catching her on the side of her head. She dropped sideways into a heap.

"Will you listen and not ask questions!" He stood over her a moment. Marie did not move. Knocked out or faking knocked out, didn't matter. He looked over at Josephine, who had backed into the corner.

"When your mama wakes up, tell her I'm in the barn. As soon as I've packed everything there, I'll bring the wagon around. I'll want to be gone before noon." The girl's frightened face gave him a pang of remorse. "And tell her I'm sorry I struck her."

Outside he took a deep breath to calm himself but it didn't work. His arms shook and he felt hot. Flynn remembered that he had promised that reb some water. Might as well do one thing right today.

Between the house and the wagon shed was the well; he stopped and slid off the cover and lowered the bucket, kneeling to peer into its depths.

This close to the river, he'd only had to dig a shallow one, twenty feet or so. He should have lined it with stones but had been in too big a rush and used planks, so the water was earthy-smelling and murky sometimes. Oh, well. So the planks would rot and the walls collapse. They'd be long gone by then.

"Lord, let me not have killed her," he whispered into the well.

He drew out a dipperful from the bucket and poured the rest back. Still cradling the shotgun, he slid his way down the riverbank to the place he had left Green Pratt.

But Green Pratt was gone.

Chapter 21

Charlotte had gone back to bed after the excitement of the predawn hours, but she hadn't been able to sleep. No one had, she imagined. She lay in the bed speculating about the jumble of shouts, the sound of horses, and the gunshots they had heard in the predawn hours after the Law and Order League had ridden off. A quarrel amongst the raiders, doubtless, but then what? It had sounded like another group had come down the hill. An ambush? An assault on Flynn's house? In the confusion of sounds it was impossible to tell.

Before sunrise she walked to the river. Flynn's farm, across and upstream, seemed quiet. Strange how the world could seem so serene after a night of violence and chaos. Strange but good, she supposed.

A man was pulling a handcart down the road, wet from his chest down. When he noticed Charlotte at the river's edge, he stopped a couple of yards away.

"I had thought I would go to the next house down the way, someplace I wouldn't cause no trouble," the man said. "But here you are, so I reckon I need to ask you for help."

"You're one of the men from last night," Charlotte said.

"Yes, ma'am." He pulled the handcart closer. There was a man in it, his clothes also soaked from the river, a broad stain of blood across his chest. "I floated him over. He's pretty bad hurt."

Charlotte stepped closer and put her fingers on the man's throat. There was the barest of pulses, and when she placed her fingertips over the man's mouth she could feel a slight breath.

His companion leaned closer. "I borrowed this cart from up the road. I ain't stealing it."

Charlotte ignored him. She felt inside the wounded man's coat. One bullet hole, no fresh blood coming out as far as she could tell.

"It was Charley Pettibone shot this man," he said. "I just want that known. That man across the river tried to run me off from him, but I snuck back. But it was Pettibone done the shooting."

"And does this man have a name?"

"This here's Green Pratt. His daddy is Parson Pratt, from up Arcadia."

"And you?"

The man thought for a moment. "I don't think that would be too wise for either of us, ma'am."

Charlotte put her lips close to Pratt's ear. "Don't be afraid," she said. "You're in good hands. Your friend is here."

"Can he hear you?"

"I think so. Hard to say."

"Well, ma'am, I need to leave you. I am wanting to be across some county lines."

Their gazes met across the body of Pratt, and she told him with her look that he had better say his good-byes. The man drew close.

"I'm going now," he spoke into the man's ear. "This lady is going to take care of you." He rubbed his hands together. "I'll send word to your family about where you're at. And all the boys, too. Meet us up on Rockpile as soon as you're able." He stepped away from the handcart. "What can you do for him, ma'am?" he said softly.

She shook her head. "Keep him company. If he lives, it won't be from anything I do."

"I'm sorry, ma'am," the man said, backing away. "I'm sorry to burden you like this."

"It's not me you need to apologize to," Charlotte said.

He turned abruptly and walked down the road, picking up speed as he went. Typical, Charlotte thought. Thunder in, make a great mess, and ask the nearest woman to fix it.

She examined Pratt again. Still a heartbeat, but not much of one. She pulled the man's coat tightly around his body and considered trying to move him inside, but decided it would only cause him pain.

The first time she had given birth, the pain had been so great at times that she had thought she would surely die. Everything had disappeared into a blur of red and black, but through it all the granny woman had talked to her, her voice a thin cord that kept her tied to the bed when she would rather have floated away. Perhaps that was what this man needed, a voice to accompany him through the darkening. So she placed her hand on Pratt's chest and spoke.

"I'm here, Mr. Pratt. Your friend will return soon." Now why say that? Better reassurance than truth, she supposed. "You're in Daybreak. Last place you ever imagined returning to, at least like this, I'm sure. You did say you'd be back. But you imagined yourself coming on horseback, guns blazing, and so did I. But now here you are, and here I am."

The sun finally crested the trees beyond the river and cast a beam across the man's face.

"My father died in battle, you know. He liked to quote the Romans. 'To the thrown stone, there is no more virtue in rising than shame in falling.' I think that was Aurelius. Fate, you know. Father found that idea comforting, that fate decides all. With no free will, you simply strive, and failure is no stain. But here in Daybreak, we are great on rising. Improvement of the human race, one life at a time. And if we fail—well, it's our own fault, or the fault of men like you. Obstacles to enlightenment. Not a pretty thought, being an obstacle. I'm sure you don't see yourself that way. You're defending a way of life. There's truth to that."

She looked down at him. His jaw had gone slack, and his breath made a faint rasp as it went in and out of his mouth. It hardly seemed the time to talk about philosophy or politics now. A life was passing from the earth. Charlotte bent closer to his ear.

"I am here," she said. "I am here. I will take care of you. Don't be afraid." The words felt inadequate to her, but she forged ahead. "I don't know why you ended up here, or why I did for that matter. I doubt it was fate, but I'd like to think it was something other than blind chance. It may not matter. The world has turned and brought us to this spot, and if I know nothing else, I know that the world turns toward the sunrise."

There was a rustling behind her. James emerged from the house and came over to see what was in the handcart. When he saw the man, he put his hand on Charlotte's shoulder.

"The leader of the gang from last night," she murmured.

"Somebody's darling." A sadness was in his voice, the sadness of a soldier who has spoken those words too often, and she reached up to touch his hand for a moment.

She realized that Pratt's breathing had stopped. They stood in silence. Then Turner jerked his chin up and squinted east into the sun. "Lots of gunfire over there last night," he said. "Seen any movement yet?"

The question brought her back to herself. "No! And that's what brought me out so early."

"I'd better check." Turner disappeared into the house, and when he emerged he was carrying the Sharps carbine and followed by Newton and Adam. They exchanged a look over the weapon. "Better safe than sorry," he said.

"Mama!" Newton called out. "Papa says I can't come along because you might need me for chores." He trembled with excitement. The next generation of boys eager to pick up a gun and fight the world.

"Your chores can wait," she said. "Adam, I need you, though. You stay here."

The younger boy looked relieved. No easy task, following in the older brother's footsteps. Charlotte smoothed down his mop of hair and directed him toward the house. "First you'll eat, then it's up to the barn for firewood." No point in his seeing the dead man. "You two be careful and don't dawdle. I'll need you back here as soon as possible." She took a last glance across the river toward Flynn's farm, quiet through the mist. After all the shooting of last night, it didn't seem likely that one grave would be all they would have to dig today. Graves to dig, a roof to fix—it would be a full day.

Chapter 22

Newton could hardly believe his luck. Finally getting to help his father on an important task, and with no snotnose Adam, either. He'd been left the man of the house when Dad went off to war. Now it was time for the two men of the house to work together. He watched the way Turner cradled the carbine in the crook of his elbow, the barrel pointed slightly down. He'd placed the cartridges in the inside pocket of his coat, to keep them dry. Newton was going to remember everything.

They walked swiftly and in silence up the road to the ford. He could see stirrings in the village, lanterns alight in the houses, a few shadows of people outside on morning errands. His father paid no attention to them. When they reached the ford, he untied the skiff and motioned for Newton to move to the bow.

"Hold this while I pole," he said in a low voice, handing him the carbine.

He had held it a few times, even gotten to shoot it once. It hadn't been so bad—the boom at his ear much louder than he'd imagined, and the kick more like a hard punch to the shoulder. Strange how the sound had seemed so much more intense than when he was standing a few feet away.

He sat backward on the bow seat of the skiff, watching Turner pole. He hardly seemed to push against the bottom, just worked his hands down the pole with a gentle push-off at the end. This was a trick to be mastered once he got taller. His father kept his eyes on the far bank as he guided the boat across the river. When it reached the shore, he said quietly, "Step out now and pull me in a little. Keep the barrel up."

Newton did as he was told, handing the carbine to his father once the skiff was secure. Turner took a cartridge from his breast pocket and loaded it into the breech.

"If anybody starts shooting, get behind a tree and don't peek out," he said.

They walked toward Flynn's cabin, Turner pausing every few steps to watch and listen. The grass along the path was trampled, and the smell of powder clung to the air. Newton longed to ask what he should be listening for as well, but knew not to speak.

"Strange," his father murmured. "Missing something."

Newton now listened for something unheard rather than heard, and it was obvious. "No cows," he said, and Turner nodded.

He had not liked coming across the river ever since Angus died. Before then, it had been an exotic place, full of brushy byways and the mystery of wild land, thickets of scouring rushes and large inexplicable tracks in the mud. But now it felt ominous. He dreamed of Angus's drowned body even though he had not been allowed to see it, dragged up at last from whatever underwater snag had held it, bobbing to the surface eyeless and accusing. Angus was over here somewhere. This was the side of the river where outlaws were buried in lonely graves, and their ghosts prowled.

By now they had reached the cabin. No smoke rose from the chimney. "We'd better look inside," Turner said. He tapped on the door. After a pause, he lifted the latch and stepped inside. Newton followed.

Josephine was kneeling on the floor in the middle of the room beside the sprawled body of her mother, bathing her face with a damp cloth. She glanced up as they entered. "He hit her with his gun barrel," she said, her voice flat.

Turner rushed to them and kneeled beside her, his hand pressed to Marie's cheek. "She's alive," he said.

Josephine had propped her against a table. Newton could see the bright red welt across her forehead where the barrel had struck. Her jaw was slack and her eyelids fluttered randomly.

"Where is he?" Turner said.

Josephine shrugged. "Out with the cows, I guess. He told us to pack everything."

"Why?"

"He never said."

Turner's brow furrowed. "We need to keep her still, and we need to fetch

Charlotte." He stroked the girl's hair. "You did well, child."

Josephine did not answer, her attention focused on Marie. Turner stood up and collected his thoughts.

"All right," Turner said. "Here's what we'll do. Marie will stay here. Newton, I will need you to take the skiff across and fetch your mother while I find Mr. Flynn. Can you do that?"

"He can, but he shan't," said a voice behind them.

Michael Flynn stood in the open doorway, a bucket in one hand and a shotgun cradled in the other. He set the bucket down and leveled the shotgun at Turner.

"We are loading up to leave, and I'll not be interfered with," he said.

"You fool," Turner said. "This woman is badly hurt, not to mention that you're the one who did it. She's not even conscious."

"I've been hurt worse," Flynn said sulkily.

"I'm sure you have, but your skull is thicker. Let's you and me talk about what happened last night while Newton goes after Charlotte."

Newton could see the man working through his thoughts. "No," he said. I can't let you leave. I'll have to take you with me."

"Seriously, what good would that do?" his father said. "You're wanting to leave in a hurry, right? So leave Marie with us and make your dash. You can send for her later."

"You'd like that, wouldn't you, whoremaster?" Flynn said. He kept the shotgun level. Newton felt a deep cold in the pit of his stomach as he realized Flynn would truly do it, he would shoot his father down right here and cold sober.

"Let's tend to the injured and settle our disputes later," said Turner, his face red.

"Boy, you can go fetch your mother," Flynn said, waving him through the door with the shotgun. "The rest I'll decide later."

Turner caught Newton's eye and nodded. Newton edged toward the door, the barrel of Flynn's shotgun gleaming huge in his sight. At the door he looked into the bucket that Flynn had been carrying. It was filled with something that looked like milk but was an odd color of pink.

"What's in the bucket?" he asked without thinking.

"Milk," he said. "I've got a calf lost its mother, and I had to drain her milk with my knife. It's bloody but it will feed."

"Couldn't you just switch it to another momma?" Newton asked.

To his shock, tears sprang from Flynn's eyes. "Ain't no momma cows," he said. "Ain't none at all. They're all dead."

No one knew what to do. Flynn stood in the door, his face working, tears rolling down his cheeks. Then he slap-wiped his face, drew back his shoulders, and scowled down. "Get the hell out of here, boy, before I change my mind," he said. "Bring your mother and don't be slow."

There was more Newton wanted to ask, about how the cattle had died, about all the shooting in the night, about the bad men who had tried to burn Dathan's cabin. But more than anything he wanted to get out from in front of that shotgun barrel. He slid past Flynn and jumped into the yard.

Newton dashed down the path to the landing. Marie's face had been so strange, her muscles alternately twitching and frighteningly still. The sight of her propped against the table, legs splayed disturbingly, hung before him.

Running full tilt, with his head down to watch his path and his mind on the scene behind him, Newton failed to see the horse until it was too late. His face smacked into its muscled flank, his feet flew out from under him, and he hit the ground hard. The smack of his nose against the horse's leg sent tears to his eyes instantly. He furiously rubbed them away, and as his vision cleared he saw that the horse's rider was Sheriff Willingham, with another rider beside him. He lay on the hard ground, waiting for his breath to return.

Willingham lifted his hat to scratch his head. "Maybe I'm shrinking. Didn't you see me, son?"

"Nosir," Newton said, sitting up. His eyes cleared. The other rider was Charley Pettibone.

"What's the hurry, then?"

Newton tried to gesture in three different ways at once. "Mrs. Marie's been hurt," he called out, trying to keep his voice calm like his daddy did. But he could hear the quaver and swallowed hard. "And Mr. Flynn's lost his mind or something and is holding a gun on my dad. But he let me go to bring Mama to help—"

A look passed between Willingham and Charley. "We just come down here to identify bodies," Willingham said. "But I reckon that'll have to wait. Pettibone, I'm gonna turn you loose here because I may need your help, but don't think that I'm done with you. And I'm keeping that gun of yours in my saddlebag." Charley held out his hands, which had been resting on his saddle horn holding the reins, and Newton realized that he was handcuffed. Willingham unlocked the cuffs and slipped them into his coat pocket. He turned his gaze to Newton again.

"So Flynn's where?"

"In their house."

"What kind of gun?"

"Shotgun. Double barrel."

"Carrying anything else?" Willingham squinted in the direction of Flynn's cabin.

"I don't know, sir. I don't think so."

Charley interrupted. "You say Marie's hurt?"

"Yessir, he smacked her across the head with his gun barrel, is what Josephine said. She's out cold on the floor, and—she didn't look right."

Charley yanked his horse's reins toward the cabin, but Willingham reached across and grabbed the bridle. "Easy, son. More harm in rushing than in thinking. Can you steer that boat across by yourself, boy?"

"Oh, yes sir!"

"Then you do that, and bring back your mama. She's got the healer's touch if anyone does. Charley and me, we'll dismount here and walk up, see what we can see. When you bring Mrs. Turner back, watch for us and don't run right in."

"Yessir." Newton ran to the skiff and stepped to the stern, hefting the pole in his hands. It was longer and heavier than he thought. He pushed away from the bank as the men tied their horses to a witch hazel bush and picked their way through the underbrush toward Flynn's house.

Then he realized that the current had already pulled him a couple of yards downstream, and the boat was drifting backward. He jammed the pole into the riverbed and pushed off with both hands, but that motion only spun the boat around so that it was now heading downriver, not across to the other bank. He fought back panic, shifting the pole to the other side to right his course. The problem, he could see now, was overcorrecting, and he gritted his teeth as he tried to find the balance he needed between force and delicacy. But the boat swung round again, and now he was ten yards downstream from the landing.

He would not cry out for help, by God. If it took him an hour, he would do this on his own. He lifted the pole, hefted it in his hands. More carefully this time. The pole down, smooth but steady, firm, find the bottom then push off, don't try to cross the river in a single stroke. Nice and easy, nice and easy....

And the boat was farther downstream yet.

The current was too strong for him.

All right, then, by God, he would turn weakness to strength, he would guide the boat slowly downstream, work it across the river going with the current, not against it. He held the pole on the bottom for a minute and let the bow of the boat drift down. Where could he take out? Easy. There was the big flat rock where his mother liked to sit and watch the river. He could slide right up onto it and jump out, drag it up a little ways and then run up the path. Heck, it was closer to their house than the landing. It would save him some time. Then the two of them could run to the crossing and find a canoe, or even swim horses if they had to. For now he could just drift.

But he had forgotten about the water wheel, turning quietly in the river, and as his flat-bottomed skiff drifted downstream, one of the paddles of the water wheel caught it by the side and drew it in. The big wheel was not powerful—only a couple of its paddles were in the river at any moment—but the strength of the current was enough to lodge the boat against it, and there it stuck, bobbing gently as the river's force pulled it down and its own buoyancy lifted it up.

Newton laid the pole in the bottom of the boat and gripped its sides with both hands, waiting to see whether the water wheel would drag him under.

It didn't.

"God damn it!" he said aloud, then said it again, louder yet. He felt a moment's thrill at cursing, himself, out in the morning dimness, using a man's swear words at a man's swearing moment. And if there ever was a swearing moment, this was it. "God damn it!" he said again. But he recalled himself. There was a dire situation to remedy, and a problem to solve. First solve the problem—get the boat loose from the water wheel—and then remedy the greater one.

He inched his way forward in the skiff, wobbly, until he reached the place where it was lodged. The paddle of the water wheel was unshakably tight against the side of the boat. He could not move it with his hands. Perhaps he could kick it loose.

Newton sat in the bottom of the boat and braced his back against a thwart, his feet against the edge of the water wheel's paddle. He pushed. Nothing. He kicked harder. Harder again.

Then there was movement, and for an instant he felt relief, until he realized that it was the skiff dipping down, not the water wheel breaking loose. His own weight, and the pull of the wheel, and his kicking, had tipped the balance, and now the bow of the boat had gone under the water. He scrambled backward, but it was too late. The thin thread of water became a rush; the wheel turned, and before he knew it the boat went under, and he floundered in the dark river.

Chapter 23

Charley Pettibone's mind would not stop racing as he worked his way through greenbriars and blackberry vines to where they could get a good look into Flynn's cabin. He tried to move quietly and focus on the sheriff's broad back as they circled around the pasture, but every step he made seemed amplified.

As soon as Charley had seen Willingham's face in the light of the match, with a troop of cavalry gathered round him, he realized they had been tracking the Law and Order League all along, probably for weeks, waiting for their chance to surprise them as a group. By then the pursuers had reached them, but the soldiers were loaded and ready, and the fight was brief and lopsided. Afterward, they had rested for a few hours at the old Indian camp, where it was obvious that no Dathan, no Cedeh, had been sleeping last night. So it was just as well that he had shot Green Pratt when he did. If Pratt hadn't shot him at the river, he would have shot him up here when their plans were foiled. Then the soldiers decided to head for town, and Willingham returned to Daybreak. And now this.

They reached the rail fence that marked the far end of Flynn's pasture. Another damned lunatic move, running fences through the woods like this. Weapon or no weapon, he'd kill the son of a bitch with his bare hands if he had to. The Mick brute, striking a woman.

Willingham squatted and motioned for Charley to do the same. "Here's the ticket," he said quietly. "We follow the fence to the barn. From the barn we can get a good look into the back door and see what old Flynn is up to."

"If I had a rifle, I could drop him from that distance and be done with it."

Willingham dropped a wad of spit between his feet. "Lordy, son, then I'd have to arrest you. We're the law and don't forget it. We ain't bushwhackers."

They crept along the fence until they reached the heap of dead cattle piled up against the rails. Willingham picked up a branch and squinted at it in the dim light.

"Here's your price of ignorance," he said. "Our boy cut them cherry sprouts and left 'em lay for the cows to eat."

"What's the matter with a cherry sprout?" Charley said, immediately regretting his own display of ignorance. Willingham cast him a sidewise glance and shrugged.

"Turns to sweet poison, is what I heard the old-timers say. They can eat it when it's on the tree, but when it's dead and curling up, it's a deadly thing. I ain't ever seen it before, but I guess it's true." He laid his hand against a steer's flank. "This is going to be a ripe old mess in a day or two." Then he shrugged again and turned toward the barn.

The barn was unworthy of the name in Charley's opinion, little more than an unchinked square of logs with a slab roof, no milking stalls or grain bins. "Calls to mind the house I lived in when I first came out here," Willingham said as they crept to the front. Charley couldn't tell if he was joking.

In the entrance, a horse stood harnessed to a wagon, tethered to a peg driven into a stanchion. It snuffled as they approached. The wagon was heaped with clothing and furniture.

"All packed and ready," Willingham murmured. "Quite a tale to learn here. This took some work."

They settled against the wall and peered through the chinks. The back door of the house was open, and in the lantern light from inside they could see Turner, sitting stiffly in a chair by the front door, and what appeared to be part of Flynn's back and arm at the table. A woman's legs and feet could be seen between them.

"She's alive, anyway," Willingham whispered. "Otherwise he'd be out of here by now."

"And what happens when Mrs. Turner and boy come back?"

They sat silent for a minute. "He won't shoot her. He ain't that crazy."

"Fact is, he's the man with the gun and he'll shoot who he wants," Charley said.

"I cain't argue that point," Willingham said. "But it's also a fact, he hates you, and he don't seem to care for James Turner. So if I had to lay odds on who ain't getting shot, I'd put my money on Mrs. Turner."

"That's reassuring," Charley said dryly. "So what's your plan?"

"It ain't exactly a plan," Willingham replied. "But I figure it this way. Old Flynn in there has messed up good, and he'll see that soon enough. A gal hurt bad on the floor, and even if it is his wife, there'll be a price to pay for that. Looks like he was loading up to move 'em all out when something interfered. So…." He rubbed his face and peered through the crack. "Either he shoots Mr. Turner, or he don't. Either way, he'll break for this wagon. And if he throws down his weapon, or if he ain't carrying it too careful, we'll knock him down and tie him up."

"And if he's still got the gun?"

Willingham squinted at him. "Then we try to quiet-talk him. He can't shoot us both without reloading."

Charley sniffed. "Some plan. You should have let me bring my pistol."

"Son, I got a family to feed, and them soldiers is long gone," Willingham said. "We ain't busting in there with guns a-blazing. If this old boy turns himself in, or somebody brings him in, it's a dollar a day to jail him up, and good money, too. But there ain't no pay in shooting and getting shot at."

They turned their attention to the house, where Turner had not moved. "Wish I knew where the child was," Willingham said. "I might venture some other little stratagem. But when there's a gun pointed at you, you're best not to take chances." He paused. "Guess I don't have to tell you that."

Charley didn't answer. He was calculating the distance from the barn to the house. With all the excitement of the day and evening before, Flynn couldn't have gotten more than a couple hours' rest. If there was some way he could signal to Turner, whose face was half-turned in their direction through the door, to let him know whether Flynn had fallen asleep, he could make his way to the house, screened by the back wall, and in a quick rush fly in and disarm him. He'd seen it during the war, men so exhausted by excitement and effort that nothing could rouse them, men sleeping even as the charge rushed toward them.

He glanced at Willingham out of the corner of his eye. He could talk him into it, if they waited here another half hour or so. But Willingham's attention seemed focused elsewhere.

"Listen," Willingham said.

"Okay."

Willingham put his fingers to his lips. "No," he said. "I mean listen."

So Charley stilled his mind and listened. And in the silence of the morning he heard a voice, a child's voice, Newton Turner's voice, away toward the river, and it was calling, "Mama! Mama!"

Chapter 24

After the skiff had been pulled under, Newton had climbed the spokes of the slowly turning wheel, desperate to stay above water, until the boat had caught on one of the pilings; with a groan and a shudder the wheel came to a stop. Now he sat atop the pitted and bird-beshitted piling, his terror gone but replaced by despair.

He had failed his endangered father and failed Mrs. Marie, who was probably dead by now. He had imagined himself a storybook hero and instead was nothing but a fool. He would jump into the river if it wasn't for his fear.

As Newton called out, he alternated between hope and further despair. People would be out doing their morning business by now; when he woke up in the morning, he usually had to run for the woods. Surely someone would hear him. But then he thought of the distance to the houses and doubted.

Then from the bank, hardly more than fifty yards downstream, a canoe emerged, skimming toward him. Where had it been? He hadn't seen anyone walk through the fields. It was as if the canoe had sprung from the bank itself, from his heart's own wish.

The boat slid close, and kneeling in the stern was Dathan. They peered at each other for a moment.

"Well, climb on down," Dathan said. "Easy now."

Newton worked his way down the spokes of the water wheel and gently lowered himself into the canoe. As Dathan paddled upstream to the landing, relief at escaping from what felt like certain death came over him, and he suddenly began to shiver.

"Took your daddy's boat out for a little play time, and now you've got some trouble ahead," Dathan said with a note of sympathy in his voice.

"Oh, Mr. Dathan!" Newton cried out. "That ain't it at all! My daddy sent me over to fetch Mama. He's at Mr. Flynn's, and Mr. Flynn is holding a shotgun on him, and he's hurt Mrs. Marie but let me come over to get Mama to tend her but won't let daddy out of his house!" He stopped his babble and covered his face with his hands to hide the threatening tears.

Dathan's tone changed. "How she hurt?"

"Mr. Flynn hit her in the head is what Josephine said. She's knocked out."

Dathan didn't speak but dug the paddle in deeper as he pushed against the current. Newton gripped the sides of the canoe, which was framed in maple, with canvas stretched over the framing and coated with thick layers of pitch so that it was a dull black, inside and out. It felt limber but solid. "What kind of boat is this?" he asked.

"Built it myself, years ago," Dathan said. "Took a long time, but it don't leak a drop. Times of trouble, like these, I go out and sleep in it. Ain't nobody find you and you can slip away, no trace."

"I never saw it before."

"Ain't nobody ever saw it. There's a bank overhang I keep it under, can't see it from above nor across." He chuckled. "Me and the muskrats gotta share the spot, but the muskrats don't seem to mind."

Before the canoe reached the landing, Dathan stepped out and lifted Newton onto the bank. "Enough chitchat," Dathan said. "Let's find your mama."

They raced through the village, and soon Newton was repeating his story to his mother, who stood frowning in front of the house with an apron full of grain for the chickens. She scattered the grain with a quick flip of her apron and turned toward the house, where Adam was standing in the doorway with his finger in his mouth.

"You," she said to him, with the ask-no-questions look that both boys recognized. "Make the beds and sweep the floor, and then wait for me at the Wickmans'. I shouldn't be long."

Adam disappeared inside.

Charlotte strode toward the crossing, her brow furrowed as they passed the other houses in the village. "So Flynn sent you to find me," she murmured.

"Yes, ma'am."

"So he's not unreasoning. And the girl? Where is she?"

"Sitting in the corner."

"Has she been harmed?"

"No, ma'am."

As they passed the last house, Charlotte stopped and looked back at the village. "No," she said to herself after a moment. "Word would spread, and the last thing we need is a crowd around that house right now." She turned to Dathan. "All right, let's cross over. And how do you come into this?"

"Just out in the morning and seen the boy, ma'am," he said.

"I see," she said.

"And the sheriff and Charley Pettibone are over there, too!" Newton rushed in. "I run right into them."

"Ran," Charlotte said.

Gingerly, they climbed into the canoe, Charlotte kneeling near the bow, Newton crouching in the middle, and with the current behind them they crossed the river in a dozen hard strokes of Dathan's paddle. As they reached the eastern bank, he stepped out quietly and guided the boat the last few feet. "Pardon," he muttered, then lifted Charlotte to the shore. He did the same for Newton, gripping him under the armpits with his large hands and putting him ashore with an almost playful toss.

"I'll wait for you here," he said. "Or close by. May tuck under some bushes."

Charlotte took a small fistful of Dathan's shirt. "Please," she said. "Come with us. I have the feeling that I will need you up ahead."

Dathan looked into the distance, as he always did when a conversation veered into troubling territory. "Ain't disagreeing," he said. "But it seems I draw as much trouble as remedy it these days."

She pulled him closer. "I will need you," she repeated. "And anyone who tries to harm you will have to harm me first. You have my word on that, and I am sorry that's all I have to give you. But that you have."

Dathan sighed. "All right, ma'am," he said. "I'll lag behind some, if you don't mind."

She nodded briefly and took Newton's shoulder. "Let's go, then."

Newton forgot his resolve to act the man, and reached up to take her hand. And hand in hand they walked down the lane to Michael Flynn's house.

Chapter 25

Flynn's mind raced. No matter how he tried to calm his thoughts or even slow them down, they circled faster and faster in the same relentless paths, like the hogs from his slaughterhouse days in St. Louis. In the wintertime he would work the slaughterhouses when railroad work dried up; the farmers would drive them into the holding pens and then go off for their pay and their dram while the hogs circled and circled, not really looking for a way out, just circling as if the movement itself could keep them from the hammer.

Now he understood their impulse, but tried to keep himself still in his chair to avoid showing fear. But the more he sat, the more impossible his situation appeared.

Marie lay at his feet, her head propped against the table leg, a bright welt creasing her forehead and running into her hairline. At least she wasn't dead, or so he supposed. Hard to tell. But no, there was a slight rise and fall of her chest.

And Turner against the wall, watching him. What to do? Shoot him? Didn't seem right, not with him just sitting there, unarmed and immobile. Not that he didn't deserve it.

Hell, they all deserved it.

The only creatures that didn't deserve it were the dead cattle out in the pasture. Wasn't that the laugh, just dumb creatures doing what cows do, grazing on whatever came to them, whatever was sweet and tasty, whether it was meadow grass or a poison branch. Born to eat and die, they were. But to die on man's schedule, not nature's. They had to die when and where we chose, not out in some lonely corner of the woods where their flesh would rot and their milk curdle inside them. It was all about the time and place, when to die, not whether.

He needed a plan.

If the woman died—

If the woman died the plan would be to run like hell and never stop. The county line would be the first mark; once he reached the county line the sheriff would have no call to pursue. From what he'd seen, this sheriff wouldn't pursue if he got past the yard fence. That old bastard knew the game. His job was to collect taxes and run the courthouse, not chase people across creation.

Now Turner—

Their eyes met across the room. Watching his every move, that one, watching for his chance. To do what? Charge him, seize the shotgun? Not likely. He could measure the distance. Watching for a chance to make the door. So why not let him go? Or just walk out the back himself, take the wagon, and go, leaving Silas Do-Good here to tend the bitch?

Because this one, this one would pursue him. Or he'd want to. He'd not let him leave in peace, he'd chase him to California if he could, out of some grand notion that he was sent to cure the ills of the world small and large.

But if she lived—

If she lived, by God, he'd set right back up and all the people in Daybreak could go straight to hell. Who were they to tell him how to run his home? If they didn't like it they could stay on their side of the river.

No, there was Ferguson and the debt. As soon as word reached town that the cattle were dead, he'd be down here seizing everything he could haul off. He'd take the land, too, or the Daybreak people would take it and throw him off. Either way, there was nothing in it for Michael Flynn but a lifetime as a tenant farmer at best and a pauper at worst. Better to light out with whatever he could take and start over somewhere else. He could send word to the woman later.

So his choices were to run like hell or to run like hell.

Flynn's head hurt and he was exhausted. A full day's work yesterday, little sleep last night, and now this. Where was that woman Charlotte? Once she got here he could turn Marie over to her and slip out, take the wagon and go.

The shotgun was too heavy to hold up any longer. He crossed one foot over his knee and laid the gun across his level shin, but that was an uncomfortable pose and he knew he couldn't hold it for long.

"Girl, fetch me that ladderback chair," he said to Josephine, still crouched in the corner. She got up slowly and slid the chair across the floor toward him from its place by the window, then backed away, her eyes never leaving him. Flynn positioned it in front of him and rested the shotgun barrel on one of the slats, aimed at Turner's chest.

But where to run? Not through town, that was sure. He'd never make it to the other side. Arkansas? Arkansas was a wasteland these days, and an Irishman coming from the north with a wagonload of goods would find himself feeding the crows. No, he'd need to head east first, get across the county line, then the state. Illinois, that would be his ticket. Once there, sell the goods, find work. Maybe the Pacific railroad. That was it. Work his way west, and once the railroad was done, settle out wherever they finished, Nebraska or wherever. They were giving away land to the veterans, he'd heard.

Now, he needed to keep his eyes open and his wits about him. The next few days would be the trial. But Lord in heaven he was tired.

Lord in heaven.

What would the Lord say to him? He'd promised Father Tucker not to strike his wife in anger, and broken that vow time and again. And here she lay, dead or dying, the sin on his head as plain as a pickaxe. He was bound for hell, no question. So was she, most likely.

Or maybe not. What was it that Father Tucker said, there is no sin for which there is no absolution. Perhaps they were not entirely lost, although he surely felt like it now. Anyway, being bound for hell didn't mean he had to rush to get there.

If only he could rest for an hour before striking out across country. They'd done it many times during the war, lie down wherever they happened to stop, post one or two sentries and sleep on the ground, no blanket or bedroll, before rising to march or fight again. A wandering soldier had once come across them in such a state after a battle and thought them all dead until the sentry began to rouse them. An hour would be all he needed. The county line was what, twenty miles away? And a hard twenty at that, swinging south to avoid the town. He'd need a day and a half, more if the horse had trouble with the wagon. And then two more counties to the river, the state line, the life he would start over.

He could feel the slackness of sleep come over him, his arms growing limp, his fingers loosening on the grip of the shotgun. If he wasn't careful, he'd fall right off the chair. Where was that woman? All he needed was for her to show up, tend to Marie, and occupy everyone while he stepped out the door. He'd be gone an hour before anyone paid mind.

His eyes fell shut. And then the girl sprang at him from the corner, wielding a carving knife that she had concealed within the folds of her dress, and the gun went off.

Chapter 26

Charley and Willingham, peering through chinks in the barn wall, leaped back at the roaring explosion from the cabin, but an instant's glance showed no flying splinters, no wounds. For a moment they paused, wondering; then Flynn burst through the back door of the cabin, running toward them, his shotgun in one hand and the other hand pressed against his face. He kicked open the barn door and rushed to the wagon.

Flynn flung a valise from the wagon, and as it hit the ground it burst open, women's clothing springing onto the packed earth of the barn floor. He grabbed a chemise from the suitcase and pressed it to the side of his face, and as he turned to climb into the wagon seat, Charley could see that he was bleeding from a long slash across his cheek and neck. And for the first time, Flynn noticed the two men standing against the wall.

He pointed the shotgun in their direction, a wild look on his face. But his voice was calm.

"I have one charge left," he said. "Who wants it?"

Willingham and Charley wordlessly raised their hands.

"I thought so," Flynn said.

He couldn't manage to climb into the wagon with the shotgun in one hand and the cloth held against his face with the other, so he finally laid down the cloth and let himself bleed while he mounted. Then he pressed it to his face again while unwrapping the reins from the brake handle.

"They're all yours," he snarled to the men. "See you in hell."

Then he chucked the reins, the horse strained against the load, and within moments he was out the door, past the house, onto the road, and turning east, away from Daybreak.

Charley dashed to the cabin, entering through the back door at the same time that Charlotte came in through the front. She too had rushed up from the river landing at the sound of the shot, and they paused, panting.

Josephine Mercadier shrank in the corner, gripping the carving knife in a small bloody hand.

Marie lay motionless in the middle of the floor.

And James Turner, knocked off his chair by the force of the blast, struggled to stand but could only manage to get to one knee. His right side was drenched in blood from the shoulder down, and his right arm dangled, limp. He tried once more to reach his feet but couldn't hold himself up, and after a second he sank to the floor, his back against the wall, and stretched out his feet with a deep sigh.

Charlotte knelt at Turner's side and loosened the collar button on his shirt. "Here, now," she murmured. "Here, now. Let's ease this up." She palpated Turner's shoulder gently. Frowning, Charlotte glanced back at Charley.

"Put your cheek to her mouth and see if she's breathing," she said, nodding toward Marie.

Charley leaned over Marie's face. He felt strange being so near to those lips he had so longed for, now motionless. Those bright eyes now closed.

As instructed he turned his cheek and waited. Was there something? There was. A breath, light but warm, unmistakable. Another.

"She's alive!" he cried.

Willingham arrived at the back door now and took in the scene. "Ma'am," he said. "Mr. Turner, you're hurt."

Charlotte didn't answer him. "Child, bring me that knife," she said. Josephine edged forward with the knife held out butt first. Charlotte took it, her lips pressed together tightly, and cut away Turner's shirtsleeve, laying the knife on the floor beside her as soon as she finished.

Turner breathed hard, sucking air through clenched teeth as Charlotte explored the wound, but although his brow was sweaty he showed no obvious sign of pain. Charlotte held her face close to his.

"You're still bleeding, and not just a little," she told him. "It won't be easy to stop. All right?"

Turner nodded and closed his eyes.

Charlotte was now gripping into Turner's shoulder with both hands. "Charley, I need you," she said. "We'll tend to Marie later."

Willingham spoke up, still in the doorway. "I'll help you how I can, ma'am."

Charlotte glanced up. "My son will be coming through the front door any minute now. You can help by keeping him calm and out of the way." She returned her focus to Turner. "Charley, in my right apron pocket is a sewing kit in a leather pouch. Thread a needle for me with a couple of feet of thread."

Charley found the kit and with trembling fingers tried to thread the needle, but his hands were too large and clumsy. He cast a wordless plea to Josephine, who stepped forward from her spot in the corner, threaded the needle, and handed it back to Charley.

"Good show, young'un," Willingham said.

"Be quiet, Mr. Willingham," said Charlotte. "I'm trying to think. All right, Charley, lean in here."

Charley peered over her shoulder. Turner's right arm was badly mangled, with bone and gristle visible beneath a sheen of bright blood. The main artery had been pierced. Charlotte had groped her way to it and was pinching it closed between her thumbs and forefingers.

"Put that needle and thread on the floor here beside me, then reach in and squeeze behind where I'm squeezing," she said. "It's slippery, so hold tight. Use both hands."

There was little room to maneuver. With Turner leaned against the wall, Charley had to stand behind him, facing Charlotte with Turner's wounded arm between them. He reached in and pinched where she had directed him, pushing aside torn flesh to find his grip.

"Do you have it?" Charlotte said.

Charley could feel the rush of blood pressing against his fingers. He nodded.

"All right." She released her grip and found the needle and thread on the floor beside her. In a dozen swift passes she sewed a tight whipstitch around the tattered end of the vessel. "Let's see how this holds. Loosen up just a bit."

Charley relaxed his fingers, and together they peered at the artery as blood flowed in. It swelled; it oozed, but it held.

A sigh of relief escaped Charley's lips, but Charlotte didn't relax. "Support that arm," she told him, and then she pressed her face close to Turner's. "James," she said, quietly but intently. "There's no more blood flowing to this arm, and the bone is broken clean through. Do you understand?"

Turner's face was the gray of the first film of ice on the river on a winter's morning. Sweat glistened on his forehead. He mouthed a "yes."

Charlotte said nothing more but picked up the carving knife where she had laid it. In two hard strokes she severed the remaining muscle and tendons, and Turner's arm sagged into Charley's hands, strangely heavy and inert all of a sudden. She leaned back on her heels and wiped her face, then untied her apron, folding it into a square which she pressed against the wound. "Take that somewhere safe, please," she said to Charley. As he rose to his feet, she looked at Willingham, standing in the doorway.

"Your belt," she said.

"Ma'am?"

"I need your belt to cinch up this compress until we make a more lasting one," she said. "I can't hold this forever."

Willingham loosened his belt and brought it over. At a nod from Charlotte, he tucked it under Turner's left armpit and pulled it around the folded apron, buckling it in front.

"Tighter," she said.

Turner stirred under the pressure of the makeshift compress and for a moment tried to rise again, but his feet kicked aimlessly as Willingham held him down. He summoned a breath.

"Why bother?" Turner said.

Charlotte took his chin in her bloody hand and lifted his face to hers.

"Oh, no you don't," she said. "No you don't. If I lose you, I'll not have it be because you lacked the will."

Turner managed a smile. "My Charlotte," he said.

"Yours indeed," she said.

She glanced up at Charley with a look that was challenging, almost angry, and he stood up, startled. He should have carried off the severed limb sooner.

"Excuse me," he said, and staggered out the back door into the bright morning with his ghastly load.

Chapter 27

There was a gap. Had he slept or lost consciousness? Was there a difference? Turner wasn't sure.

He was at home now, propped up on pillows, his wound packed and tightly bound. He couldn't remember crossing the river. But here he was, home to die.

He knew they all wanted him to heal up and go on. He could see Charlotte standing at a table in the corner, mashing boiled slippery elm bark and folding it into squares of cloth for fresh poultices. Couldn't blame her. He didn't want to die. But from somewhere in the middle of his body, he felt—*what?* Not cold exactly. Just … absent. Not there.

Dead.

That's all they'd wanted during the war, the chance to die the way a man should, at home, surrounded by family, with a few words to share. So many men had been denied that—blown to smithereens, or trampled in a charge, or simply groaning their way to eternity in a field hospital with no one to hear their final words but a passing aide or, if they were fortunate, a comrade. So he was a lucky man.

His arm—or the place where his arm ought to be—didn't feel dead, though. It burned and prickled fiercely. He yearned to scratch it but didn't have the strength. Fool, to think he could scratch what wasn't even there.

Adam was hovering nearby and Newton lingered in the doorway. He needed to talk to them. He needed words. He needed breath.

A face came out of the blur at the edge of his vision. Harley Willingham.

"I sent Charley Pettibone to see if he couldn't find that fella before he got lost in the woods somewhere," Willingham said. As if it mattered to Turner what happened to Flynn. "Just wondering, was that there an accident or did he mean to shoot you?"

He turned his head to the left to get Willingham out of his view and tried to wave him away. Accidental or intentional? What did it matter? Flynn had been wanting to shoot him for years, and it finally happened. Perhaps in all accidents there was some intent, and in all deliberate deeds some amount of accident. He didn't want to think about it.

What was it that old Newton Carr used to say? The thrown stone. That was him all right. Flung up high and bright, and now falling, about to make his little splash and sink to the bottom of the pond with hardly more than a ripple.

Newton Carr. He watched Charlotte laboring over her poultices. There was a woman who had borne her share of grief. Sister, mother, father, now him.

And Adam. Adam Cabot.

Jealousy had long since burned out of him, leaving only the ache of loss. Of course Adam had loved Charlotte. Who wouldn't? Old loves and old losses, washed downstream now like an early season flood, leaving only the driftwood lodged high in the trees as a sign of its passing.

For some reason Turner's own father came into his mind. He could barely remember what he looked like now—just a blurry assemblage of a thick beard, intense eyes, and the smell of tobacco. The spring he had turned nine, his father had taken him overland in the wagon to Shawneetown and from there by boat to Cincinnati, three days' travel, to hear the debate between Robert Owen and Alexander Campbell over the existence of God and the truth of the Bible. For nine days, the Welsh atheist, brought upriver from New Harmony, stood on one side of the platform and the frontier theologian on the other. A shiver of repugnance ran through the crowd every time Owen got up to speak, repugnance that turned to grudging admiration as he detailed the ills of society, ills he was personally working to remedy. Then he would offhandedly deny some deep truth of the Bible—not argue against it, just deny it, as if it were the merest of fairy tales—and the crowd would groan and cry out. Campbell would rise, his bony face solemn. He recited passages in the original language to show how they had been misunderstood over the centuries. No orator, he had to be prompted to speak up from time to time. Turner had thrilled at the two debaters, the sway of the crowd packed into the pews, the arguments flying over his head like swallows.

That was where it had all begun, he supposed. The love of oratory, the thrill of the lecture circuit, the fascination with grand ideas that he could never entirely comprehend. The ambition. The hunger for applause, which now felt so vain and ephemeral. All from a childhood trip with his father.

What would his children remember of him? What had he done that would shape their lives? He would never know. Newton, slouched against the door-frame, frowning at the floor—what was he thinking? And Adam, lingering but afraid to come too close, unable to take his eyes off the bandaged absence that was once his right arm. Would he remember anything of him besides that?

And Josephine. Where was Josephine?

"She's here," Charlotte said from the corner. "Right outside the room. I think she's a little shy to come in."

Had he been speaking aloud? He hadn't realized. And for how long? The borders between inside and outside were getting blurry.

He wondered about Marie but was afraid to ask. But Charlotte sensed his need and walked over to the bed. "Marie's still alive," she murmured. "Not conscious yet, but her breathing is regular. We'll see how she comes out." She turned to her work but paused. "Your going over there probably stopped him from killing her, I imagine."

Well, that was good. Better alive than dead. His feeling of relief should have been greater, it seemed to him, but somehow he could manage nothing more than a sense of mild satisfaction. Emotions were bleaching from him once again. That was how they had made it through the war, by tamping down their emotions with the idea that they weren't losing them, but rather banking them for the future. When the war was over, they would all return to feeling again, to normality, to the simple joys and sadnesses of the life before.

The war. That's what would shape those children, the violence and privation, not anything he had done. His meager efforts to change the world had been washed away by that great tide. He couldn't foresee who was going to inherit the earth, but it wasn't the meek.

"Children," he said. Charlotte divined his meaning and pushed the boys toward him, on the left side of the bed so they wouldn't have to come too close to his wounded side. She disappeared into the front room and brought out Josephine, holding her hand, reluctant but yielding.

That man on the hill, the hate in his eyes as he charged him with his bayonet fixed. He had to have known he was racing toward death, but hate had overpowered his need to live. They'd all done it, that rush toward the cold embrace, and it had marked them. The ordinary sensations had not been banked, but lost. His generation had become like whiskey barrels, smooth and regular on the outside, but with an interior that was charred, hollow, scoured, shiny black. It was just as well they all die off, to clear some space for the next generation. Clear the stumps so the crops could grow.

The children shuffled nervously before him, and he returned to the present moment. What was there to say to them that was worth a damn?

"I've been the man killing, and I've been the man killed," he said, and it felt as if his breath had left him altogether. "This is better."

His gaze wandered to the window. He couldn't see much from this angle—a slice of sky and a blotch of tree. That was enough. When his attention came back to the room, the children had gone.

Charlotte in the corner, folding, pressing, stacking, her every movement an exercise in controlled ferocity. As if she could stave off inevitability through labor. Turner waited until he was sure he had enough breath for his words to carry across the room.

"Stop working. Come sit with me and hold my hand."

She looked up, startled. Then her face softened and she came over, wiping her hands on her apron. She sat on the stool beside the bed that the children had just vacated and took his hand, her hair glowing in the windowlight, and Turner could see that her eyes were glistening.

They held their silence for a while.

"You're not finished," she said.

Turner didn't answer. There seemed no point in arguing, and he'd been wrong before. But he felt finished. The work—the work would never be finished. There was work enough for the centuries if they chose it. But inside, he felt a growing emptiness.

He had so much he wanted to say. Always his condition, too many words and not enough time. Her hair, floating like a vapor. The faint freckles on her cheeks. Her pale blue eyes, so penetrating and intense at times, so luminous now, soft as air. How could he ever bear to lose sight of these things? How could he tell her all this, now, so late, with so few words left?

"I love you," he said.

"I love you, too," she replied.

There was more to say. There was so much more to say.

He closed his eyes.

Chapter 28

Charley Pettibone, riding the five-year-old mare that was the best of the Daybreak stable, had no trouble following Flynn's wagon by the trail of castoffs that led up the hill—chairs, trunks, a splitting maul and wedges, clothing. When the road leveled off at the top, the wagon's path was still easy to mark. Flynn had turned off the main road at the Indian camp, where the old trail to the southeast branched out through the forest, and even the poorest of woodsmen could track the bent saplings and broken weed stalks.

Before striking out on his chase, Charley had reclaimed his revolver from Willingham and stopped at his cabin to fetch his Enfield rifle, which the Federals had let him keep after the Surrender. His pistol wasn't the true Connecticut Colt revolver, just one of the Southern copies, and he doubted its accuracy at any sort of range. But the weight of it in his belt was reassuring. He'd stared down the barrel of Flynn's shotgun unarmed once and didn't care to repeat the experience.

He figured Flynn had gotten a three-hour head start or more, by the time he'd finished helping get Turner across the river, cleaned up, equipped himself, and saddled a horse. Flynn would be pushing to cross the county line, no doubt, but he surely couldn't make it before nightfall. He'd have to stop somewhere. Charley had made a silent bargain with himself. If Flynn stopped to rest before the county line, be it house or barn or roadside wagon camp, he'd wait until he was sound asleep and then creep up on him, bring him back for Willingham and the course of the law. But if he had made it out of Willingham's jurisdiction—well then, too bad for Michael Flynn. There was more than one reason people tried to get across boundary lines.

After a couple of hours the trail reached a better road, or at least some ruts that weren't as overgrown in the middle, and Charley paused to think. Flynn would be avoiding the towns. So he wouldn't have turned left, toward Fredericktown. Charley bore right, though the road drifted south over the next couple of miles, and he guessed that Flynn would take his next opportunity to head east again.

Another mile, and he passed the remains of a cornfield, with an old man gleaning grains from the ground. It was going to be a hard winter ahead.

"Did a man with a wagon pass by here earlier? Loaded down?" he called out.

The man looked up. "I expect so."

"How long ago?"

The old man squinted at the sky. "Couple of hours, maybe. It was past noon for sure. I was in that hayfield yonder when he passed, and I didn't get there till noon or more."

"I don't need your life story. Did he say where he was going?"

"He didn't say, and I didn't ask. He didn't look like a man who wanted asking. Had a big bandage around his head."

Charley nodded. If Charley had had any food to share, he'd have left it with the man, but he'd only tossed some salted potatoes and slices of bread into his satchel before leaving. He nudged his horse on.

Another mile down the road, and he developed the sense of being followed. Not that Flynn was crafty enough to circle out and wait; but something in the falling afternoon made him uneasy. So the next time he topped a ridge, he quickly reined out into the woods as soon as he was below the hilltop. He trotted his horse into a clump of cedars, tied it there, and hunch-walked back to where he could see the road behind. He sat down to wait behind a good-sized oak tree, the Enfield across his knees.

It didn't take long. In eight minutes he could hear the creaking of a saddle, and two minutes later the rider came into view, rocking nonchalantly with the movement of his mount as if he were out for a Sunday ride in the park.

Another minute and Charley could tell it was Dathan. He stepped into the road as the man drew close.

"I don't need your help," Charley said.

"Ain't offering," replied Dathan.

He was unarmed and wore his field work clothes—heavy canvas pants, a collarless shirt with the sleeves half torn off, and a shapeless felt hat that appeared to have come from a different century. His mount, one of the Daybreak stable, smelled its stallmate nearby and snuffed in recognition. Charley's horse answered with a nicker from its hiding place behind the cedars.

"So what the hell are you doing out here?" Charley asked.

"Riding this horse."

"I'll not be interfered with."

"Don't intend to," Dathan said. "Fact is, I'm not sure you're up to the task."

"Oh, yeah? There's many a Federal soldier might have thought that way, once upon a time."

Dathan looked down at him impassively. "Ain't it just like a man, to boast when there's work to be done."

Charley spun on his heel, furious, and untied his horse. He had not come this far in his life to be lectured to, spoken or unspoken. He lashed the rifle into place behind him, returned to the road and urged his horse to a trot. Dathan kept pace.

They rode in silence, Charley trying to stay a foot or two ahead. But that pace wasn't natural for his horse, so after a few minutes he settled back to a walk. At the next fork in the road, Charley took the eastward branch, and Dathan didn't question him.

It was on this road, which wound alongside a small creek and gradually led uphill, that Charley realized they were heading up the valley toward Rockpile Mountain. In another half mile the surrounding forest would thin out as they reached the scanty-soiled slopes, and in a mile the two of them would be shining like beacons above the scrub grass and granite outcrops. He reined up.

"Listen," he said to Dathan. "You ever been up this way before?"

"Time or two, chasing rabbits and whatnot," Dathan said, suspicious. "Ain't much game farther on."

"Yeah," Charley said. "Up ahead—" He wasn't sure what to say. Might as well go straight to it. "Up ahead is where we always used to meet. And by 'we' I mean—"

"I know who you mean," Dathan said. He squinted into the distance. The two men sat and considered.

Charley untied the Enfield from his saddle and handed it over. "Follow as far behind me as you can without losing sight. You might want to walk it until we see what's what."

Dathan nodded and dismounted, tying his horse to a pawpaw tree beside the creek. Dathan appeared familiar with the rifle, so Charley didn't press him. He handed him a box of cartridges from his saddlebag and rode away.

He came upon Flynn's wagon where the road skirted Rockpile before turning east again. It had been ransacked, items strewn across the ground for ten feet in all directions. There was blood on the seat, but Charley couldn't tell if it was fresh.

"Well," Charley said into the air. "So there's this." He pondered for a moment, then dismounted and tied his horse to Flynn's wagon. He'd come this far. Charley headed up the hill, shifting his pistol to his back, under his coat. No sense inviting a confrontation.

If he had the leisure to think about it, he'd wonder what the hell he was doing here, chasing a man he hated with a man he didn't trust, on behalf of a woman who might well be dead and who had never cared much for him anyway. But those were thoughts for another time. He needed to keep his mind on the task at hand, which was getting up this mountain and coming down again alive.

Halfway to the top, a voice called out. "Far enough, Pettibone. State your business."

"I'm in pursuit of this man Michael Flynn."

There was a chuckle. "You're headed in the wrong direction. Last I saw, he was down by the creek. But come on. We want to talk to you."

Charley picked his way up the slope. There was no real path, only level places between the rocks where he could see his way to the next level place higher up. Maybe he should go back to Arkansas, leave these rocky hills to the lizards and the wild hogs. He could take up riverboating again. No, riverboating was done for. Railroading was the thing now. Well, he could railroad along with the best of them.

And then he was in the clearing on top of the mountain, where four of the Law and Order League—Horace Landsome, the Barker brothers from up in the Flatwoods, and a new recruit whose name he had not yet learned—squatted around a pile of farm tools and cooking pots from Flynn's wagon.

Landsome barely looked up from under a short-billed cap. "That was a dirty trick you pulled on Green Pratt back there, shooting him like you did."

Charley folded his arms. "Almost as bad as the trick he was about to pull on me. At least I shot him front to front."

Landsome raised his head and glared at him full in the face. "That you did. I seen the wound myself and tried to stanch the blood. But it couldn't be stanched because it were too close and too deep. Ain't that always the case, that the mortal wounds are the ones from closest in?"

Charley didn't answer. His pistol scratched the small of his back, but as long as none of these men looked to draw a weapon, it would stay there.

"So you're looking for Michael Flynn," one of the Barker boys said.

"Yes," Charley said, keeping his voice low to avoid sounding too nervous or aggressive. "He went on a tear back at his house, pert near killed his wife, shot Mr. Turner. Don't know whether either of them will live."

"Ain't that hell," Landsome said. "So now you're the one out after him."

"More or less."

"The hell with this Flynn," said Landsome. "Where's my horse?"

"Soldiers took him. I'm gonna have to buy you a new one."

The unknown man butted in. "Some of the boys think you were working with those soldiers all along. Think you led 'em right to us. What do you say to that?"

Charley turned to face him. "Anybody who says so is a liar. What do you say to that?"

"Easy, boys," Landsome said. "We've already lost more good men than we can afford. Charley, I don't doubt your word. Jesse, you don't know Charley here like I do. He fought for the Cause from the very start. Charley's word is good."

"I'm in no mood to be trifled with, Horace," Charley said. "I'm here for Michael Flynn."

"He's back down the hill," Landsome said, pointing with a hand scythe that he had been inspecting. "We got the jump on him, but he cost us dear. Killed old Zebo right out, and that after he'd been shot a time or two. Put some lead into Willie Loudon, too, had to take Willie to Greenville to get fixed up. He was reloading when we got him."

"I thought the idea was to punish the lawbreaker, not to go back to bushwhacking."

Landsome winked. "Sometimes they look about the same."

"I'll take him back and bury him, if you all don't mind. He's got family."

Landsome stood up, and the other men followed. "Suit yourself. But I have to tell you." He stretched his arms, and Charley placed his hands on his hips in case he needed to reach his pistol. "You fought for the Cause, so you get a pass this time. I understand what you say about Green, one or the other of you was going to be down in the dirt. And that horse was not my best mount, so with the one we just confiscated we can call it an even trade. But you ain't part of the League no more, and if you cross our path again, you might find yourself on our list."

"All right," said Charley.

"Some of Quantrill's old bunch are going to be through here before long, and they might not be as forgiving. Just want you to know that."

"Appreciate it." Charley walked away but did not turn his back entirely, in case one of the men had a second thought. But no one moved, and soon Charley was back at the wagon.

He followed a trail of crushed weeds downhill and soon enough came across Flynn's body, face up beside a small creek. He counted a dozen pistol wounds in the chest and head, more than enough to kill, and some smaller ones made by a knife. "Those were just for sport," he said to himself. But in a moment, Dathan was beside him, shaking his head, and Charley knew he had heard. They said nothing more but started to work dragging Flynn back to the wagon. Since the bushwhackers had taken Flynn's horse, Charley harnessed the Daybreak mare between the traces. They hefted Flynn's body into the wagon, threw the spare saddle blanket over it, and turned to the west, stopping to tie Dathan's horse to the back of the wagon.

"Long trip home," Dathan said after a while.

"Well, I ain't stopping to camp, not with you up here beside me and a dead man in the back," Charley said.

"Wasn't recommending it," Dathan said, unperturbed. "Just thinking about how often we ought to switch out the horses."

"Oh, now you're a horse driver?"

"Not my trade, no. But I've done my share of teamstering."

Charley knew he probably had, so he held his tongue. But Dathan's air of superior knowledge galled him. Uppity son of a bitch.

They passed the old man's farm, the fields now empty, and turned toward Daybreak. "Michael Flynn, buried in the Daybreak cemetery," Charley mused. "Now there's a laugh. He hated them people."

"Hated *you* people, you mean."

"All right," Charley said. "I suppose. Guess we could bury him on his place, but he'd hate that even more, to be planted next to a rebel. We could put him next to his son if we knew where he was buried, but I think old Flynn took that knowledge with him."

As if by unspoken agreement, Charley stopped the wagon, and they stepped down to switch out the horses. Charley flipped back the saddle blanket for a moment to view Flynn's corpse. His eyelids had begun to draw back, and Charley wished he had placed pennies on them earlier. If he'd had some. The slash wound across his jaw from Josephine's knife, which had launched this whole disaster, now seemed little more than a scratch.

Across the wagon bed from him, Dathan leaned forward, his lips pursed as if he were ginning himself up to make a declaration about something, and rested his elbows on the side panel.

"There's another graveyard on that land," Dathan said. "I been fixing to tell somebody one of these days, and it might as well be you. We might could put him there. He wouldn't like the company no better, but at least it wouldn't be a fronting to the ones left alive."

Charley was astonished. "What are you talking about?"

"It's just down from where you all had your rope mill, between the road and the river. Ain't no markers left on it, what ones were there to begin with, 'cause they were wood and I imagine they washed away long ago. But it's there, all right. I been cleaning it up in the odd days."

Charley knew the place, a patch of level ground with nothing much to distinguish it, some nice open space between sycamore trees.

"A graveyard? That's the beatenest thing I ever heard," Charley said. "How do you know that?"

Dathan averted his eyes. "That's the slave graveyard there, what it is."

Charley snorted in disbelief.

"You don't think so?" Dathan retorted. "Son, you know less than you think you do."

"I ain't your son."

"That's for damn sure. Now you think for a minute. You knew old George Webb, didn't you?"

"Most certainly."

"Ask yourself this. Even in his prime, you think George Webb could have farmed a thousand acres by himself? Or with that son of his?"

Charley was silent. He'd never considered the matter.

Dathan went on. "When George Webb sent for his bride out from Louisville, she brought a dozen slaves. Men, women and children. Five years later, that was up to twenty, by purchase and natural increase. That's how that farm got built up, man—slave labor."

"George never mentioned anything about slaves!"

"Ashamed of it, is my guess. When the missus left him, she took 'em all with her since they were her dower. All but the ones who had died and were buried there."

In Charley's dumbfounded silence, they climbed back onto the wagon and got into motion again. But Dathan was not finished. "And yes, two of them people were my mother and father. Slaves to the missus and to her mother before that. I was born on that farm. Later on, Mr. Webb wrote Mrs. Mary Ellen that it was his desire to buy my freedom, being as how I was a young boy with no real connection to her, but she warn't about to give him that satisfaction. It took the war to do that."

"So you knew George Webb?"

"Just the way a young boy knows his slavemaster. He was a kind man, and you could tell that the ownership made him uneasy. But he was a man with big ideas for a big plot of ground, and a crew of slaves to work the fields was the fast way to make those ideas come to pass. His boy Harp was a few years younger than me. We would have been playmates except I had to work most times."

"Where did you live?"

"We had cabins in back of the house. That old stillhouse is one of 'em. The rest got tore down and used for something else, I reckon. Barn building or firewood."

Charley found himself rethinking everything he had ever known. Daybreak, the community of dreams, built on a foundation of slave labor. Old Mr. Webb a reformer and a slaver. Could a man be both? Could a community grow a dream of equality from such a rootstock?

Strangely, the more he thought over these questions, the more at home he felt with Daybreak. He was not such an outcast after all, the man who fought for the wrong side. It turned out that they all had their own blend of impurities.

They rode in silence for miles until they reached the Indian camp. "Cedeh was a child here, too," Dathan said. "I used to come up here on Sundays with goods to trade, and we'd roam the woods. I never forgot that little gal."

They had reached the steep descent into the river valley, and Dathan stepped down to walk beside the lead horse. "So you see," he said before moving out of earshot. "I got as much right to live here as you do. More, maybe. And if we don't want to bury old Flynn in the Daybreak cemetery, we can put him down with my people."

"All right," Charley said. "Ain't no better nor worse than any other burying spot on the earth."

At the river's edge, Dathan parted from him wordlessly, walking away to who knows where, and Charley ferried the wagon across by himself. The first cabin up from the river was where Jenny, Mrs. Smith's former serving girl, had taken up residence. She stepped out of her door as he approached. She was barefoot, wearing a faded calico print dress, and in her hand was a spoon. Charley stopped the wagon.

"Mr. Turner's passed," she said.

Charley took off his hat and placed it on his lap. He closed his eyes for a moment.

"Well, that is a bad end to a bad week," he said. "Can't say I didn't see it coming. But it is sad news even so."

Jenny nodded solemnly, and they faced each other in the quiet. "Mrs. Turner told us how you tried to save them, him and Mrs. Flynn, and how you went out after Mr. Flynn."

Charley glanced over his shoulder. "Flynn's back here," he said. "Wasn't my doing, but I figured he would need buried somewhere."

"You are right about that," she said. "You can't deny a man his six-by-two." She looked down at the spoon. "I've been making soup."

Charley could think of little else to say and was about to chuck the reins on his horse again, but Jenny spoke up again. "I don't mean to be forward," she said.

"That's all right. You're not being forward."

"No, I mean with what I am about to say."

Charley waited in puzzlement.

"This is the first time I've ever had so much as a room to myself, much less a house," she went on. "Before this I had half a room and half a bed in the fourth floor of Mr. and Mrs. Smith's house, which I shared with another girl. And before that just a spot on the floor with me brothers and sisters." Charley smiled to himself at the faint Irish tone that had crept into Jenny's voice with the memory. "So now here I am with a two-room house, with a stove of my own, and a mountain to see out my front door and a river to see out my back. You folks may have gotten used to this, but to me it feels impossibly grand."

The simplicity of her feelings cheered Charley's heart. "Yes, ma'am, you are right about that," he said. "I forget what we have here that—"

She cut him off. "Don't 'ma'am' me yet, please," she said. "I am simple Jenny, and hope to stay that way for a long time to come."

"All right," Charley said. "If you think it proper."

"What's proper and improper is not for me to judge," Jenny said, turning away slightly. "I am no lady." She paused. "Sometimes, when Mrs. Smith was away, the old man—Mr. Smith—would call one of us girls down to his rooms. It was none of it to our liking, but what could you do if you didn't want to be turned out into the street? So I was in no haste to return to Philadelphia."

She looked him in the face. "These past years have damaged us all," she said. "Me as much as anyone. And here you are, an old rebel at your age and an outcast to many, yet trying to help the neighbor and correct what wrongs you see. And in my calculation that's a fine thing, whatever side you fought on in the past. For I am leaving my past behind and plan on doing the same with all who can do it as well. Let the dead bury the dead, as the Good Book says."

She smiled, and Charley could feel himself blush. "I have a fine two-room house, Mr. Pettibone, and in the afternoon I will make tea. And on Sundays I will be pleased to go walking, and if you should come by I would like to serve you tea and walk out with you."

Charley's usual loquaciousness failed him. "What time?" he finally managed.

"Any time you please, Mr. Pettibone." She stepped into her door again. "Now excuse me, I need to stir my soup."

Chapter 29

The grave from which Lysander Smith's body had been taken was still open, so on a warm afternoon two days after he passed, they buried James Turner in it. Frances Wickman did not leave Charlotte alone until bedtime for those days, and Charlotte was glad of it, although she didn't feel that she "needed someone with her" in the way that they sometimes spoke of grief-stricken widows. But she was exhausted, the children were fearful and moody, and Frances' presence was a relief. They rarely spoke. But her calmness, and the simple way she set about the tasks of the day, were settling.

More dead, always more dead. James up the hill, Flynn down by the river. Two brothers of Green Pratt, lean and bearded, had shown up to retrieve his body. No one knew how they had learned where it was, but learn they did, arriving from Ironton in the late morning with a team of mules and a wagon with a hastily built coffin in the back, glumly refusing offers to eat a meal or spend the night. "Daddy will want to have him home," one of them said. "He'll want to sit up with him and then preach the funeral."

"Your daddy is a preacher, then," Charlotte said.

"Yes, ma'am. A preacher and a fighter. You ain't never heard of Parson Pratt? He fit all up and down this part of the state, and Arkansas, too. All us boys fit, and only one didn't come back."

"Not counting Green, here," the other one said.

Charlotte turned away. Any more talk of fighting and she would vomit. She'd preach them a funeral, all right, one about waste and loss and the price women paid when men couldn't stop fighting. She'd draw her text from Ecclesiastes and preach about vanity.

As Charlotte walked toward the village, she heard the Pratt boys whistle to their mule team and head south toward French Mills. She didn't look back.

Frances could manage the children, or they could manage themselves. She needed to walk.

She remembered when she had found an arrowhead in the cornfields in the predawn moonlight, years ago, and imagined to herself how enriching it was to live on ground that had been inhabited for centuries, the civilizations that had come and gone, the ancient lives beneath her feet. Now as she walked northward, Daybreak and the whole valley felt like a great graveyard, where it was impossible to set foot without treading on a corpse.

They had ferried Marie Mercadier—by unspoken compact, everyone had stopped calling her Marie Flynn—across the river to her father's old house, where she had lain in bed for the past two days. She appeared to be coming around little by little, taking nourishment by spoonful, though her eyes were unfocused and glassy. When Charlotte stopped by her door, she was propped up in a chair by the window, with Josephine behind her brushing her hair and Dathan sitting close by with a towel to wipe her face.

"How's she doing today?" Charlotte asked quietly.

"Better," Josephine said, in a voice that was too bright and loud. "She's been trying to talk most of the morning. I'm real encouraged." Marie's eyes drifted toward the sound of Josephine's voice.

"That's good to hear," Charlotte said. She wasn't convinced, herself. Marie might come back to them, but the longer she stayed in this deadened state, fed by hand, soiling herself like a baby, the more Charlotte doubted it. Still, stranger things had happened.

That reminded her of something else. She touched Dathan's forearm. "Those cattle across the river."

"Yes, ma'am, I been thinking about them. We brought that little calf up to our milk cow, and they got along fine with a little encouragement. But all them others are still out there."

"It'll take quite the pile of firewood to burn those carcasses, but once we get them going, we need to finish them all the way. Perhaps you and a couple of the others could gather all the dry wood that's over there, and any drift you find along the riverbank, too."

Dathan nodded. "Don't you wonder about it none, ma'am. We'll figure it out."

Marie leaned forward in her chair, her eyes rolling. Her lips smacked together. Charlotte could see what Josephine had meant about her trying to speak.

"Buh … buh … buh … buh," Marie said.

"Yes, Mama?" Josephine said. "It's all right, don't hurry."

Charlotte stepped back, wondering if her presence had agitated her.

Marie's expression grew more intent, a gathered frown that compressed her entire being into her eyes and lips.

"Buh … burn the house!" she exploded.

Charlotte and Dathan exchanged looks. Dathan leaned close to her. "You got it, Miss Marie," he said. "That old house will have plenty of wood to burn up them cattle, once and for all. Won't be nothing left but a scorch."

Marie leaned back and her eyes lost their wildness. "Burn," she repeated.

Charlotte opened the front door. "I'm going up to visit your father," she said to Josephine. "Come along with me, why don't you."

The girl glanced at her mother, whose eyes were now closed with fatigue. "All right," she said. "Mama'll be sleeping for a while now."

Charlotte took her hand and they walked up the valley past the Temple of Community. The neglect of the war years had taken its toll on the Temple. Its stonework, so carefully overseen by her father, had grown mold on the shady side, and the broken windows had gone unrepaired for so many years that the thin planks they had wedged into the frame to keep out the wind now seemed like part of the original design. More work to be done, by her or someone.

Turner's words came back to her all of a sudden. "Stop working and sit with me. Hold my hand."

How much she now wished she had done more of that—more sitting, more handholding, less force and fury. She had not been destined to be one of those happy helpmeets from *Godey's*, she knew that—but a little more softness from time to time, what would that have hurt? All Turner's flaws and failings were buried with him now, and she was left with recollections. That first moment in Leavenworth, when she had seen him speak. The grindings of life out here in the hills, their hopes and their failures. She had never imagined him dying and leaving her behind, even during the war. He was always going to come back, and they would reshape Daybreak, rebuild it to its imagined possibility, but the war had taken that away. Her old Turner had never come back, and the Turner that had returned was not that man, no matter how much they had wished for it. Perhaps she should have been easier on this new, broken Turner. Perhaps they should have chucked it all, headed west, rebuilt themselves instead of their dreamed-of community.

And as she walked to the cemetery, holding the hand of a child who was not her own, she felt for the first time that she was alone, utterly and entirely alone, with no one living to hold her hand and give her reassurance, only those who needed reassurance from her when she had none left to give. They all sought strength from her. But where could she go for strength of her own? Nowhere. And with her free hand she wiped her face, and it was wet with tears.

They reached the fresh mound.

"Your father was a good man," she told Josephine. "I hope you remember him as such."

Charlotte cast a glance up the hill at Adam Cabot's grave. The bittersweet she had planted five years ago had vined its way into the small oaks at the edge of the forest. She could see the seed clusters forming on the underside of the vines, dull orange showing through the green covering, faintly hinting at the explosion of color to come in the fall.

Josephine said nothing. Always the observer, that one. How could a child have developed such an air of judgmental watching, at her age? Hard to fathom.

Charlotte went on. "Whatever happens, I want you to know that you'll always have us. You'll always have me, and the boys, and the people of Daybreak."

"I don't want you," Josephine said. "I want my mother."

Charlotte let go of her hand, stung.

"There's no need to be harsh, child," she said.

"I'll prefer harsh over false any day," said Josephine.

Anger blurred Charlotte's eyes but she didn't speak. So these were the children of the new dispensation, the children of the war, tough-talking, as hard-shelled as a black walnut, closed off to the romantic ideals of her generation. Perhaps it was just as well.

"As would I," she replied, and said no more.

As she stood with the child, gazing but not gazing at the graves before her, her eyes blurred and her mind in flux, Charlotte grew aware of another pair of eyes on her. A whitetail deer had come out of forest across the hollow from the graveyard and begun to graze at the shoots along the edge. Their voices had caught the deer's attention, and now it had jerked its head up and was watching her, its ears spread wide, its nostrils open, its eyes protruding like knobs from the sides of its narrow head.

She didn't know why, but for some reason she immediately thought of

Caroline, her sister, dead now—what? Ten years? Eleven? Could it be that long? Apparently so. Perhaps it was the way the deer had lifted its head, swiftly but gracefully, that reminded her of a similar movement Caroline used to make; her habit of listening with her head slightly turned, favoring her better ear or maybe showing a prettier profile. Or perhaps it was the air of fragility that Caroline always possessed, despite her *joie de vivre* and coquettish ways. Caroline would be the one to die earliest, of course. She had weighed so lightly on the earth that it was easy for her to float off.

Charlotte gazed at the deer. The deer gazed back.

Or perhaps Adam Cabot's spirit was in the deer, or James's, newly flown. Crossing the bar of eternity had placed them both beyond the reach of talk, and fighting, and daily care, and despite the anguish of the last few days she felt herself beyond its reach as well. What was there left to fear after this?

No, it was not Adam, nor James. Over the years she had tried to conjure up Adam's presence, here on the hillside, and if he had ever returned to her she would have known it. And James—any uncanny sensation would not come from sensing his presence, but from feeling an absence. How could she not know his presence? She had talked with him almost daily during his years away, in the privacy of her own mind, to the point that he was always with her in thoughts regardless of distance. If James wanted to communicate with her, he wouldn't need to inhabit the body of a deer. He could simply speak to her inside her thoughts.

The Widow Turner. She was now the Widow Turner. This would take some getting used to. The Turner inside her mind, the one she had grown used to over the years, the one, she had to admit, whom she sometimes preferred to the actual Mr. Turner—would he fade and disappear? Would he stay, or would she be forced to make do with the lesser comfort of memory?

The deer's eyes were immense and watery, and the thought flitted through Charlotte's mind that if only she had brought a rifle with her she could have fed the colony for a week with this animal. As if sensing that thought, the deer shook its head slowly from side to side.

That action gave Charlotte an eerie feeling. She felt the hair rise on the back of her neck. Was that deer really reading her thoughts? Impossible. But the longer it stood there, and the longer they locked eyes, the stranger she felt. It was as if the deer had come to tell her something. And a name came to her mind.

"Angus?" she said, tentative but loud enough to hear.

In an instant the deer bounded away, its white tail flying, and was out of sight before she had time to blink. The spell was broken.

ℰℛ

As it turned out, there were enough split rails from Michael Flynn's prodigious fence-building labor to pile onto the carcasses of the cattle. The men spent a day heaping them over the bodies, camphor-soaked handkerchiefs pressed against their faces to counter the smell. Newton joined them after being repeatedly warned to watch for snakes in the shady underbrush. By the end of the day they were ready to burn. In the evening, Dathan stopped by the house to talk, standing in the yard under the maple tree.

"Ain't looking for much wind tomorrow," he told Charlotte. "That fire's going to be hotter than the hinges of you-know-where, though."

"That's all right," Charlotte said. "We've got a river running by. We'll not run short of water to put out sparks."

"I'm gonna need both your boys. Newton to scour for flare-ups, and Adam to stay at the landing and keep all the buckets full. It ain't lack of water that concerns me, but lack of buckets to hold it and men to take it where it needs to go."

Charlotte nodded. Adam seemed young to be joining in such an effort, but dipping water at the river crossing seemed safe enough.

They gazed into the darkness across the river.

"Wind'll be from the west," he said.

"That's good." The stench of the burning carcasses would be carried away. There was more to say.

"We don't have to burn that house if we don't want to," Dathan said.

"I know," said Charlotte. She considered for a moment. "Do you want it?"

"No, ma'am! I wouldn't live in that house. But somebody might."

She shook her head. "Promises were made." Dathan nodded in agreement. Charlotte realized that the direction of their gaze was not only to the Flynn house, and the site of their latest disasters, but also to the slave cemetery on their own side of the river, where Flynn now lay. "How many people are buried in that cemetery down there?" she asked.

"Ten that I know of, eleven now, I guess," Dathan said.

"You have their names?"

"Oh, yes."

"We should mark them."

"That would be a fine thing," he said. "Some of the old folks, I just know their first name, or their name and what we called them, like Stinkpot."

"Stinkpot?"

Dathan chuckled. "Yes, ma'am. I was real small when Stinkpot died, but I remember him. Stinkpot was a field hand, name of James. To a boy, everyone looks old, but he was the oldest of the old. And I don't know how to say this politely, but you didn't want to work downwind from old Stinkpot."

They shared a laugh, and for the first time in several days Charlotte felt better. So they were walking on the bones of the dead. Who wasn't, all around the world? Perhaps her answer was not to flee the graveyards of the world, but to consecrate it somehow.

In the morning they started early, and within a couple of hours two plumes—one the bright ferocious flame of a burning house, all dry timbers, floorboards and shingles, and the other, fifty yards to the south, a thick, low-hanging, black boil of smoke from the burning cattle—rose above the forest. They had brought Marie out in the street to watch, loosely tied into her chair with a sheet so she wouldn't slide out. Just before lunchtime the house collapsed. Marie let out a groan that Charlotte took to mean satisfaction, and the men scrambled with buckets of water as sparks flew fifty feet into the air and settled into the fields and woods.

By midafternoon it was done, although Newton and Dathan stayed across the river to patrol for flare-ups. The rest of them settled into the shade of the trees near the Temple with jugs of cold water from the springhouse.

"Charley, you've been a veritable ironclad through this whole mess," Charlotte said as they relaxed on the grass. "I'm going to put you up for president of the Daybreak community in October."

Charley smiled and looked away. "Mrs. Turner, you know I don't have the brains for that."

"You think I'm joking, but I'm not," she said. "When I saw you ride out after Flynn, and then Dathan ride out after the both of you, I figured somebody would be bringing back somebody for burial. I just couldn't figure out who and how many. We're fortunate it turned out the way it did."

She leaned closer and spoke in a low voice. "That man across the river has earned some estimation, too. I know this goes against your upbringing, but come next meeting, I'm going to nominate him for membership in the community. I'd appreciate your support."

"What if I can't give it?"

"Then I'd have to choose between you, and I'd hate for that to happen."

Charley kicked at a clump of weeds and didn't answer.

They all seemed to notice the stranger on the road across the river at the same time. He emerged from the screen of underbrush, reached the crossing, paused, then urged his horse forward. All conversation stopped.

"I heard tell that some of the old irregulars might be passing through here," Charley said softly. "That might be the famous Frank James. I heard say he was a stocky sort."

The man was wearing a gray slouch hat and a brown duckcloth duster that floated out behind him as he swum his horse across the river. He carried no visible weapon. His face was broad and he wore a thick Maltese beard that completely covered his mouth.

"Where's your rifle, Charley?" Charlotte said.

"In my cabin."

"All right. If he tries to push past me, knock him down."

They stood up and walked in their separate directions, Charley toward his cabin and Charlotte out to the edge of the village. She stood in the sun and waited.

The man let his horse shake dry for a few seconds and then urged it toward the village, ignoring the drifting plumes of smoke from Flynn's old place. When he reached Charlotte, he tipped his hat and drew up his horse, dripping water.

"Good afternoon, ma'am," he said. His accent was odd. Charlotte could not place it.

"Good afternoon."

"Is this Daybreak ahead? I'm looking for Daybreak."

"It is." She did not move.

He looked toward it and squinted. "Good." There was no sound but that of water dripping on dry ground.

The man returned his gaze to her. "Begging your pardon, my name is Nordhoff. I am looking for Mr. Mercadier of Daybreak. Do you know him?"

With the mention of his name, Charlotte recognized the man's accent as vaguely German, and she relaxed a bit, although his question was confusing. "Mercadier?"

"Yes. Emile Mercadier." He dug into his pocket and pulled out a sheaf of letters. "We have been corresponding for some time." He held them out.

"Perhaps you know me. I am Nordhoff of the *Evening Post*."

"What *Evening Post*?"

"The *New York Evening Post*, of course, ma'am. You've not heard of me?"

"Sorry, no."

"Ah. My editors take great interest in communities such as yours, and I have pursued that interest at their direction, and of my own great interest as well. Your Mr. Mercadier, he and I have exchanged letters for years now, and he has told me all about Daybreak. I am interested in doing a series of articles about your community."

"And what has he told you?"

Nordhoff wiped his brow. "That Daybreak is small and struggling in its outward appearance, but well led, and rich in the greatness of the souls who inhabit it."

Charlotte smiled. "That sounds like Emile, all right. I am sorry to tell you that Mr. Mercadier has died. But he was of considerable age, and his passing was peaceful." Nordhoff removed his hat.

She reached up to shake his hand. "I am Charlotte Turner. Let's dry you off and get some feed and rest for your horse."

She turned and led the way into Daybreak.

~ The End ~

Book Club Questions

1. What makes Marie Mercadier accept Michael Flynn's proposal?

2. Are there common threads in the ways that the main characters have been changed by the war, or do they change in different ways?

3. When Kathleen Mercadier leaves the community, she tells Marie to keep looking ahead, saying, "Take what life gives you, but do not try to hold on to it." Do you see merit in her philosophy?

4. Was Turner right in trying to withhold the details about Colonel Carr's death from Charlotte?

5. As he wrestles with his divided loyalties, Charley Pettibone sometimes wonders if he should have returned to Daybreak after the war. What do you think?

6. Learn about the "Drake Constitution" of Missouri, which was in effect from 1865 until 1875. How do you see that constitution influencing the actions of the characters in the novel?

Acknowledgements

The post-Civil War era in Missouri was a confusing time full of abrupt shifts in popular sentiment and public policy. Victors became outcasts; the defeated found themselves returning to power; and old wounds never healed. Understanding this period of history is a challenge, even for the professional historians. Those who wish to learn more about the actual history of the state during this time (as opposed to the fictional version I offer in this book) would do well to begin with William Parrish's *A History of Missouri* (Vol. 3), one of the University of Missouri Press' series. That press has also just come out with a collection of essays, *The Ozarks in Missouri History*, well worth the reading.

Sam Hildebrand, who was one of the few guerrillas who not only survived the war but dictated his memoirs, figures in this novel as well as in *Slant of Light*, my first volume. I freely confess to taking liberties with Hildebrand's life story in this novel, particularly in the timing of events. Then again, Hildebrand took his own liberties, and I recommend you take a look at the University of Arkansas Press' *Autobiography of Samuel S. Hildebrand*, magnificently edited by Kirby Ross, if you'd like to sort out the facts of the matter. For those who are looking for something connected to this era that is even grimmer, try Harriet C. Frazier's *Lynchings in Missouri*, published by McFarland.

Immense gratitude goes to the folks at Blank Slate Press for their care in editing and creativity in design. Publishing is an act of faith, and authors are always fortunate when a publisher expresses faith in them—faith that their work is worthy and that it will find an audience. My partnership with Blank Slate has been rewarding on many levels.

Gratitude as well for those perceptive folks who have read the manuscript versions of this book and offered their comments and suggestions. It's hard to know how well a book is working until you see it through someone else's eyes.

And finally, thanks to all who read *Slant of Light* and kept peppering me with questions about what was going to happen next! There's no motivation as powerful as the interest of readers. I hope you enjoy *This Old World* and pepper me with questions about what happens next!

About the Author

Steve Wiegenstein grew up in the eastern Missouri Ozarks and roams its back roads every chance he gets. The Black River and the Annapolis Branch Library were his two main haunts as a kid, and they remain his Mecca and Medina to this day. He is a longtime scholar of the 19th century Icarian movement in America, which provided the inspiration for *Slant of Light*. He particularly enjoyed weaving the real-life story of Sam Hildebrand—the notorious Confederate bushwhacker who murdered one of Steve's ancestors—into the novel. Steve and his wife, Sharon Buzzard, both academics, live in Columbia, Missouri. *Slant of Light*, the first book in his Daybreak series, is his first novel.

CPSIA information can be obtained at www.ICGtesting.com
Printed in the USA
LVOW07s0426010814

397053LV00007B/9/P